F.
Kristeva,
Julia

M

◆ P O S S E S S I O N S ◆

◆POSSESSIONS◆

a novel by Julia Kristeva

Translated from the French by Barbara Bray

columbia university press
NEW YORK

Columbia University Press

Publishers Since 1893

New York   Chichester, West Sussex

Copyright © Librairie Arthème Fayard, 1996

Translation copyright © 1998 Columbia University Press

Library of Congress Cataloging-in-Publication Data

Kristeva, Julia, 1941–

[Possessions. English]

Possessions : a novel / by Julia Kristeva : translated from the
French by Barbara Bray.

p.   cm.

ISBN 0–231–10998–9

I. Bray, Barbara.   II. Title.

PQ2671.R547P6713   1998

843'.914—dc21   97–29554

Casebound editions of Columbia University Press books are
printed on permanent and durable acid-free paper.

Printed in the United States of America

c 10 9 8 7 6 5 4 3 2 1

And, you know, lowering your eyes is totally
unbecoming to you: unnatural, ridiculous, and
affected, and to give satisfaction for my rudeness
I will tell you seriously and brazenly: I believe
in the demon, believe canonically in a personal
demon, not an allegory, and I have no need to
elicit anything from anyone, there you have it.
You must be terribly glad.

—Dostoyevsky, *Demons*

·POSSESSIONS·

◆ PART I ◆
A Beheading

◆ CHAPTER ONE ◆

Gloria was lying in a pool of blood with her head cut off. The ivory satin evening dress, the rounded arms, the long manicured hands, the Cartier watch, the diamond on the ring finger of the left hand, the sun-tanned legs, the shoes matching the dress—no doubt about it, that was Gloria. There was nothing missing except the head. "My sexual organ," as she laughingly used to call it, referring to the cerebral pleasure she got out of her work as a translator and the equally intense pain she suffered from her headaches. Sometimes she'd amend the description and call her head "the tool of her trade." And now here she was, bereft of her organ or tool, and so made almost anonymous. But only almost. For, head or no head, Gloria Harrison was easily recognizable. True, her auburn hair and sea-green eyes were no longer there to prove who she was, but the strong fingers, the shapely gymnast's thighs, the slim ankles, and above all the arrogant breasts that she flaunted so openly, even if they had started to sag these last few years, were evidence enough that it was she. And that unmistakable bosom was encased, perfectly as usual, in the bodice of an ivory satin evening dress, on the left side of which spread a crimson stain. It looked like a knife wound.

Nothing is heavier than a dead body. And it weighs even more when the head's missing. A face—whether peaceful, purple, or distorted by death—gives meaning to a corpse and so makes it lighter. Eyes, even if they're dull, staring, or protruding; lips, even if they're twisted, bloodstained, or swollen; hair, even if it's torn out, plastered down, or disheveled—all necessarily convey what we suppose to be the expression of death. But without eyes or mouth, head or hair, a corpse is no more than a hunk of butcher's meat. Its once erotic contours, pinned down implacably by gravity and lacking the only means that could have given acephalic distress a voice, are reduced to mere pragmatic pointlessness. Deprived of a death mask's baleful exuberance, the dead are dead twice over. It's not that the victim has lost his or her humanity or even personality; on the contrary, humanity and personality both survive, minutely present even in the headless trunk, the crooked limbs, the frantic disarray of the body. But the madness that is the mark of what is human, and that is revealed in the face, becomes literally invisible when that vital clue is missing. A decapitated corpse is a substance that has thrown off its own consubstantial insanity. Or rather retracted that quintessence into an anatomical and visceral landscape hitherto concealed by clothing, which is a continuation of the face. Yet here, either because of or despite all this, the cropped neck and the bleeding hole within it were evidence that a genuinely, if horribly, human act had been committed—an act inspired by dementia in another human being very similar to the one whose canceled flesh now lay before me so cruelly shorn of the signs of its own insanity that it presented a woefully inadequate idea of the human condition. In short, all that remained of Gloria was a motionless heap lying on the ground, bereft through some mysterious catastrophe even of the expression of terror she must have worn as she saw a deed of madness about to be performed on her by one of her fellowmen. A deed all the more human because it was anonymous and therefore universal. As you can see, I was completely baffled.

"And of course nobody's seen the head!"

The grumble came from Northrop Rilsky, who always expressed himself in platitudes. But he failed to attract my attention.

A decollation—that's what it was: the word's at once broad and precise. There are natural examples of the phenomenon. Dione and Aphrodite, both beloved by Phidias, both lost their heads, though they did so when they left the pediment of the Parthenon for the cavernous recesses of the British Museum. I prefer them to the Winged Victory of Samothrace, another decapitee: she'll never fly away from the Louvre. How could she, without a head? Anyway, that particular beauty richly deserves both the place she has landed in and her punishment; she's so ardent and self-important—quite different from Gloria. But those now headless mistresses from the past appeal to my imagination; they don't move me. Their mutilation, at the hands of History, was relatively bloodless. Premeditated violence is the prerogative of human beings. Doomed to be ruled by time—or at least so they think—they do their best to abolish it, and often they do so through hatred, which belongs not to time but to desire. Or to revulsion, its shameful obverse. Disgust and passion can cut short hours of happiness: you have to be out of time to scheme someone out of life.

"What a lousy setup, boss! I've never seen anything like it in all my goddam days!"

The chief of police and his assistant had drawn up outside the gate in a black unmarked car, its ceiling light switched on. The garden was full of cops, but as yet no one had alerted my colleagues, the press. I loathe that mob with their notebooks and tape recorders, drawn like flies to wounds and blood, so to avoid being taken for another salacious reporter I mingled with the medics and the forensic experts. All too soon the dazzle of TV projectors would join the red and blue flashes pulsating from the patrol cars, and poor old Gloria would become a media star. Served up on the news by way of dessert; for a few seconds, perhaps a minute or two. For a decapitation you can hardly do less. Was it the work of a serial killer? A crime of passion? I was there to try to solve that bizarre problem, a task clearly beyond the scope of the worthy Rilsky.

Amid all the hassle that follows a crime, a sensitive soul like me likes to pause for thought. For two thousand years the gory neck of St. John the Baptist, the Forerunner, has been advancing toward us from the shores of the Dead Sea. The preparer of the way of the Lord is wearing a camel-hair tunic and carrying a lamb that bears a cross. He himself holds another cross made of reeds—and sometimes too his own severed head. He was arrested by Herod but was really destroyed through the machinations of Herod's wife, Herodias, who when her daughter, Salome, had pleased the king with her lascivious dancing told the girl to ask for the prophet's head on a charger as a reward. Centuries later Mallarmé, before his own life came, so to speak, to a glottal stop, took pleasure in—as he put it in an elliptic and prophetic pun—imagining an end to his "former quarrel with the corporeal" that would reenact John the Baptist's fate in his own body. Then there was the master of mosaic in Venice, delighting in his work as he illustrated the same story in the baptistery at St. Mark's, using the pallid gilt tones so apt for severed Byzantine heads. He developed the Gospel magic further by showing the saint putting his head in an urn with his own hands, while further on in the same strip cartoon Salome puts the jar on *her* head to perform a tête-à-tête dance that will remain unique forever, unrivaled by even the steamiest cheek-to-cheek.

Venice reminds me of Tiepolo in Bergamo, depicting the saint's gaping neck like an overturned pitcher spilling a flood of red paint at which the bystanders pretend to be terrified. Not to mention Caravaggio! Or Leonardo da Vinci! Or Raphael!

Painters' eyes, whether like pitch-dark silk, or green with flecks of ice, or misty, fierce, and brown, or a frankly timorous blue, are, unlike most people's eyes, covered with a sensitive skin made up of receptive dots like tiny satellite dishes. Emanations from external objects or other living beings converge on the dots' damp surfaces, as do pulsations of sound, touch, smell, and biological cataclysms of all kinds coming from within the orb itself. And the painter's eye transmutes all these minute, chaotic stimuli into little visual correlatives. It is at once mouth, skin, ear, penis, vagina, anus, throat, and all the rest: for a painter's eye covers first the five senses, then the incalculable rest of the body, with a thin film that makes visible what cannot be seen. A moral wound, for example, or a dagger blow to the heart, or a breath or a hope cut short, become, through the luminous membrane of the artist's slightly narrowed or boldly staring eye, a tempest of red paint, a shattered face, an unnaturally long limb, or better still one that has been lopped off. And because it transforms sensation into spectacle, the felt into the seen, the painter's eye doesn't merely reach but flies swift as an arrow to the invisible heart of the spectacle of murder—murder of a man or a woman. It is through a kind of hypersensitivity that the greatest artists have a taste for anatomy and butchery. Gloria's own sea-green eyes, flecked with black and narrowed shortsightedly, used to shine with the tension characteristic of painters or great readers. And there, then, standing by her dead body, I could easily imagine she might have seen herself as one of them would have felt, then seen her: as a challenging headless shape, perhaps by Caravaggio.

How the choleric Caravaggio likes lighting up his theatrical faces *a giorno*! To say he loves severed heads is putting it mildly; he adores them, worships them. He deserves a prize for gruesomeness with his series of waxwork horrors: heroic Judith recoiling from a Holofernes whose gaping maw emits a skein of stiff red wool; Isaac, innocent as Bluebeard, shrieking in the grip of an Abraham deaf and blind to the finger of the Angel as it points in vain to the providential ram. And though the melancholy head of his Baptist, beginning to lose its freshness as it lies there on the salver, may leave Salome cold, it still strikes terror into the artless slave girl clutching at the holy man's locks. Nor does the vagabond Caravaggio, when depicting dread Goliath's head in David's dismayed hands, shrink from giving the giant his own features, modeled on a criminal's mask hired from the commedia dell'arte's prop department.

The only exception to such antics is the beheading of St. John in Malta. I breathe again: the killing itself occupies only the left half of the huge picture, while the shadowy right holds the spectators—you and me—imprisoned behind the bars of their curiosity. And as the executioner turns to show off his manly torso, and the blood of the

Baptist, his body limp, is transfused into the painter himself, who has seen fit to write his name in the crimson stream—whose head are you really cutting off, Signor Caravaggio?—an old peasant woman stops her ears. But a decapitation is meant to be heard, not seen! *All* painting ought to be heard. But how?

A decapitation marks the limit of the visible. The show is over, ladies and gentlemen, move along, please! There's nothing to see! Open your ears instead, if they're not too sensitive. The deepest depths of horror can't be seen, though perhaps they may be heard. Put away the palettes? Hear, hear!

In a word, there's nothing like a good beheading for showing the bad taste of an artist fretting over his impotence, or perhaps over the impotence of art. Rodin is an exception of course. His *Walking Man*, with both hands over his sex organs, is a supreme example of how to lose one's head—the opposite of *The Thinker*. I make another exception of Degas, a sculptor in love with the bosoms of his dancers, who after the show have discarded their heads as unnecessary. It's a well-known fact that it's perfectly possible for a man to walk and a dancer to do her tricks without a head.

Right. Despite the similarities between the Santa Varvara carnage in its luxurious setting and the famous images jostling in my mind to try to shelter me from the horror before my eyes, *I*'m doing my best to keep a cool head. The present situation is more urgent than ever. So I concentrate on the differences.

John the Baptist was a saint, and a man, and he began the Christian era before Jesus Christ himself, having baptized him in the waters of the Jordan. All the more reason for understanding, though of course not excusing, the pleasure Herodias and the rest derived from the episode. But Gloria was a woman. Not a "mere" or "poor" woman, because she was wealthy, or rather her family was. But all the same she was just a woman, a translator living in Santa Varvara. Easier said than done, for what's the point of translating when no one (except computers) writes any more, and no one reads any more (except women alone at the seashore, and there aren't all that many of them)? Aggravating circumstances, no doubt, but not enough to make a modern Herod, Herodias, or Salome commit the crime of decapitation, an act that mingles sophistication with a kind of crude enjoyment. A gross, low pleasure, with no conceivable future. I can't imagine any ambition that could have been punished, let alone furthered, by such a vile crime. All it did was present poor old Captain Rilsky with a first-class headache!

I admit my pictorial reminiscences might strike some readers as literary and irrelevant, perhaps to the point of obscenity. But what use is art if it can't help us look death in the face? My purpose in remembering museum encounters with painters and sculptors is to be able to draw on them when I'm confronted with macabre experiences. Such ordeals aren't all that rare in Santa Varvara, and here more than anywhere I need art to help me see my way, to retain my common sense, and, if you'll forgive the expression, to keep my head.

For the present just one thing is sure: It *is* Gloria Harrison. No one has expressed the slightest doubt about the identity of the corpse, with or without its head. Poor Gloria, whom life humiliated so much and who was proud only of her head—according to what she herself said, ironically but with a certain amount of reason. The black humor of destiny willed that at the fatal moment she should be deprived of her ultimate fetish and depart bereft of any consolation.

"No head of course!"

Rilsky repeated his irrelevant "of course." I still wouldn't look at him. For my mind, bent on trying to recover from the sight of all that carnage, went on passing in review other images, images closer in time and without allusion to God, that had haunted my imagination when I was a child. Gloria's bloody torso somehow summoned up the guillotine: it too aimed at the head, though *it* went in for mass production. Terror, Virtue and Terror, Concord! "I shall drink the cup to the dregs." "Do your duty." "One moment more, Monsieur the executioner!" Men's heads, women's heads, heads noble and heads less noble, all whipped off by the blade and sent rolling in the sawdust: Madame Roland, Charlotte Corday, to mention but a few. You'd rather not think about it? Personally, I *do* think about it. The operator of the guillotine is inevitably some efficient male. The zealous professor of anatomy who perfected the sinister blade insisted until he died on his good intentions. He merely wanted to shorten the suffering of the victims. But the explanation is so reasonable it's hard to believe in it. I find this foretaste of modern times particularly amusing. And I can't understand the women who according to Stendhal were so besotted with their executed lovers that they did their pious best to reclaim their severed heads: one stole the poll of the marquis de La Mole in the sixteenth century, while Stendhal's own Mathilde de La Mole, her descendant in *The Red and the Black*, caressed that of Julien Sorel. It seems a shrink recently caused a stir at a symposium by claiming that one out of every ten dreams dreamed by women has to do with a severed head; one of his female patients, he said, always dreams she's carrying one through a landscape of ruins as if it were a baby. An illustration of the extremity of desire, perhaps!. But I shouldn't like to be the head on that analyst's shoulders. Are we supposed to believe that women, eternal mourners over castrated corpses, can feel passion only for a guilty (*sic*) phallus? Maybe. I see what he means. But I must admit I doubt it. Whether seen from the point of view of the cutter or the cut, the guillotine and all that goes with it is foreign to feminine sensibility as I see it. My modesty or, if you prefer, my repression can't go along with it. The topped and gory remains of Gloria Harrison, lying at my feet exposed to the impotent curiosity of the police captain of Santa Varvara, shocked as much as it intrigued me. And try as I might to call painters and sculptors, the Terror and '93 to the rescue, such cultural digressions solved strictly nothing.

Did I hate the monster who'd killed Gloria? Of course. What other answer could there be to the appalling question posed by that act? On

the fear emanating from it I had to heap all the hates deserved by meanness, pettiness, slander, jealousy, all kinds of hypocrisy; the treachery
of friends, lovers, husbands, and wives; blows below the belt, sly
blows, glancing blows, stabs in the back; denunciation, sabotage, cen-
soriousness, malicious criticism, gossip; disparagement, rivalry, humiliation; wrecked passions, children thwarted, loves made impossible. I
had to shatter at last the decency that reduced my pain to passive pride
and made me what I was, a lonely hunter, a traveler, a journalist.

Hatred works in silence or expresses itself in short, breathless sentences: slang and a line of dots. I knew all about it; I'd experienced it,
I felt it so much I'd have liked to be nothing but hate. But in me it was
only partial. In me it was mingled with an inexplicable tolerance that
loosened hatred's grip and made my loathing veer toward sardonic
laughter. In the same way some detective story writers rub your nose
in horror while adopting a tone that's gruff, naive, and even dim, as if
to apologize for being much more intelligent than the characters, with
their paltry tricks, who represent knowledge and the law. Perhaps too
to booby-trap the supposed intelligence of the sophisticated reader,
condescending to amuse himself with a form of literature often
regarded as mindless and stupid. Like such writers I too indulged in
hatred, only under cover of the mockery supposed to be appropriate
to minor accidents and petty crime as well as to hatred and to those,
including myself, who harbor it. This ambiguous and, I assure you,
unconscious attitude unfortunately watered down my physical perception of Gloria's murder and turned it into a party piece for which
I was the only audience. At the same time it had the great advantage
of placing me at a distance from what had happened and enabling me
to see it more clearly. A satisfactory hatred is bound to blind you to
some extent; only irony may occasionally lead to something worthwhile. Meanwhile people took fingerprints, put hairs and buttons and
other bits and pieces away in bottles or plastic envelopes, took photos
and videos, were indignant, looked grave, put on professional airs.
All this under the gratified and competent eye of Captain Rilsky,

though at the same time he was very put out. He took off his glasses with a touch of guile and much solemnity.

"Clues aren't always false—only irrelevant," I remarked cheekily, but with some circumspection.

"Of course," said Rilsky in his musical voice, glad to have got my attention at last; he was basically a humanist. Poor Gloria!

I knew some humanists in Paris. They told me one ought to fight against social "exclusion" and that the object of life, now the Wall was down, was "assimilation." They weren't very sure into what, but they *were* certain that one had to "assimilate" rather than "exclude." They uttered the word *exclusion* with a mixture of surprise and complacency that lent their love of mankind a force at once gauche and menacing. Rilsky, for his part, was rather cynical. In Santa Varvara the Mafia operated in broad daylight, and he couldn't have cared less about people suffering from too much exclusion or not enough assimilation. Music contained the only beauty he believed in, and then only if it could be shared. "Music ought to be listened to together," he always told me. He regarded painting as a slow art and tried to get me to share the ecstasies he experienced at concerts in between investigations into low-down crimes. As a postmodern humanist, believing everything has its price, he thought the sublimity of Bach amply compensated for a bunch of wretches shedding a few pints of blood. "A necessary counterpoint, human nature being what it is," he'd conclude with some satisfaction between concerts, while busy flushing out some murderers. He rightly regarded himself as an aesthete who was also a lucid yet persevering humanist.

Watching him go about his work I couldn't help reflecting, without undue indulgence but not without some pity, on what a mess Gloria's life had been. Like that of so many women, to put it mildly! Not to put it mildly would be another story. I knew she was hated, a foreigner, almost a writer, and the heroine of some public successes: she had distinguished herself as the translator of Faulkner into Santavarvaran and then fallen back on being the official translator of Philip Roth.

Quite a visible life, in short, of the kind that doesn't attract much sympathy in Santa Varvara—or anywhere else, for that matter. Slander, treachery, and gossip were no news to me, and I knew they'd stopped surprising Gloria long ago. I'd even have admitted, despite the humanity mistakenly attributed to human beings, to women, and sometimes to journalists, that the dagger plunged into her chest and then used to cut off her head didn't strike me as far-fetched or even uncalled-for. The deed, carried out, as the forensic expert would demonstrate, by means of a knife with a sharpened blade and point, might well be the natural result of the feelings of rejection that Gloria always caused, in this case in someone who was mentally unstable. The bottle of Rohypnol found lying beside the glass of champagne suggested she was under the influence of drugs at the time of the murder. Was this really true? The medical tests would soon throw light on the matter. But what dark passion, coursing through the veins of what psychopath, could have guided the hand that cut away with such delicate skill the flesh of the neck, the larynx, and the spine and left the smooth wide stream, the red mirror, the dreadful crimson edge outlining the corpse where the head should have been? That was where the mystery lay, at least as far as I, Stephanie Delacour, was concerned, having just arrived yet again in this cursed country. Moreover I'd had dinner at Gloria's house only two days before. And when I'd kissed her good-bye at the door at thirty-five minutes past midnight on Sunday, October 16, she'd still been quite all there.

Who? Who could it be?

Nothing I knew of Gloria suggested any such monstrous technician hovering in the background. That left the possibilities of a motiveless crime, a sex maniac, or one of the innumerable kinds of delectation discussed in the books on psychiatry that Rilsky knew like the back of his hand—and that I was ready to bet he'd secretly consulted again in his office before setting out to confront the enemy. Why that butchery, that pointless ferocity? For I knew enough to realize Gloria had been dead *before* she was decapitated. The pool of blood was relatively small, the head nowhere to be seen. Who had done this, between 12:35 A.M. on the night when the blue dark bathed my face as I left after the dinner party, Gloria's cheek just brushing mine ("I'll phone you." "Thanks for a lovely evening!"), between then and five past ten today? Today, Monday, October 17, when I'd had the pleasure of being woken up by Captain Rilsky's typical music-lover's voice, telling me how glad he was our paths had crossed once more, and on a case where I was lucky enough to be an important witness. Our shared admiration for Yehudi Menuhin naturally prevented Rilsky from putting it any more strongly for the moment, but from the strictly legal point of view, Ms. Delacour must admit it was a very odd situation, and the last people to have seen the victim alive were always ipso facto suspect. In short, it was between those two points in time that a passion, a madness, or a deranged artist had gone to work.

As Rilsky spoke I thought I could hear the third movement of Bach's Concerto for Two Violins and Orchestra in the background: the violins, followed by the other instruments, climbed dizzy heights; the allegro, repeated, swelled up until the strings formed a grid across the sun itself, which exploded in a shower of crystal particles. I was right: when Northrop wasn't actually on the scene of a crime, his staple diet was music.

"See you there in an hour."

As usual I had to interrupt him. Then I showered and took a taxi to the house I'd left only thirty-six hours earlier. Assailed by a reek of salt, ozone, and seaweed, persecuted by dusty flies and bees drunk on privet, I felt as if all the sultry intrigues and criminal passions in Santa Varvara were targeted on me.

CHAPTER TWO

It was less than a week since the Air France plane had brought me back here, and I had the usual feeling that I'd never really been away; the sense of a physical yet shameful affinity with some kind of wickedness, as in one of those dreams that herald a stomach upset—or another of my editor's fits of hysterics!

It's as though I were inhabited by another person, vague but impossible to get rid of, whom I'd rather ignore but who in fact possesses me; someone who likes these dirty streets, the painfully slow pedestrians jostling one another to give themselves the impression they're in a hurry to get somewhere, the skyscrapers reflecting only emptiness, the restaurants perched on top of forty stories of plastic from which the lights of the shanty towns and the lamps on the bridges look like strings of fireflies.

Santa Varvara has changed since I was here last: it's become even more modern, even more violent. But I don't really know the place. I wasn't born here. I only lived here for a few years. But of course they send me here whenever some squalid incident occurs; in other words, quite often. Is it the memory of the childhood I spent here, when my father was alive and posted to "the back of beyond," that comes back and makes me feel like another person? Or is it a certain closeness to the worst kind of abjectness—the enlightened variety? An intimacy that my friends in Paris know nothing about, and that I myself don't wish to go into. I prefer not to know the answer to that question.

The first thing I did was hang up my clothes in the dressing room of Bob's absurdly large loft, which he let me borrow as much through apathy as friendship. Like me he spends most of his time going back and forth all over the world. The idea of "home" means nothing to him, so he isn't bothered about lending his place to me or anyone else. Still, I appreciate the gesture.

I have been here before. I say that, but I know it's not true: this is the first time I've lived in this apartment crammed with carpets and objects of every kind, all daubed with orange now by the sunset on the other side of the river. I loathe all the junk Bob feels obliged to bring back from wherever he goes. But I can't throw off a feeling of déjà vu. *Have* I slept in this bedroom before? Used this bathroom? When? In what life? In whose life?

Traveling makes me dizzy. It makes me face up to the inner dizziness I'm usually so good at keeping under. Let's not go into that.

There's a ring at the door. Probably Brian. Along with his apartment, Bob lent me his and Gloria's assistant. "You'll see, he's very efficient. You'll need someone who knows the ropes, someone who belongs here." So he thinks I don't belong! I don't know whether I ought to feel grateful or resentful.

Brian is rather short, with a greasy skin, dark glasses, and a mustache that fails to conceal a greedy mouth. If he's not gay he's deceiving himself. Oh, I know: everyone deceives himself or herself on that score. He's almost invisible behind a bouquet bursting with blazing roses, purple peonies, crimson-flecked carnations, and dark mauve tulips, all surrounded with crisp green leaves and giving off a heady perfume. Brian's offering might seem in rather crude taste were the lounge not filled with the amaranthine rays of the declining sun. As its russet waves lap against the flowers, the late afternoon is draped in a silken dazzle as ceremonious as a matador's cape. "All we need is the bull!" I tell myself; my imagination, together with the quality of the light, helps me resist the charm of Brian's scarlet tribute.

"Brian Watt." (He, obsequiously.)

"Coffee?" (I, without enthusiasm.)

"With pleasure. That is, it's a great pleasure to meet Stephanie Delacour." (He, saying his piece as if we were taking part in a TV debate.)

I realize there's no more to be said. I go off to make the coffee.

Meanwhile, my visitor's oily complexion has gone blotchy and red. Could he be sexually aroused? I hand him the sugar. He flings his hand out and overturns not only the sugar bowl, the coffeepot, and his cup but also the Chinese table brought back by Bob from some trip or other. My visitor's feet play havoc with the antique carpet, then scrape against the Empire chaise longue onto which he finally flops, sending vases of flowers flying right across the room. He's racked with spasms, he fights for breath, loses consciousness, then falls onto the floor, his back arched, his body quivering. All this hullabaloo ends in a lull, followed by a muffled groan. Has he had a catatonic attack or a fit of epilepsy?

Santa Varvara always gives me a spectacular reception, but this time it has excelled itself. "They" must have wanted to test me. Well, "they" underestimate me. They ought to know by now the sort of person they have to deal with. I refer of course to the secret services by whom both Bob and Northrop Rilsky are manipulated. I decide to wait for a quarter of an hour before calling an ambulance. After eight minutes and fifty-three seconds Brian utters a few syllables and tries to sit up. I mumble something reassuring and help him totter to the maid's room. Did Bob really intend it to be put to this use?

Make yourself at home, Mr. Watt! I feel I know him already too. Of course that's impossible. But nothing surprises me in Santa Varvara, including epilepsy. I'm sure I've lived through this scene before. But in what life?

The real nub of this kind of situation, as of most others, is loneliness. "People" don't exist; there are only different varieties of loneliness. Brian knows something is happening to him that he doesn't understand and never will understand, and that scares everyone else. The fit he's just had, which is really just an example of the awesome strangeness that belongs to all of us, seems to him just a tide sweep-

ing him away from the rest of humanity, and at a deeper level breaking the links between him and himself. I almost warm to him when I
think of the inhuman loneliness of a self bereft of itself. But no, I
don't want anything to do with him: my own loneliness is enough for
me. As I look at his disintegration, my own solitude seems narrow but
admirable. As natural as the snow on the Alps. That's how it is.

Brian resurfaces and burbles his excuses: he must have had too
much to drink, he's terribly sorry, he hopes I'll forgive him, he's still
at my service, it was only a slight indisposition, nothing serious, and
we'll be meeting again on Saturday at Gloria Harrison's dinner
party, she'll call up and tell me the time, yes, that's right, until
Saturday, then.

I don't believe in omens, but no one would call this a promising
beginning. Santa Varvara is greeting me with convulsions and other
signs of the devil. No time to get bored—oh no, that would be too
aristocratic a feeling for this town. Here people spy on one another
and dish all the dirt they can find about their neighbors. To whom?
Oh, to anybody; to all their other neighbors. Everyone's fair game
for everyone else. "All men are slaves and equal in slavery. Slander
and murder are approved of. The thing to remember is that all men
are equal. This entails complete depersonalization and unquestion-
ing obedience, apart from the odd upheaval that's allowed every
thirty years or so." I read that somewhere. But there's nothing to
stop an individual indulging in a little attack slightly more often than
that, to avoid getting too bored. Just like Brian. You start by not dar-
ing to kill yourself, or to suffer, or to desire. And in the end all action
becomes impossible. You go on living just out of fear. Until the
explosion occurs, and an attack of some kind causes you pain, the
real undeniable pain that can impart a bit of intelligence even to an
idiot. A fierce, destructive, unostentatious intelligence. Only tem-
porary of course. So I understand Brian. Yes, in a way I include
him in myself; I possess him. Though in reality he's completely alien
to me.

For my (false) feeling of déjà vu is accompanied by an impression of opaqueness. Of inscrutable faces, prefabricated smiles, flagrant but obstinate inefficiency. For out of laziness, hostility, or incompetence, the Santavarvarians like to shut themselves up. There's no reciprocity, no interchange of feelings or ideas, no mutual consent. ¡No pasarán! They shall not pass! All those crowds milling around distraughtly are opaque. All the things in the shops, luxury goods as well as necessities, are heaped up anyhow on the shelves: opaque. There's no guide, no intermediary to help you; the salesclerks use their computers or smile into their telephones: opaque. Even the orange light from the other side of the river that lends my studio its charm is the same: it's now turning crimson, and as it hits the grimy windows it transforms Bob's apartment into a gaudy, impenetrable, opaque polyester cube. Am I inside, or on top of, some building in a video game? Yes, I'm inside one, here at Bob's place on the sixth story of an apartment block equipped with a janitor, an elevator, locks and bolts, burglar alarms, surveillance cameras, and all that the heart could desire. Or dread. A shining prison bombarded from outside, a rainbow cell closed in on its own reflections, an opaque replica of the general opacity. I keep close to the walls, but they're not walls, they're screens, letting through the rays that pour down on me relentlessly from the other side of the river with an unvarying force that finally fills me with exasperation. They're opaque too, these walls, but without substance; the hostility they seem to project is a mere play of light. I am being rejected by nothing. By the arrogance of nothing.

I switch on the radio, the TV, the cassette player, the hi-fi—all the gadgets Bob has plugged in everywhere. "You won't be lonely at my place—every nook and cranny is inhabited." There's even a radio in the john and a telephone right by the toilet. No way of escaping the barrage of Santavarvaran. So I dive into it, immerse myself in it, get drunk on it. I thought I knew the language well but find I can't understand a word. Every time I come here it's the same: it takes me at least a week to be able to make out a few intelligible syllables from amid the meaningless din, a few words I seem to remember learning but that now elude me.

And yet I once spoke the language. Or at least I listened to it a lot and knew it passively. Once. When? In my mother's womb? Anyhow, someone used it on my behalf, in the past, at a distance. A man or a woman, I don't know which. But the harshness of those liquids is not unfamiliar to me, nor is the sleepy drawl of the vowels, nor the greedy dentals exploding under pressure built up in the digestive tract. For it's a language that, like American, gesticulates from the throat and the guts, excluding the respiratory system. So Santavarvarian lungs weaken, the vocal cords grow strained, people's voices are always hoarse. But all that's no longer familiar to me, I've got ties elsewhere, I've adopted the high-pitched delivery, the clipped and prettily mannered tones of French. And yet the rougher music of the local barrel organs, glancing off the corners of my laser cube, sounds welcoming. I'm sure I'm one of them. Or was, in another life. But I don't understand.

There's nothing more tiring than not being able to understand. After a long time spent vainly listening, I fall from acute frustration into a kind of numbness. But now I can catch three words out of every twenty. In this interlude of relative relaxation I'm able to spy on the locals. I move among them in a state of musical osmosis, X-raying the erogenous zones that their language, like all others, reveals if you listen to it in the way you take a sauna: languidly, with all your pores dilated. I'm on the brink of sleep or of a coma. For if lack of understanding doesn't finish you off first, the lost language, the tongue you think you once knew but that has abandoned you, gradually recovers its power to embody meaning. And you wake up one fine day to find yourself in it, with another throat, different lips and stomach, and even a sex not quite the same as it is in your usual language, which only a few days ago possessed you entirely.

But for the moment I'm in the process of transition, in the middle of a kind of transvestism. Santavarvaran might turn out to be only a mask for me; so many people do wear false beards, artificial breasts, false selves. But Stephanie Delacour likes to do things properly, and she really reincarnates herself in Santavarvaran. And as I put on another language I practice a kind of transsexualism. To everyone his or her own sadomasochism. If I don't actually feel pain I invent it. I live in a state of trauma. To me everything is trauma, shock, upheaval. Starting with language itself. Santavarvaran or French? A red language or a white one?

Without even thinking about it I ruled out the big double bed, intended for nights of gladness. In Bob's study there's a Victorian mahogany divan, standing strangely and majestically high off the floor. This, I discovered, was because it had a drawer underneath that was a sort of pullout bed, and when I opened it I found it contained a mattress, sheets, a comforter, and pillows. Exactly what I needed. The same as I had at home, in the rue du Cherche-Midi, in Paris. I love that kind of bed; I can only sleep well in a drawer. Like a rabbit in its warren, a mole digging its burrow below the surface on which humans think they can sleep. Our nightlife, that splendid negotiation between sleep and the umbilicus of dream, should never make do with exposed surfaces. My pullout couch transports me to the other side of innocence; I sink straight down into something better than the sleep of the just. In the damp warmth of my shell I feed on the russet smells of wood, the variegated scents of my body, the certainty of being nowhere, yet safe. I'm camping, sailing, the boat pitches and tosses, I'm a migrant. Some people sleep; I am in transit. Conscious or dreaming, I have no definable place. To "have a roof over your head"—the ultimate form of property! But it's not for me. The depths of our nights are unconsciously modeled on our lives. So mine is a place of passage; I am always passing through. This drawer is also a coffin. Not because sleep is a gentler form of death but because there are lives in which, as in a painting by Poussin, death has already taken place. My father's life, for instance, and no doubt many others before that. It's also like when I learned to travel through different languages, dying every time I crossed a frontier, then being reborn elsewhere. But that's enough sensibility from stuck-up Stephanie, the well-known bluestocking!

I'm really more inclined to laugh at the cave I hide deep inside me and carry about with me and encounter in the form of a pullout bed all over the world, like one of a nest of Russian dolls. Immature Stephanie Delacour who imagines she's left the womb! But no, like everyone else she needs a giantess to shelter, reassure, or ultimately swallow her. Ah, there we have it, our intrepid globe-trotter's fantasy: the folklore character with swarms of children coming out from under her skirts. Dream or nightmare? Same difference. And what if the secret sofa were the primitive couch where the Mother, the mother doll, the Old Woman Who Lived in a Shoe, disported herself: the refuge of suppressed agonies, the hiding place of negative orgies, a collage of ingrown fears, impossible longings, clammy furies? If that's the way it is, so be it!

I get up. Push the drawer back under the visible layer of the mahogany divan, so impassive and British. The night I seek is nowhere to be found. Do you think Stephanie Delacour can sleep? Not on your life! She passes through, she moves around, she observes—she's a reporter, that's all. No point in looking any further. Her bed? She carries it around inside her, like her sex organs and her dreams, no one any the wiser. Click!—there, it's tucked away all neat and tidy. Until this evening, then. Until tonight. Until we meet again in invisibility.

◆ CHAPTER THREE ◆

The dinner party Brian referred to duly took place, and I was quite glad to meet Bob's sister and her circle again. Gloria entertained a good deal, though she did so with indifference, if that's not a contradiction in terms, and her invitations lacked warmth. But even "indifference" doesn't entirely convey the formality tinged with anxiety that prevailed at such gatherings.

The house was a mixture of Victorian and Santavarvaran. Gloria's grandparents had built it in memory of the old England they should never have left yet where no truly rigorous-minded person, no one brought up in the puritan tradition that exists only to separate individuals from themselves, could really survive. But at the end of the last century Santa Varvara, while not exactly a paradise for elephant hunters, did offer what might be regarded as virgin soil. Not a territory to be conquered, true, but one that could certainly be educated, developed, and emancipated. Very little had changed in the house itself since the days of the first civilizing migrants, despite the passing of several generations and regardless of political upheavals as inevitable in this part of the world as elsewhere.

The Harrison residence narrowed toward the top like a pyramid, and the uppermost of the three stories had been converted from what was once an attic. The building was L-shaped. On one side a narrow lane led down to a park that must have been a wood a hundred years ago, while on the other side a now well-to-do but discreet residential thoroughfare was called, appropriately enough, England Street. The house virtually turned its back the street, however, for although the main entrance was on that side, an imposing hall with a floor of black and white tiles formed a kind of barricade against undue curiosity from without. A small lawn acted as a foil to a brick facade of such elegant proportions that it could be appreciated only by connoisseurs. A wrought-iron gate and matching railings, together with an old stone wall, seemed designed to act as a bridge between the house they guarded and the more rustic style of the local architecture.

The really comfortable part of the house was safely stowed away at the back, out of sight of passersby. Here, finally, you came upon a huge terraced garden dotted with Italian columns entwined with purple wisteria. Tall orange trees grew in baroque stone urns; beds of roses and lilies filled the air with fragrance all the year round. The whole thing, sloping almost imperceptibly down toward a showy graveled courtyard, recalled the European travels of Gloria's forebears. At the far end of the property, isolating it from the rest of the world, groves of lilac, maple, and hazel grew right down to the bank of the river—the same river whose crimson reflections, to the north, on the other bank, flooded my own laser cube.

Unfortunately the world hadn't stood still during the past century, and through the trees could be glimpsed not merely the inevitable electric pylons and a few old-fashioned dwellings but also the hideous structures of the New Town. According to Gloria there was only one thing to be done: plant more trees and make the wood denser so as to protect this miraculous haven from the tentacles of modernity. Such measures were all the more necessary because a road had already been built beside the river; it wasn't a highway yet, but it soon would be. People already used it to reach the house by car on the garden side. As there could be no question of putting up actual fortifications to shut out the view of the road, a low wall had been built with a tall gate to admit visitors who preferred to avoid driving through the narrow streets of the old quarter of the town. To cut off the house even more thoroughly from the road and also to take advantage of the clement Santavarvaran climate, the old lilac, maple, and hazel trees had been reinforced by others. Acacias, silver poplars, mimosas, oaks, privets, and even fig trees, eucalyptuses, limes, lemons, and bougainvilleas had been planted between the river and the graveled courtyard, to mingle their various rich aromas and their different shades of green. Whether to enclose or to plant was a constant dilemma, one more problem for the mistress of the house to cope with, on top of her professional worries and many other cares the reader either knows or can divine.

The house itself, though not unduly luxurious, was far from easy to run, with all its sitting rooms, studies, bedrooms, staircases, and changes of floor level, together with numerous arrangements origi- nally designed to protect the "privacy" of all Harrisons present and to come. So Gloria was in charge of a veritable labyrinth.

Luckily the labyrinth had a center: the main sitting room and its adjoining dining room, entered via the black-and-white-tiled hall. Leaving the sitting room through a door on the left, you found your- self in what was known as the "green corridor," full of potted plants and other more or less outmoded curiosities; this passage was at right angles to the hall and parallel to the anonymous lane outside. Three interconnected rooms opened off the green corridor. First, Gloria's study, separated from the sitting room by a wall covered in raw silk and hung with an inordinate number of Stan's pictures, which had to be admired by the guests at the ritual dinner parties; a sumptuous pair of French windows led out to the wisterias on the terrace. Next came a bedroom. Third a smaller bedroom, fitted out for the baby soon after it was born. All three rooms gave on to the same inner terrace overlooking the graveled courtyard and with a view of the wood, the river, and the rest of the grounds.

On the second floor, which was much smaller in area than the first floor and linked to the sitting room by a spiral staircase, was the library that had belonged to Gloria's father, a banker as well as a polyglot with a genuine passion for books. To the right of this bibliophile's dream with its endlessly fascinating treasures was Bob's room, kept ready for him permanently "out of fairness and family feeling" (Gloria). But it remained shut up and unused; Gloria's roving brother took no interest in the Harrison heritage and never slept there. To the left of the library Stan had set up his studio; it occupied two floors. The ceiling was level with the roof of the attic, and tall windows let in plenty of the iridescent light so conducive to the painter's art. The corner of the left wing of the house was Jerry's domain: study, bedroom, and bathroom. But it was seldom occupied, as his mother preferred to keep an eye on him in the room prepared as a nursery on the ground floor.

On the third story the part of the attic not included in the studio had been turned into a room for the maid. She was very glad of the independence afforded her by the back stairs leading up from between the kitchen and the dining room in the right wing.

The left wing ended in a circular annex, once intended for the caretaker but now modestly known as the "guest room," though in fact it was a small two-roomed apartment much appreciated by friends visiting in couples or with their families.

But no visitor was staying in the Harrison house that night. It was just an ordinary dinner party. Odile, a Frenchwoman, was an old schoolfriend of Gloria's. Her long gaunt body was clad in a diaphanous red gown with so many frills and flounces she looked like a tree shedding its leaves. She was on "a business trip" with her husband, Pascal: "Pascal Allart of Allart Perfumes." Gloria introduced him to me for the umpteenth time. Her tone implied that while firms like Pascal's were of no importance whatever, that was what people always said, and when you entertain you're supposed to say what people always say.

"Do you know Professor Igor Zorin?"

Did I know him! A loyal worshiper at Gloria's shrine, affecting to be in love with our hostess so as to avoid having to pay attention to any other woman. His appearance, impeccable considering he was a sixty-year-old bachelor, suggested a status higher than that attaching to his job, though that was lofty enough: he was head of the child psychiatry department at St. Ambrose's Hospital. Gloria's son, Jeremy, was one of his private patients.

Larry Smirnoff, editor of the Santa Varvara *Morning Star* and an inveterate womanizer, recently divorced, was given the task of squiring me for the evening.

Brian Watt, seated at the lower end of the table, showed little embarrassment at the uncomfortable scene he had recently inflicted on me but knew his place as a relatively humble member of the staff. He was almost as pink now as he had been during the episode in Bob's apartment, though this time he was flushed with gratitude at my friend Gloria's generosity—or was it charity?

The circle was completed by a gray lady wearing an immaculately tailored gray suit over a white silk blouse. She seemed to be in her fifties, but apart from some streaks of silver in her chignon she seemed little touched by the years. Her eyes were gray; her glance strong and unwavering.

"Pauline Gadeau, Jerry's speech therapist. I've often told you about her. She's my lifeline." (Gloria.)

I was prepared to believe it. With young Jerry, poor Gloria certainly needed a lifeline. But I didn't think I'd ever heard her mention Ms. Gadeau before. Maybe I'd simply forgotten—Gloria chattered away at such a rate after her second glass of champagne. As for speech therapy, I wasn't sure I was all that interested, especially after *my* second glass of champagne. What was the relationship between speech therapy and, for example, phonetics and rhetoric? Not the sort of question to ask Larry Smirnoff. He was probably as inexpert as I in this field—I knew he was ignorant in many others. What can you expect of a journalist? As for Professor Zorin, he was already launched into his act as an elderly beau dancing attendance on Gloria: no chance, obviously, of *his* giving anyone else the benefit of his knowledge of linguistics.

As usual, Jerry put in a brief appearance to say hello to the guests, and once again I was disturbed by the child's inexplicable beauty. He had huge gray—almost black—eyes, amazing beneath a short, neatly

Julia Kristeva

trimmed crop of flaxen hair. The dark eyes lit up features as fine as Chinese calligraphy. His face grew animated as he spoke a few conventional words in his mechanical, rehabilitated voice. ("Child," did I call him? How old was he? Fifteen? He didn't look more than twelve.) Though he'd been born deaf, Jerry overcame his handicap with a natural, mocking gaiety. He looked like a mischievous Pinocchio offering his mother's guests a cocktail mixing freshness with unease.

This ritual out of the way, we settled down around the big oval table. Candles added a touch of old-fashioned intimacy but this was canceled out by the harsh glare of the halogen lamps. Hester served the salmon and the blinis. "Served" is hardly the word, for as usual Mrs. Harrison's maid-cum-housekeeper wore the glummest possible expression. The periwinkle blue eyes and blond curls that might have lent her charm only accentuated her pasty face and unhealthy complexion, while her whole demeanor suggested she hated her job. In her eyes, handing round dishes to a gang of self-satisfied guests was the worst kind of humiliation. Hester Bellini loathed such people, all of them without exception. She hated life itself. And perhaps she hated Gloria most of all. I never understood why Gloria insisted on keeping her on. She was sly and surly, with the sort of criminal look you get in passport photos. Was I contaminated by her malevolence? Be that as it may, I'd never been able to stand her.

Fortunately Gloria's majestic but icy manner lent an air of unreality to everything that moved, lived, ate, or drank beneath her roof. All I had to do was go along with the rest and put away my slice of roast lamb, feel Larry's right knee pressing against my left thigh, and be soothed by his ingratiating prattle. Or rather by its winsome sound, for the subject itself was serious. He'd recently been unearthing the latest financial scandal in Santavarvaran government circles, and the story was about to break. "Believe me, it'll damage the reputation of the president himself!" I didn't need *him* to tell me of such goings-on. Still, though he didn't really like me he regarded himself as an irresistible lover, and I did need the tips he could give me. "Details, please, Larry. Details!"

It was the usual kind of dinner party. Gloria did her best to divert herself, preferably with people from abroad who were passing through. She clung to her own little circle as if hoping it might help her—not to forget everyday life but rather to incorporate it into the grandiose picture she painted of things in order to detach herself more completely. Both from everyday life itself and from the picture.

"Michael sends his apologies. He had to leave at the last minute. An urgent appointment—a gallery in London." (Gloria wanted to convince herself her affair with Michael Fish was so official and like a marriage that to the rest of us his presence at the dinner party seemed inevitable and his absence therefore incongruous.)

No one reacted to what she said. In any case, the tone she used— peremptory and slightly ironical, or perhaps merely artificial—canceled her words out even as she spoke.

Michael Fish was a vulgar businessman who'd dabbled in risky speculations without ever getting caught at anything illegal and who'd lived, as is usually the case, way beyond his means. That is, until he met Gloria and discovered the possibilities of modern art. He then turned himself into a dealer and with considerable profit to himself launched the hitherto unknown and unrecognized work of Gloria's late husband, Stan Novak.

I'd liked Stanislas and went on admiring those of his paintings that still hung in Gloria's sitting room and in all the other rooms in the house. I'd liked his quiet shyness, his clumsiness, and the deep-set green eyes that never met mine except in a sudden riveting stab, after which they'd be lowered again. He used to make me laugh with his mania for painting distorted female faces reminiscent of Willem de Kooning. But Stan added touches derived from Santavarvaran sorcery that made his pictures less comic and more angry-looking than de Kooning's airy visions. When Novak took a rest from his female vampires, he dreamed in landscapes of sandy yellow with intermittent flashes of emerald green or dark red. I wasn't sure what I admired most about these pictures—their strength or their gentleness. One of them hung over the piano, on the wall covered with raw silk, some distance away from where I was now sitting. Stan hadn't been the married type, and it had taken all Gloria's snobbishness and obstinate pragmatism to make their union appear more or less normal. Nor had Jerry's birth improved matters. After it, Stan was seen more and more rarely at Gloria's dinner parties. In the end she heard he'd died of an overdose in some Indian ashram where he'd been living with an old mistress, whether ancient or former wasn't clear.

My friend had met this news with the indifference that had been typical of her for I don't know how long—a neutrality just tinged with arrogance. But this didn't stop her making a confidante of me whenever I was around. Indifference, whether true or assumed, lets a person speak of what's impossible as if it were nothing out of the ordinary. So I knew everything, including a lot of stuff that was far from interesting.

Before Stan died the two of them had arrived at the stage of enmity where, amid the incurable debris left by reckless desire, a still active hostility takes the form of smoldering blankness. This state of affairs might be thought monotonous and boring. Not so. Gloria savored the whole range of feelings that can be generated by a passion damaged but not yet spent. A childlike affection did still survive between the two; the former lovers sometimes indulged in the old infantile caresses. But this bland felicity gradually froze, closed in on itself as if they were dead to one another. Neither could see or hear any message emanating from his or her ex-partner. Both their transmitters went on functioning, but the bulletins they issued, though sent out within close range, were indecipherable. For each of them a kind of negative hallucination, a fragment made up of images and sounds, took the place of what had once been Stan or Gloria. They hadn't made love for years. His infidelities and her self-sufficiency, not to mention the problems of snoring and putting on weight, ended in a tacit agreement to sleep in separate rooms. The separate rooms were like a kind of cold store containing a complicity that had once burned with the flames of excess but that now, while not regretting those early fires, was not prepared to pay the price they involve. Except . . . perhaps . . . why not? . . . with someone else. For the surprise, for the novelty, for something to do. Okay . . . if the occasion arose . . . in certain circumstances . . . maybe . . .

This delicate balance was so fragile it deceived neither of them. A word out of place, a touch of fatigue, even a faraway look caused by some outside conflict but lingering on at home—even such trifles told them their peaceful coexistence was founded on dead desire. Or perhaps on pride—on a contest as to who could best contain his or her contempt for the other. Stan never asked Gloria any questions. He didn't inquire about her work (what are you translating? how is it going?). Or about herself (her health, makeup, dress, blouse, shoes—so many details are really important in a woman's life). Or about her mother or her brother. Still less about her father, whom he'd never met (old man Harrison had been dead for ten years. But even so . . .). Nor about Jerry, for of course it was all so painful for a sensitive artist—that was quite understandable, wasn't it? Gloria, on the other hand, never stopped interrogating Stan about the awesome and mysterious world of art. But her questions always struck him as incongruous, irrelevant, and naive, especially as she always posed them in the strident schoolmarmy voice she adopted in order to quell the frightened little girl cowering inside her. Stan hadn't the time to work out the meaning of such exchanges and wrote Gloria off as tactless, loud, insufferable. In short, like all mature couples and settled families, they no longer had anything to say to one another.

That was the situation when Stan, without warning, died, and Gloria was left a widow. A funny kind of widow, people said, and she did her best to live up to the description. She owed it to Stan, with his love of gambling, his quest for amusement, his nonchalance. Wouldn't he have been proud of a wife who enjoyed her bereave-

ment? It was her duty to be a merry widow. Liberated at last—but
from what?—she was obscenely arrogant. I couldn't quite understand all this, but then I wasn't really interested in understanding it
and lent only a vague ear to rumor.

Michael Fish was invented soon afterward, and Gloria set her mind on
transforming that unattractive Bloch into an enviable Charles Swann.
But the results didn't come up to her expectations. The character
involved wasn't capable of change. For Gloria's friends, only Fish's
success at selling Stan's pictures and turning him into a star at last
really justified, if justification were needed, the elegant translator's
attachment to the playboy-cum-businessman. "He's an excellent
lover and very attractive to women," Gloria would explain with a per-
functory grimace, imagining people would think it typically amusing
of her to explain the reasons for her penchant for Michael Fish, which
Santa Varvara society regarded as a complete mystery. It shocked
people for a while, then, like everything else, was absorbed into the
general boredom.

"He just phoned. He sends his regards and asks you to act just as if
he were here." (We were clearly inclined to forget all about Michael,
and this was Gloria's way of reminding us of his existence.)

"That's hardly necessary, is it, darling? Professor Zorin fills in for
him perfectly!" (Odile, caustic.)

"You might be more tactful, my dear!" (Pascal Allart, jealous.)

"I was referring to his place at the table, my sweet. As for the rest,
you've always had too much imagination. And I didn't know you
were still so interested." (Odile, growing increasingly sour. She'd
had too much to drink and was alluding to an old flirtation between
Gloria and her husband.)

"And there was I hoping to have dinner at last with the perfect
couple!" (Larry always spoke quite audibly when he supposed he was
whispering to me. And he couldn't tell the difference between humor
and caricature.)

"You must be joking, darling. But perhaps you were talking about Gloria?" (Odile, adding treachery to acrimony.)

"Gloria will always be an apple of discord. How could it be otherwise?—she's so beautiful! She'll have us fighting duels over her one of these days, and it will all end in a bloodbath—mark my words! Charm like hers is a sort of witchcraft." (Igor Zorin, ignoring the Frenchwoman, was playing the doting lover who tries at the same time to be detached. It seems psychoanalysts have taken to blurting out their own bloodthirsty instincts. They bottle themselves up in their consulting rooms only to let rip at dinner parties!)

"I prefer suicide to murder. In love, honor is an internal matter. Jealousy is a personal defect converted into hatred of the other." (Brian, on the strength of his own irreproachable angst, was trying to raise the level of the debate.)

"You may be right, philosophically speaking. But as a woman I don't reason like that. Perhaps I don't reason at all. I simply loathe any woman who's being made love to instead of me!" (Odile, with one of her usual birdlike glances, came and sat next to me at the other side of the table.)

"That's a fine version of feminism, I must say! What do you say, Pascal?" (Larry, always unable to resist a joke and glad to cause trouble between any couple who thought their partnership could last longer than his own.)

"Who's talking about feminism? Perhaps it's just a question of passion." (Professor Zorin, whose theories were as inflexible as his posture, was trying to open our ears to the truth and spare us the private psychodrama.) "Passion between women, I mean! Anyway, all passion is homosexual. 'Both sexes will die, but separately.' Who said that, Miss Delacour?"

"Proust, perhaps?" (Me, not very sure of myself, and more and more oppressed by the disagreeable atmosphere hanging over the dinner party.)

"Alfred de Vigny, in *The Wrath of Samson*, if my memory serves." (Good grief, the gray speech therapist had a strange taste in reading matter! She spoke as if relating some spicy item of gossip, which had the effect of melting the gray ice of her usual demeanor. But I didn't have time to be surprised. Nor did anyone else pay any attention to Pauline Gadeau's erudition; people who sit at the foot of the dinner table are supposed to be seen and not heard.)

"But of course someone who looks like a man can really be a woman deep down. And that, you'll admit, rather complicates the professor's theory." (Brian, sly and self-important.)

"I know what you're getting at, young man. Don't think I don't know about my own feminine side. I'll even tell you a secret: it's the woman in me that loves women." (Zorin, being provocative.)

"Watch out, my dear Igor—you're pushing it a bit far! If you mean to say you love Gloria as one woman loves another, and if we also take Odile's confession into account, you could also hate our hostess more fiercely than a man would who *didn't*, to use your expression, know about his own feminine side." (Larry, as aggressive as ever.)

"Nothing escapes our expert on the rights of man, does it, Larry? I'm an analyst, don't forget, so I've been analyzed myself. I know both what you know and what you don't know. But I personally don't need to give way to my instincts." (Zorin.)

"*I* do. But I keep it secret. And that adds to the pleasure, I assure you. Odile agrees with me, don't you, darling? On the other hand, Professor, I'm afraid your restraint must be very dull. I feel quite sorry for you." (Pascal Allart.)

"There's no such thing as secrecy these days, my dear; everything gets known somehow. You're perverse, that's all (notice that I don't say perverted). And it suits you beautifully." (Gloria, being coquettish.)

"I'd leave you to it and go home to bed if the roast lamb wasn't so delicious!" (Odile, being accommodating.)

"Everything either is known or will be known." (Brian, regretfully, with a meaning glance at Gloria.)

I look over at a landscape, blue and yellow and streaked with emerald green, and concentrate on enjoying the upside-down apple tart. I don't join in the chitchat or even think about Stan Novak or Michael Fish. It's another of those times when I'm overcome with under-standing—in a kind of mental sauna that anesthetizes disgust. Our access to what other people experience, whether they're men or women, living or dead, is bound to be fragmentary, limited to the ves-tiges they leave behind in colors, sounds, or words. We can't appre-hend them unless we're lucky enough to be able to forget our own pre-occupations, large or small, and to touch not another body, nor even another name hiding in- or outside ourselves, but a vibration that's usually unattainable and that no personal pronoun can convey. The ocher sunshine that lit the mornings of my childhood, punctuated by a beloved velvet voice: I'm dreaming in Stan's picture. Champagne inclines me to passion, or else to metaphysics. But this doesn't affect the conversation. That's taking its natural course.

"In any group there are always two or three males who act as studs, if you see what I mean. Ambitious women make use of them and pass them around, setting up more or less secret links among themselves by means of these unconscious carriers of sperm and fashionable ideas, who are thus also circulators of power." (Under the influence of alcohol Brian tended to see things on the grand scale.)

"But the opposite is equally true. In Santa Varvara as in Versailles—if you'll pardon the presumptuous comparison—men make use of cer-tain influential women—and women *are* getting more and more influ-ential, aren't they? Here, just as at the French court (making all due allowances), power is merely a fiction. Where the men are reduced to performing administrative chores instead of participating in real rep-resentative democracy, a country is governed by public opinion. In other words, by the women. By women journalists, for example. You see what I mean?" (Professor Zorin's lecture on sociology was a polite way of saying feminization is inherent in any society, ancient or mod-ern, that values show more than reality.)

"Just a minute, Professor! What you're implying is that the media govern everything nowadays because they mold public opinion—is that right? I couldn't agree with you more. But if I may say so I think I've noticed a few men in the media. Am I imagining that I have met some male journalists. What do you say, Larry?" (Pascal Allart, with the air of bright impartiality affected by male spies.)

"Don't be deceived by appearances! Fundamentally we're completely feminized. There aren't any men left! There'll never be any again! But don't think I'm complaining! Certainly not! I'm like Zorin—I love the feminine part of my personality." (Larry Smirnoff, not content with playing ordinary footsie under the table, was now positively grinding my toes into the floor.)

"In a nutshell, gentlemen, you believe the only choice is still *catins* or *Catons*—between scrubbers and statesmen—as they used to say in Paris?" (Me, calmly putting my oar in despite the assaults of my neighbor and adding the translation to make sure everyone got the pun.)

Silence. One of those moments when it's clear a dinner's drawing to a close.

"Well, well! I don't know if I understand you correctly, Stephanie dear, but I think you'll agree that men start by telling us we rule the world and end up stealing our own qualities! What's really putting the modern world in a tizzy is that the gentlemen are envious of the ladies! Q.E.D!" (Odile, with her silent crow of satisfaction that's almost a yawn.)

Spent the night with Larry. Passable. No more than that. His reputation is of course exaggerated. Slept till brunch in the big double bed. I wasn't going to have *him* in my mahogany drawer. We could have spent the afternoon together; he would have liked nothing better than a chance to improve on the previous night's performance, which had suffered from the effects of the dinner party. But I had things to read and wanted to be on my own.

I like spending an idle Sunday afternoon in Santa Varvara, in my cube of light by the river, targeted by the steady rays of the sun as it sets over the far bank. I don't need anything, and nobody needs me.

What could be better? A hot bath, some Vivaldi, then an early bed with a Christa Wolf novel to kid myself I'm clever, the world is grim, and I can sleep without having to take any pills. The rights of man as they exist in Santa Varvara, or rather as they don't, can wait till tomorrow, and so can my editor. If he tries to get in touch with me the answering machine is on. I won't bother with the fax until Monday morning, after I've had a nice cup of tea.

But why should the paper be obsessed with me? Where did I get that idea from?

There isn't any message from the paper on Monday morning, October 17. But there is Northrop Rilsky's music-lover's voice.

And I rush round to Gloria's place.

◆ CHAPTER FOUR ◆

I was sure my father had loved me. He always seemed busy with his own affairs and wanted me to do boring or impossible things like ice skating or becoming a chess champion. But when he looked look at me out of those misty blue eyes, he seemed to be gazing inside himself at someone amazingly intelligent, perhaps even beautiful, someone who was worthy of immeasurable affection. In the absence of other evidence and given my mother's self-effacing nature, I'd concluded at an early age that the idol I could see reflected from those wondering eyes could only be myself, Stephanie Delacour. Since my father's death I'd always consulted him mentally about any question with two or more possible answers. And now once again, as I expected, my father approved of my decision. He agreed it was quite possible to be both a detective and a journalist. The fact that I was a woman meant I had two advantages: intuition and perseverance.

So once more my path was crossing that of Northrop Rilsky. That wasn't very surprising, seeing I'd deliberately chosen to stick my nose into what was none of my business. But this time it concerned Gloria. Why Gloria, for heavens' sake? "Fate's always striking at the same people—usually those who are depressed," said the captain. Not content with playing the violin as a hobby, he also prided himself on his knowledge of psychology and even of psychoanalysis.

Right. Gloria's mistakes were common knowledge, even though attempts had been made to cover them up. There was her absurd marriage to Stanislas Novak, "the local artistic genius, the Leonardo da Vinci and Don Juan of Santa Varvara" (Rilsky). Then there was Jerry, the shock of his birth "or rather the trauma, the devotion, the passion" (Rilsky again). Lastly, "the ridiculous Michael Fish" (Rilsky, as always). Gloria would never be able to pass Fish off as a connoisseur, especially to someone like me, who knew Proust by heart and could tell the difference between the sublime Swann and a mere art dealer, however sexy, who on top of everything else was a native of Santa Varvara. In short, the whole story was either vulgar or tragic according to your point of view. In any case it did nothing to explain Gloria's murder. Still less the savagery with which one or more people had mutilated her corpse.

"I presume you've questioned the neighbors?" (Rilsky, offhandedly.)

"Two of the houses in the alley behind the Harrison place are closed up and empty. And the third belongs to a retired couple who didn't hear anything out of the ordinary during the day and who wear earplugs at night. The kindergarten in England Street, just opposite, is shut on the weekend. Nothing to report in the little square, naturally. And the gas station closes at ten P.M. on Saturday. So we haven't got anywhere so far, sir. It was only to be expected." (Popov, phlegmatic, chewing gum.)

"Stabbed in the left breast. Sudden attack. Wound widest at point of impact. Write everything down, Popov, needless to say." (Rilsky, cleaning his spectacles with a mauve silk handkerchief.)

"Right you are, sir." (Rilsky's assistant followed him like a shadow, as in every self-respecting detective story.)

"We'll get the trajectory of the blow and a cross section of the wound from the lab when they've dissected the pectoral muscle. But—tell me later if I turn out to be wrong—I'm already as certain of their verdict as if I had the photos here in front of me: an oval orifice between the ribs, near the sternum, made by a very sharp blade; considerable infiltration of blood."

"Very possible, sir. And therefore probable."

"Not probable, Popov—certain! And you'll move heaven and earth to find that very sharp blade. Needless to say."

"Right you are, sir."

"It's our job—or yours, rather, Popov—to find both the weapon and the hand that wielded it. It goes without saying."

"Just so, sir."

"And I can tell you now there's another oval-shaped puncture in the pericardium—smaller but vitally important. And near this smaller wound there must be a big bruise on the thorax, because there are a lot of blood vessels in that part of the body."

Rilsky went on mentally probing the wound in Gloria's left breast, beneath the torn and blood-soaked bodice of her splendid satin gown. As he did so he threw several triumphant glances at the forensic expert, whose efforts he happily wrote off as useless there and then. For Santa Varvara's chief detective was a master of all specialities, especially those of other people. However, he seldom succeeded in his own, which was supposed to consist in finding the guilty party.

Rilsky evidently fancied himself in the clothes he was wearing, chosen as if for a visit to the theater. His perfectly cut suit, à la Cary Grant, was of dark gray alpaca with a lighter stripe and obviously just back from the cleaner. Out of his many shirts, ranging cautiously from white to pastel shades, he'd selected for today, the seventeenth of October, the pale pink one. It was set off by a paisley necktie: scarlet curlicues on a navy blue ground. His spruce appearance, which usually clashed horribly with the grim affairs he was supposed to unravel, was today strangely in harmony with the dramatic scene of Gloria's decollation. Rather than making him look like an intellectual, as he hoped, his thick-lensed horn-rimmed spectacles gave him an air of stupefaction that reflected his timorous nature. I saw this as a sign of the professional inadequacies fate had sent me to help him avoid. His assistant, Andrew Popov, unable to compete with his boss's elegance, allowed himself a provocative gesture: he was wearing jeans along with a sweatshirt and a leather jacket. This ultranegligent—or ultramodern—get-up lent Popov's apparently obsequious words a tinge of irony. He'd already covered the whole room with his camcorder, including every visible detail of the headless corpse.

"As you'll see in due course, there'll be another wound, smaller than the other two, in the right ventricle, near the sternum. This will confirm that the murder weapon was a sharp knife. The wound must have proved fatal because the blood flowed into the pericardium and slowed down the functioning of the heart. Do you follow me, Popov?"

"Yes, sir."

"If you were more open-minded, less ready to agree with what other people say, you could have objected that the victim might have been dead before she was stabbed, as the wound indicates. She might, for instance, have taken an overdose of sleeping pills or some other drug, as suggested by the bottle found beside the body. Don't touch it—I'd rather the doc sealed it up like the rest of the clues. Needless to say."

"Right you are, sir."

"Or she could have been strangled. For since the head is missing, as you'll have noticed, my dear Popov—"

"Yes, I did notice that, sir."

"—we don't know if there were any marks on the neck. So we can't for the moment say whether death occurred before or after the knife attack. That's why I need you and your lab, Doc, after all. The amount of blood you find in the pericardium will give us the answer. Of course I don't rule out the possibility of sudden death from inhibitory shock, in which case the results of the autopsy and any other tests will be hopelessly normal."

This idea rather appealed to me. If anyone in the world was likely to have died from "inhibitory shock"—and the term was apt from several points of view—it was certainly Gloria! Rilsky would diagnose it as sudden death due to "vagal stimulation": overstimulation of a sensitive area (such as the skin, larynx, genital organs, neck of the uterus, eardrums, solar plexus, or the like) caused by some psychological or emotional disturbance. And who would be more emotional than

Gloria, terrified by an assailant? Even if she hadn't been attacked she was an easy prey to fear: fear repressed, vagal, vaginal, urethral, carotidal, or solar. Fear takes an infinite number of forms. Not that that makes the murderer any less responsible. Far from it. Even so . . .

The forensic expert, used to working with Rilsky and not particularly bothered by his colleague's omniscience, was now conscientiously stowing away his samples in bottles, test tubes, and little plastic bags.

"A professional job, I'd say." (The expert bent over for one last look at the neat decapitation.) "Carried out several hours after death, judging by the very moderate loss of blood from the upper part of the torso. You'll have noticed that granulation has started around the wound in the chest, which means the stabbing must have been done about two days ago. Whereas neither fibroplastic fibers nor capillaries are observable in the region of the neck, or rather the absence of neck, so the decapitation is definitely more recent than the death."

Granulation or not, recent or otherwise, the word *moderate* seemed inappropriate in connection with such carnage, an act of butchery of which the perpetrator had airily, as if by chance, removed what for me was the essential and by no means a "moderate" part of the person concerned, not at all just "the upper part of the torso." And it seemed to me there was plenty of blood around, given the saturated carpet and the stained gown. Where the famous sharp blade had struck all the left half of the bodice was turning purple.

"It would be good practice for the anatomy class at the university! If the circumstances hadn't been so far from academic, Northrop, I'd have suggested all this might be just a medical students' prank!" (The quack, with the bad taste usual in members of his profession, was having a little fun at the cop's expense.)

"You're rather short on imagination, Doc, needless to say!" (Northrop Rilsky, the vexed humanist.)

"You're right there, sir." (Popov, sardonic.)

"As for the theory that there were two assailants, allow me to congratulate you! That really does beat the band! I won't keep you any longer, Doctor. Thanks in advance for the results of your tests. Needless to say I'll await them with interest." (Rilsky to the doctor, who was already slamming the door.)

At last Captain Rilsky, who'd already tried several times to catch my eye, only to turn away whenever he succeeded, affected to notice my presence.

"Well, Miss Delacour, what a surprise—and, I must add, what luck!—to see you back in Santa Varvara! You seem to turn up at every dramatic moment in our history, and heaven knows there are plenty of them! No, no—the pleasure's entirely mine! I've thought about you a lot lately. Was it yesterday? Or the day before? I'm quite serious—I'd have liked to play you Yehudi Menuhin's latest recording— someone just sent it to me from London, and I know you admire him almost as much as I do. But fate deprives us of that pleasure, at least for the moment. You'll forgive me if I take a statement from you as a witness, won't you? Not as a suspect, no question of that, even though it might strike someone else as quite an interesting idea—though not me, needless to say. So just as a witness, then, like all the other guests at the dinner party on Saturday the fifteenth that I understand pre- ceded the events with which we're concerned. You *were* at the dinner party, if I'm not mistaken?"

Rilsky enjoyed spinning out all these phrases, trying simultane- ously to pull the wool over my eyes and make an old-fashioned but genuine pass.

I went along with it.

CHAPTER FIVE

Okay, Gloria might have committed suicide. She *should* have committed suicide (I would have done so if I'd been her): blotted out Jerry's sufferings by blotting out Jerry in person and then done away with herself, the perpetrator of the crime. I'm sure she thought about it more than once; I could tell from her averted eyes, from the livid mask that would suddenly replace for a moment her usual calm indifference. Not that she ever mentioned such a thing in my presence. I wasn't even sure she'd confided in Odile. Anyway, now was the time to check it out. Gloria wasn't one of those women who are emancipated postfeminists in the morning and in the afternoon try to persuade themselves the ultimate magic of the second sex resides—surprise, surprise—in the pleasures of the bedchamber, the conquest of young men, or the exquisite depressions they suffer deep inside themselves. Whether because of an atavistic Russian influence that reached her by way of her mother or from the hypnotic effect of reading Dostoyevsky, Gloria believed suffering, pleasure, and boredom were the special prerogative of aristocratic souls. But she also knew that pain can burn infinite time down to an infinitely small speck: pain is the truth of time and becomes identical with it by assuming the right to suspend it. Should she flee from the world and retreat with Jerry into a convent? It wasn't impossible; she must always have been prepared to do that, but first she risked one last folly, the Michael Fish escapade. Or should she just swallow the contents of a container of sleeping pills, of the empty bottle that Lieutenant Popov filmed in close-up on the bedside table by the headless corpse? Had her assailants attacked her body when she herself was already gone? But who? And why? Or had she been sound asleep, unconscious, stupefied, incapable of resistance, but aware, in the depths of her toxic slumber, of the aggressors' hatred? A hatred that must have reassured her as a physical confirmation of the distress the world had inflicted on her all her life but that she'd stubbornly defied day after day until she no longer knew whether it was real or a hallucination. But there was no doubt in that fatal fraction of a second when she was face to face with hate incarnate. Evil outside time. Death.

Just as she was at the end of her tether she became pregnant. It was the first time and probably the last, so she had to keep the baby. Never was a woman so happy as Gloria during the nine months she was carrying Jerry. A solitude for two, Bernini's ecstasy with the future added on. So the trauma that followed was all the more cruel. When the baby was born, the midwife's jubilation was forced. The doctor stammered out a few superlatives. As you may imagine, Stan couldn't be present at the birth: he was at one of the twice-weekly meetings of the sect of which he was now an influential member and that ably supported both his inspiration and his sales. He was very pleased by the birth of his son but wasn't around much afterward. You know how it is with artists: a sudden irresistible need to work with the current favorite model; lunch to a with-it lady reporter; or a TV interview for the coming presidential campaign (in Santa Varvara the artist's point of view is so much sought after at election time). And somehow such things always coincide with a doctor's appointment, a visit to the social security office, a birth, a fit of anxiety. On the third day Jerry was placed under observation. Nothing definite, medicine isn't an exact science, and a trauma, contrary to common belief, may strike like lightning but slowly become permanent. Eventually Jerry was diagnosed as deaf. Eventually Gloria was told. He couldn't hear, he never would be able to hear, and he wouldn't be able to speak either. There was always physiotherapy of course. Specialists could perform miracles these days. It would be unreasonable, and above all premature, to panic.

The specialists tried to be reassuring: "It's just an average case, you know. A shortfall of between forty and seventy decibels. We'll give him a special aid, and everything will be fine, you'll see. He won't even need to use sign language; he'll be able to talk and go to an ordinary school." She listened avidly; she hoped. Then, in the end, she stopped listening. All she could hear was Jerry's monotonous little voice with its strange nasal twang and its words sometimes rapped out fast and sometimes drawled. His dreadful toneless singsong rose at the end of words and sentences as if he was asking a question, always the same one, a continual plea. Shrill tones, almost no low ones: the voice of a girl interrogating a speechless sphinx. Gloria realized he'd have to be taught everything. First it would be necessary to enter into his senses: his eyes and what they saw, his lips and what they tasted, his nostrils and what they smelled. Then this shared universe would have to be named, and spoken language constructed as if it was a foreign tongue. Translated. But, after all, that was her profession, her vocation, her fate. Like Stan, Jerry was an optical glutton. He devoured images with his eyes and soon began drawing nourishment from pictures, either from the originals that he and Gloria used to look at together or from the reproductions she kept him supplied with. In their sensory communion, painting became their first foreign language: their German, their Russian, their Chinese. Then she'd transpose everything into words. Jerry took it all in, smiled, waited. She guessed from the beginning it was no use hoping he'd ask questions, and he never did. So she anticipated them, imagining what he wanted to know when he brought out his jerky, shapeless phrases, which nevertheless always had a rising tension suggesting a desire, a quest. I question you, you question me, and the game we play teaches you the question that's in your voice but not in your words. I play, you play; I translate, you learn; we play, you speak; it's happened, it's always happening; it will never happen, but it's coming, better and better; you give me pleasure, it gives you pleasure; we'll go on, we'll never part; I'll translate you till the end. You will endlessly translate.

Gloria didn't panic. She clung on to poor little Jerry. A love. Her love. The only one. The only one that was certain. That was forever. People say babies cling to their mothers as monkeys do. Not true. It's the opposite. If Gloria hadn't had Jerry to cling to she wouldn't have survived. Survived what? Life, Santa Varvara, childhood memories, all the things that are really unimportant. Not forgetting Stan, her genius: the Catholic, alcoholic, polygamous artist she adored above all else. She wouldn't have been able to take it without Jerry. Jerry was a gift from Heaven, her complement, her crutch. She devoted herself to him body and soul, as they say. Was she a saint? Nothing of the sort. Devotion is a kind of devouring. Gloria lavished on Jerry attentions that no man, or woman, had ever bestowed on her. So much so that Jerry, disadvantaged from birth, had trouble coping with it. Physiological handicap plus an anxious, overprotective mother: the pediatricians, child psychiatrists, and other gifted neurologists were baffled. To Gloria's great despair, which was also a kind of rejoicing. It was clear you couldn't rely on anyone but yourself. And that "self" of yours was everything for Jerry—mother, father, grandfather, grandmother, aunt, boy cousin, girl cousin, godfather, godmother, doctor, shrink, friend, lover, matrix, womb, ears, mouth, stomach, anus, God—and that wasn't all. The responsibility was enough to fill a life already busy enough, in particular with translations, for in addition to everything else it fell to Gloria to try to keep the wolf from the door. It's common knowledge that geniuses like Stan are by definition at odds with society (and vice versa) and therefore not very good providers. Luckily there was the Harrison residence, inherited from Gloria's highly respectable family, a luxurious mansion that was the envy of all their friends and that no one would have dreamed of selling at any price.

Stanislas was traumatized too, in his way. He'd never wanted to be a father—he thought parenthood unaesthetic—and could never see that the unfortunate infant had anything in common with him. The child seemed to suffer terribly, which was utterly out of keeping with the well-being supposed to emanate from the work of a true artist, whose relaxed and happy nature isn't meant to have to endure life's common hardships. To Stan, women's desires and men's ambitions never seemed so incompatible as when he was confronted with young Jerry.

On such occasions Stan's fair round cheeks would grow hollow and his eyes look stern, with that painter's gaze that doesn't simply look at things but bores into them so as to extract a movement, a motion, that has always tormented the artist's own flesh but is now given form. And with form, temporarily, peace. As he looked at Jerry, Stan's expression became at once appealing and angry, like that of a hungry baby. His son's misfortunes reached out to him from within, from a secret wound that hitherto he'd been able to ignore but that now without warning burst forth into the light. Was it his own fault, Stan wondered, or did the aggression come from other people? If so, who were they? He'd have liked to ask for help—for the first and last time in his life to ask other people for help. But who was he to turn to? In such situations there's never anyone there. In any situation, for that matter. And Gloria, who liked understanding things and didn't often deny herself the pleasure, realized it was no use asking Stan for anything. "Everything to do with our marriage is a perfect match," she'd say jokingly to her friend Odile, "except our characters." And a little while later, again quoting a famous marquise: "I share quite a common misfortune, but I'm not entirely sure whether it's that I don't love my husband or that he doesn't love me."

Stan was the kind of man whose erotic pleasure depended on his partner's refusal to comply. This bleak situation came as a shock to Gloria, but eventually she learned to make the best of it. If you can't rely on the person you love, you don't rely on anyone. Instead you acquire the fragile but unconquerable strength of sand. The years go by, and the sand, a vast and hopeless solitude, still relies only on itself. Until one day a friend of no particular consequence offers to save you time by parking your car for you, or a neighbor you hardly know says, for no special reason, that she'll look after Jerry for a few hours. Then suddenly the sand sees that it has been piling up for ten years on a dead planet, while all the time, somewhere else, close by, there was another life that was simple and possible. But how are you to reach it when you're deep in a desert of isolation, a waste where the grains of sand have lost the habit of mutual support? It would have taken a tidal wave or torrents of rain to turn that sand into a friendly, malleable solid. But floods like that never happen except in myths. So Gloria would return to her wilderness more friable and frail than ever.

How is it some people seem to lack depth? Without lapsing into undue pessimism, Gloria concluded that what's called depth is the ability to suffer tactfully. She didn't want to flatter herself, but in her opinion what was really needed was a quiet strength. Some weak people collapse; others close up the shutters of their souls and run away. Stan, who was flayed alive by the slightest adversity, protected himself by exposing his soul in his paintings. This got rid of suffering, but with it went depth and even the soul itself. It's a well-known fact that painters have no soul: they exist only on the surface. Except for geniuses, who by giving depth to what is visible open the eyes of our souls, and incidentally those of our bodies too.

In the end Gloria found herself alone with the child. For anyone else he'd have been a burden, but for her he was her only chance. "To be of use to someone. To achieve the impossible. Perhaps that's what love is. What do you think, Pauline?" she'd naively ask Jerry's speech therapist. Pauline would smile good-naturedly and say nothing. She knew very well that in terms of Gloria's definition very few people could claim to "love" or "be loved." But self-denial is a delusion of grandeur disguising trauma. Pauline was in a good position to know this, but her job was to make others speak, not to speak herself; still less to speak about herself.

Meanwhile Gloria learned all anyone needed to know about transforming a "handicapped" child into a "normal" one. Careful to avoid using either word, she taught Jerry to struggle to live among other people. Her love for her son didn't really blind her to his handicaps, but it did make her idealize him to such a degree that she sometimes forgot the things that made him different from other people's children. In spite of all the physiotherapy, the little deaf boy's speech was hesitant, the thoughts it reflected rudimentary. But the pitying or hostile looks that greeted them only produced in Gloria the kind of bitterness that increases pride and love. True suffering is silent. Gloria had no use either for the overdone compassion of neighbors, the cold sanctimoniousness of fellow parishioners, or the unease of ordinary children when they found themselves alone for a moment with Jerry's strangeness. (She called them "ordinary" children because she disliked the word "normal"; what does it mean, anyway?) She tried to avoid those charitable souls, perverted Samaritans, who are always ready to do good to others but present a hefty bill for their kindness. She learned to look not into but above people's eyes and to think only of the things she could still try to do to help Jerry.

"He thinks I think he doesn't suffer." "She thinks I'm just like everybody else." Perhaps both mother and son played at not understanding one another, and as a result Jerry did gradually come to be like everyone else. Almost. And Gloria, so confident of her own self-control, sometimes forgot to be careful. Then those steady eyes of hers would mist over.

But she and Jerry were not to remain walled up in their solitude for long. Pauline Gadeau soon brought into their world her professional competence, her perfect but unobtrusive tact. It was a great stroke of luck for Gloria. Pauline understood and faced up to things. This gave Jerry more space, and he used it to breathe more freely or, in pedagogical terms, to "make progress."

◆ CHAPTER SIX ◆

In the end the child came to possess Gloria. Her whole world—sex, ambition, personal appeal, professional success, feminine charm, sessions at the gym, riding, visits to the hairdresser, outings, dinner parties, cocktail parties, social contacts of all kinds—virtually everything had gone, disappeared. There was nothing left. But Gloria hardly noticed. She had no regrets. She was living her life to the full. Possession can take the form of a single love absorbing the entire universe. Absorbing you as well; whether that leaves you in the world or outside it, it makes no difference. There *is* no more "you." When you're possessed you're ruled not by external forces but by inner self-evident necessity. Jerry didn't force Gloria to do anything; no one asked anything of her. On the contrary. Lots of mothers whose children "have difficulties" send them to special institutions. ("Difficulties"—that's how people put it now that everyone's against racism and distinction is regarded as discrimination.) There are plenty of these places, all more or less satisfactory. Anyhow, what does it matter? To every man his own fate, and devil take the hindmost. "It's congenital," old Mrs. Harrison used to say; she simply didn't understand her daughter's obsession. "You ought to think of yourself a bit. Have you considered those places in Switzerland? They're very well spoken of. And really, you should be more modern: I was reading a book the other day that said there's no such thing as the maternal instinct. The author proves it conclusively, and she's a young woman just like you. You ought to read that book. Move with the times, get a breath of fresh air, take up a cause, be a feminist—*do* something or other!"

But as often happens with "traditional" couples belonging to our parents' generation, who never spend a night apart in fifty years of married life, Mrs. Harrison, who hadn't known what sickness was till then, started suffering from asthma when she was widowed and died two years after her husband. Then there was no one left to give poor Gloria the benefit of a little common sense.

But she hadn't even noticed her mother's insensitivity, still less resented it.

Her possession had no trace of resentment in it. It was just a kind of concentration; humiliation converted into serenity. When a wound changes into a shield you become invulnerable. But how had Gloria attained that refinement of trauma where it can be savored like iced vodka: with no sense of either pleasure or intoxication? "The Super-ego!" declared Professor Igor Zorin, Jerry's shrink. "Of course," said Gloria, less to please him than because she was fond of theories. Still, were all that many father's daughters incapable of such blank folly, such bloodless passion, such kosher discipline? The pleasure of renunciation nourishes anorexic saints as often as it produces heroines. It can undermine a woman's customary reserve and make her dance to a tune by Ray Charles, alone, in a mauve dress, on a deserted dance floor. In the dark, her eyes looking inward. Inaccessible, unshakable. Ready for anything. Or nothing. A twin of death, a colored version of death. Until Michael Fish comes on the scene.

Great sportsmen and virtuosi experience this ultimate absorption of the self when they're possessed by what's called technique. This is really a paradoxical passion in which the whole personality is transposed into something else: a code, a language, rituals, rules. Being's self outside the self.

One sorrow made a breach in Gloria's citadel. Though Jerry's speech was admittedly improved and better and better constructed thanks to Pauline Gadeau—nor of course should Gloria's efforts be forgotten—his words had no real content. Jerry never told his mother anything she hadn't already told him, anything she hadn't expected, foreseen, programmed. Every word, phrase, or story was merely a kind of prosthesis, rarely containing the surprises that give parents so much delight, the sudden flashes of brilliance that make mothers and fathers think their offspring will turn out to be geniuses. Jerry was reliable enough. He sometimes returned the ball very neatly. But he never came up and smashed from the net. Though he was extremely sensitive to mood and to variations in nature, animals, and people, when it came to exchanging ideas his intelligence seemed very limited and lacking in invention. Gloria had no partner for the verbal joustings, literary fireworks, and philosophical flights she'd once hoped to enjoy with the people around her. Certainly Stanislas, preoccupied with his painting and under the thumb of his female admirers, did nothing to enliven the pleasant but restricted universe that Gloria and Jerry inhabited and that was such a strain on both mother and son. Even Jerry's rages, which were bound to grow worse when he reached his teens, were expressed in clichés borrowed from TV ads, though he often followed up a fit of bad temper with a disarming but equally trite attempt to get around her. So Gloria swallowed her frustration over Jerry's unsatisfactory words and marveled at how he'd learned to compensate for his lack of reasoning power by the extraordinary lucidity of his affection.

She had to cope with the demands of everyday life. An endless series of details, large and small, to be dealt with: social security, school, ailments, doctors, taxes, parking, gasoline, breakdowns, plumbing, electricity, accountants, mailmen, checkbooks, telephone, bakery, butcher shop, dry cleaner's, stationer's, more schools, more doctors, more things to be repaired in the house, a spot of gym, a drop of perfume, a game of tennis, fitness classes, a translation, two translations, three translations, a publisher, two publishers, three publishers, a lunch, two cocktail parties, three dinner parties, train or plane tickets, two one-ways, three round-trips, are you sure, yes, we're sure, please do your best, I am, let's go, we're off. Agencies of all kinds: travel agencies, rental agencies, agencies for hiring staff, for finding real estate, for moving your furniture into it. Buying, maintaining, escorting, earning, spending, coping. Deadly dull? Not really. Gloria had attained the numb efficiency of matter moving at supersonic speed. Once past Mach 2.9, motion is subject to more and more incidents, but there's no surface resistance by which to measure the stress. It was as simple as that: she carried out her tasks with the ease of a robot operating beyond the sound barrier. For in fact it wasn't "she" anymore. But if not, who was it? Didn't such interstellar anonymity conceal disturbance, alienation, even madness? But by some miracle Gloria managed to quell any demons that may have inhabited her, without ever letting them emerge into the light of day.

A trauma thus consumed generates an elation that accepts everything because everything's already reduced to nothing. "She's got no soul—that's why I married her" (Stan's irony masqueraded as a compliment and allowed him, equally soullessly, to pursue a number of mistresses). "She's a masochist, that's the explanation" (Odile Allart, who had good reason to know that what is called a couple may be merely a whited sepulcher concealing exhausting conflict). Gloria greeted such comments with a knowing smile, as if she agreed with their reasoning. But all the time she was pursuing her own unreason. Perhaps Jerry was merely a pretext. Perhaps if he hadn't existed she'd have had to invent him in order to reach the point where action reduces anguish to placidity.

She was forever nursing an invisible wound. Perhaps "nursing" wasn't the right word, but she couldn't think of a better. It was a question of adding to human life the kind of other life that was her son's. His life could certainly not be described as animal, still less as vegetable, but it could only stand and stammer when it came to speech, to what's regarded as the threshold of the human condition. Gloria crossed that sacred frontier in order to raise Jerry up to the level where normally constituted people operate. He often gave her the slip, because he liked it where he was: below, or was it beyond, everyone else. It was a world she had to learn to manage, as he did: a world of smell, saliva, color, touch, all insulated by unrelenting silence. She followed him there in order to snatch him away from that quiet acceptance. To bring him back, ultimately, to the words and rules of others.

It was really Gloria who was the handicapped child. On Jerry's behalf she slowly learned what she was supposed to know already but what she had never really possessed. *Can* you possess something bestowed on you merely as a matter of routine? For Jerry, with Jerry, she taught herself the names of scents and sounds, the logic of stories and their digressions, the secret of imitating ordinary attitudes: how to behave, how to stand up straight, to be correct, honorable, considerate, charming. Also to be angry—why not?—but not too angry. To discuss, argue, suffer, endure, despise, enjoy, live. None of all this could be taken for granted with Jerry; none of it was innate. He had to learn, she had to learn to teach him, and to do that she had to learn for herself, to rediscover, no, to discover the taste of ordinary things and of the words that go with them.

Mothers give birth only once to each son or daughter. But to Gloria the physiological event had come to seem animal-like and oversimple. Every day, every minute, every second she struggled to create a bridge between Jerry's dungeon and the sound-filled light of humanity. Some incomplete biological process, some lesion undetectable by any scanner, some horribly painful injury had marked his infant face with a grimace of fear and rejection that he himself had gradually changed into serenity. Perhaps he'd learned to be sure that with Gloria there was no need to be afraid? That helplessness you could share was helplessness no longer? Gloria was a refuge, a permanent balm for a permanent wound. For years, as his mother, she stood on the border between his inadequate genes and her own amorous senses. Both guilty and responsible. A perpetual, continuous, unique childbirth: her own private mysticism.

It took her some time to admit that Jerry was different. Love prevents you from looking things in the face; love only makes you hope.

It also took her some time to recognize that she herself might have taken everything away from him because—it didn't matter when or by whom—everything had been taken away from her. A craven excuse. Gloria, incapable of revenge, turned in on herself, listened to her own heart, a heart worn away and shattered. The mysterious vitality of which all mothers are made had in her case turned to ashes. How could she, with all those internal wounds, have brought forth a child like other children? She had handed her own invisible disaster on to him like a poisoned chalice. In Jerry she loved her own unsuspected weakness, her own hidden, affectionate frailty.

"You're just wasting your life and your talent while Stan produces works of art and fools around, if what people say is true." (Odile was trying to persuade her to be more practical.)

Works of art? Fooling around? You could tell Odile had no children. Playing such games. Which is more important, an intellectual bloodstain that all the perfumes of Arabia can't wash away (as is well known) or a child dying of hunger? You'd need to share the French worship of literature, to enthuse with the romantics, even to go on guilt trips with the profs, to dream up such a dire alternative. That wasn't the point; it didn't even occur to you when you'd experienced *it*, the real thing. I suppose we should be tolerant of people who devote themselves to art, the unknowns as well as the successes. It's an activity that encourages the apotheosis of the self, secular religion, and the conversion of civilizations into museums. But that path was too self-regarding, too exhibitionistic for Gloria. Nor was the embryonic seclusion of lovers in some ashram, tabernacle, or Vatican the answer for her. People who were always talking about the absolute never had the slightest inkling of *it*, the real thing.

It? The dark liquid light of those amazing, tenacious great eyes, drowning you as in the circle of water at the bottom of a well. *It?* As a child she'd been frightened by a story in a book her mother had given her, but she'd read it over and over again, curled up inside one of those shell-like retreats where you hide from yourself. It was a moving story, Russian or Slav, what's the difference. From the very first line it made you weep over the unhappy fate of a mother with an incurably sick child. For a long time she implores God to save him: in vain of course. Then she has the bright idea of offering God her own life, and then He condescends to revive her son. The story was called *The Sacrifice*, no less, and Gloria innocently reveled in the title. The tale itself struck her as full of mystery and terribly, irresistibly beautiful. She kept quoting it to her parents, dismaying them with her enthusiasm. She drank in its words as if they were the honeyed juice of the quinces that grew by the window in the story, their ripening aided even more by the mother's devotion than by the son's resurrection. On her deathbed old Mrs. Harrison, milder at last and not so strictly rational as usual, reminded Gloria about the story: "You've been doomed ever since you were a child. Do you remember how you used to recite *The Sacrifice* by heart? It used to worry your father. Such an extreme passion—it must have been your fate."

It? Suffering? It's out of place nowadays except in novels about the third world. People have had enough of it here. They're fed up with having their feelings exploited by victims. And Gloria, like the rest of us, laughs at the old idea of the Madonna taking herself for Christ! Just like you and me, Gloria is looking for something light—it doesn't matter whether it's fast or slow, noxious or harmless. Take your pick, draw the curtains, zap from one channel to another! Politics, metaphysics, aesthetics, aerobics, robotics—anything but *it*. No proud scars, please; no pale dignities or clammy palms clutching the hand of a child who's different and gives you the impression, the false impression, that he holds the entire universe in an invisible, unshed tear. *Anything but it!* Stand up straight. To think there are people who've no idea how hard it can be to stand up straight! To keep your eyes wide open and strangely absent-looking and never show a sign of weariness. All that's there is worry about Jerry's worries. Meanwhile he's suspended up in the sky like some crystal clam, like a leaden sword lit up by a merciless sun, with no before or after. Just the unending moment of a contained concern. A happiness that, if it existed, would be the death of sorrow. Almost a joy.

Gloria couldn't put all this into words; she could only "act." The Christians were right: the only way to encounter the divine, the ultimate "other," is to become as a little child. To become its mother, father, brother, sister; the ultimate nearest and dearest, the comprehensive neighbor of the child king, the Divine Child. Everyone can do it? Maybe, but not everyone knows what he or she is doing, and it's absolutely necessary that there should be something unexpected, anomalous, a Jerry for example, to jog you out of the domestic lethargy and remind you of the bolt from the blue.

But lightning is usually accompanied by thunder, and on the occasions when Jerry appeared particularly and impossibly dim, Gloria could be incredibly violent. Reproach and remorse being equally impossible, she simply exploded. All her devotion would suddenly collapse, and a fury out of some antique tragedy fell on her bewildered victim. Jerry just accepted the insults and blows—completely speechless, numb, guilty. He knew this witchlike figure had reasons for behaving as she did. There was nothing she wouldn't do for him, but he was hopeless, his stupidity knew no bounds, and he deserved to die just as much as his mother did. Because everything came from her, or so she thought, and therefore he thought the same. So there was she, like a tragic actress with her shrieking and tears; and there was he, nauseous and dumb, the helpless victim of a mother's rage that was really directed against herself.

There was no shelter from the storm. Hester was its only witness, but though she was upset she was also helpless and hampered further by not knowing whether what she felt for mother and son was love or loathing. When the boy tried to complain to his father, Stan, exasperated, slammed the door of the studio in his face and told him to go to bed. So Pauline had become his valued confidante. Her slow gentleness couldn't shield him from Gloria's black possession—anyhow, Jerry would never have dreamed of exposing his mother to Ms. Gadeau's reproaches—but she did provide him with a refuge where, like a beaten puppy, he could lick his wounds and wait for the next bout of devotion or ferocity.

Putting myself in Gloria's place, I was ready to admit she lived through all this feeling as if she'd been stabbed through the heart or grabbed by the throat. As if. But usually there's a distance between words and things, and even in this case that gap seemed to me unbridgeable. Most people have had to a greater or lesser degree the feeling commonly expressed by such phrases as "God, he (or she) was killing me!" But that a sick woman could, through an obscure form of autoprojection, transform such an impression into an actual stab wound or slit throat— well, no. That would have been an incarnation spectacular enough to challenge all the stigmata and crucifixions in the history of art and religion. Ridiculous! That's where you ended up if you were an oversensitive reporter and took other people's troubles too much to heart, especially when they were women. And if you tried to usurp the already suspect role of a detective in a godforsaken place like Santa Varvara.

Monday, October 17, 4:55 P.M. I'd already been prowling around the wisteria-clad Harrison house for some time: going to and fro in the grounds, returning to the terrace, approaching the body and skirting around it, on the lookout for some clue or memory. Captain Rilsky, mocking, almost unpleasant, but absorbed by his own routine chores, let me do as I pleased. The stain on the bodice of Gloria's ivory satin gown, which had been crimson that morning, was now dark purple and would soon be only a blackish crust of no definable color. The neck, on the other hand, more obscene than I'd seen in my worst nightmares, still presented the same gaping hole edged as if with red paint. Tiepolo attacking John the Baptist in Bergamo and Caravaggio murdering Holofernes were really only trying to lend beauty to the bloodthirsty passion that now lay, for real, before my very eyes. Murder wasn't repulsive to them; it was an excuse for studying proportion. An apple might serve the same purpose. Similarly, for a police chief, murder was an excuse for producing theories. But count me out, please. I took one last look. The gore, and the cadaverous limbs of what on Saturday had still been a woman, reminded me of the bronze-glinting Salome dancing eternally over the mosaics at St. Mark's in Venice. A deep and ruthless wickedness was grinning out of the heart of this disaster. Enough! I had to get out of there. A dozen or so detectives were lifting fingerprints and collecting every hair they could find that was anywhere near the murdered woman; they couldn't have cared less about my conjectures as to Gloria Harrison's misfortunes. Any more than they cared about my troubles, for that matter. That only made them fit more naturally into the general picture. They too were indifferent, unfeeling, becoming stiff and theatrical. Extreme brutality makes people unreal. I'd have liked Rilsky to invite me to the concert that was to take place that evening. The Santa Varvara Philharmonic, with a galaxy of famous singers, was going to perform extracts from Haydn's operas, those highly unreal masterpieces of frivolous cruelty. But no, the worthy Northrop was pretending to include me among the suspects, or at least among the witnesses. And now, having rubbed my nose in some butchery that after all was none of my business, he was keeping me at a distance. After ordering that the doors and windows be sealed, he escorted me in deathly silence to the nearest taxi stand. I had no intention of regaling him with my thoughts of Degas's decapitated dancers, whose delightful shapes were now beginning to replace the lugubrious images that had been weighing on my mind for so long, though they were probably of no interest to anybody but me. Anyway, Rilsky didn't care for either painting or sculpture.

I was hungry. I needed some peace, some warm, ordinary, comfortable peace. I needed a cup of tea.

• PART II •

Virtual Crime

◆ CHAPTER SEVEN ◆

Tuesday, October 18, 5:30 P.M. Waiting around, confrontation of witnesses, interrogations. Rilsky wasn't under any illusions about the results, but he knew from experience that it can be useful to talk to the last people to have seen the victim alive. The nearest and dearest always have some thoughts if not deeds to reproach themselves with when one of their group meets with a violent death—or when nothing happens at all, for that matter. The consequent embarrassment is almost sure to reveal the guilt so delightfully inseparable from the human soul, and this the captain proceeded to track down as a rudimentary sign of bad conscience, despite the fact that the misconceived secularism of our contemporaries makes them strenuously deny that any such thing exists.

All the witnesses waited in Gloria's main drawing room. Rilsky thought it important to question them at the scene of the crime. That usually got a case off to a good start.

The seals on the doors and windows had just been removed, and the house was vaguely coming back to life, like a body still dazed and racked with nausea after an anesthetic. The dry, dusty air seemed to cake your nostrils and make it difficult to breathe. The Chinese Buddha Gloria had salvaged from the family junk room sat sunbathing on a Victorian chest of drawers, its eyes lowered in modesty or irony, depending on the observer's character or religion. Green moiré taffeta draperies were drawn over windows shut against the heat, except for one wide open on a cluster of wisteria whose scent and delicacy no one noticed now. On the left wall of the room a huge canvas painted by Stan in the manner of one of de Kooning's monstrous females seemed poised to spring some unpleasant surprise on whoever looked at it. It was ridiculous of course to entertain such fancies. But all our minds were influenced by the thought of Gloria's corpse.

On the other side of the wall with the picture was Gloria's study, where Rilsky had set out his papers on the carved hazelwood desk. Gloria, the translator, used to stroke its cool, reassuring surface every morning before confronting the blankness that precedes the problematical effort to shift the meaning of words adequately from one language to another. As if to show he was taking possession of the premises, Rilsky tossed his briefcase carelessly onto the dark blue velvet divan, The case was full of reference books unlikely to be relevant, but he always carried them about with him "in case they came in handy," Then—the ultimate sign that he was making himself at home—he threw the jacket of his Cary Grant suit onto the divan too. Then he went over to the window and opened it carefully. An orange tree grew just outside, in an enormous terracotta pot on the terrace. A bee flew out of its branches and made for the left wing of the house and the guest room. The captain peered out at some improbable tire marks on the gravel, looked down the slope and through the little wood to the almost imperceptible glitter of the river, then let his eyes come to rest on the wisteria growing rather too profusely over the right wing of the Harrison residence, probably to conceal the staff's quarters. It gave Rilsky a certain pleasure to think of the dinner-party guests waiting anxiously in the drawing room. He slowly polished his glasses—sign of a self-satisfaction that was nothing to be proud of. He glanced at the bound volumes of Shakespeare, Thackeray, Browning, and suchlike that adorned the bookshelves at shoulder height (evidently they were the deceased's favorite authors). Then he strolled along the green corridor and appeared in the doorway of the drawing room. Naturally he was going to start with the person who'd found the body.

The epileptic student poured out once more what he'd told the police already and what they'd observed for themselves when they answered his summons. He'd had an awful shock—how could it have been otherwise?—but he'd had the presence of mind to call up the nearest police station. Rilsky's crime squad had been informed immediately; they were responsible for both homicides and sexual offenses in Santa Varvara. This was clearly an extraordinary case even in a country familiar with murder and scandal. So Rilsky was the man of the moment. He decided to hear his first witness in private.

He'd gathered that epileptics, like pedants, express themselves in a kind of telegraphese, a barrage of staccato, allusive, unorganized phrases. Brian now confirmed this belief: French window open onto the garden, front door bolted, victim stabbed and beheaded; work session between the translator and her assistant forgotten, a nightmare, only one idea: to call for help. Watt's uneasy manner and disordered, sketchy utterances might have awakened suspicion if they hadn't reflected real shock and hinted at an imminent attack. He did in fact have a fit soon after the interview. Rilsky, to avoid the disagreeable task of having to bring him round, cut the interrogation short. He'd make do with such minor evidence as the student had volunteered of his own accord, together with details of his movements that Popov and his four sergeants had already established.

Watt and the maid had been alone in the house on the night in question. He slept in the guest room in the left wing, so as to be easily available for Mrs. Harrison while she was working on her translation of Shakespeare's sonnets. (To this weighty task had been added an urgent demand for a version of Philip Roth's novel *The Breast*.) Brian felt obliged to reveal everything about his activities since the fateful dinner party: an assignation with the maid; sleeping till noon on Sunday, October 16; lunch with friends, after which they'd had a game of chess (the friends confirmed this, together with what followed); a visit to the Film Theater ("I wouldn't miss the Eisenstein festival for anything! As you know, Captain, one hardly ever gets the chance to see that sort of thing—television's killing the cinema!"). Then dinner, a night club, and home at two in the morning—Monday morning. The house was plunged in darkness, which was only natural: everyone's in bed and asleep at that hour. "I only have a cup of coffee for breakfast, and I make it for myself in my room. I like to have a coffee at different times of the day, and it's not worth bothering Hester. Well, in due course I presented myself at the front door on England Street, at nine o'clock as usual; I sleep in the annex, but I'm not a member of the staff: I'm just a colleague, a freelancer, and like Mrs. Harrison herself I prefer to keep things formal. Or rather I preferred. She gets up very early . . . I'm sorry—she used to get up very early, and by nine o'clock she'd already have done a lot of work: arrangements for the house, instructions to the maid, orders from the stores, Jerry's appointments. Sometimes she'd have scribbled down a few pages of translation in bed when she couldn't sleep. Of course she had trouble sleeping—she led such a stressful life. . . . No, not really difficult—never raised her voice; always polite and careful to ask after my health before we started work—but liked to have her own way. Finicky. And, yes, demanding. But—you feel these things even if you don't necessarily say them—I think she valued me. I really believe she did, though you mustn't suppose there was anything . . . Anyway, I ring the bell. No answer. I ring again. Not a sound. I wait. I press the bell again. No answer again. Has something happened? Is someone ill? Jerry? I go around to the right wing of the house, by the kitchen: Hester will know what's up. But there isn't any sign of Hester. I go back to the England Street side and look through the window: the black-and-white tiles, the cold empty hall its usual dreary self. Like a sort of barricade to keep people out, have you noticed? I scurried back and forth two or three times by the back way between the front door and the kitchen, like an insect before a storm. And finally I heard—I can hear it still—a silence. Not a sound, not a whisper, not a leaf stirring. The silence before the revelation: lucid, absolute. Imagine what the neurones of animals must be like! I'm not superstitious, but I really did have a presentiment of disaster. I take a deep breath, walk around the house yet again. Through the garden. Onto the terrace. Call out, knock on the French windows opening into the study. No one. Then I push the windows ajar, Captain, these windows here, but from the outside . . ."

"From the outside." (Rilsky, without expression.)

"They'd been left open." (Brian doesn't take up Rilsky's hint.) "But I felt there was something there. A sort of presence. Something alien. Intimidating."

"You say you sensed a kind of presence. While you were still outside." (Rilsky, going along with his witness.)

"The air seems to come alive when you're in a panic—haven't you ever had that experience, Captain? Inexplicable rushings and swirls. Yes, I did think I felt a presence. But it might just have been the orange tree outside the window. Extraordinary how threatening the fruit can seem: so heavy yet never really ripe. A sort of moldy head. You can't tell from the color if it's maturing or just going moldy. Unnatural. A tree in the wrong climate is like a kind of degenerate . . ." (Brian, in no hurry to get to the point.)

"So it might have been the orange tree?" (Rilsky, suspicious of the suspect.)

"I'd like to see how *you*'d have reacted in my place! You always arrive when it's all over, long after the witnesses! And then you just keep on at them! Much easier than looking for whoever really did it!" (Brian checked himself: his sudden furies made him lose his self-control, and this was no time for recklessness.) "As I said, I was outside the French windows. Then I pushed them wide open—and you know the rest." (He was almost fainting.) "I'm sure it must have been Hester. If not, why would she have run away? She told me she hadn't been getting along with Mrs. Harrison lately; in fact she said she hated her. Hester was a nonentity. Jealous. Capable of anything."

Watt was at the end of his tether. The captain summoned a sergeant to take him away and calm him down.

This was certainly a case for the homicide squad. Premeditated murder. That much was clear without the student's evidence. The detailed and determined way the crime was carried out showed it to be the work of a psychopath. Or else the result of some old, terrible, insane grudge. A crazy passion, white-hot and surgically precise. But was it a sex crime or mere blood lust? And was the killer someone known to the victim or just some passing nutcase? Detecting is a surgical passion too.

Stephanie Delacour sat around with the others. This was just a grotesque charade, she thought. She loathed waiting. Especially in the very room where the horror had taken place. To wait in the presence of the horror was both criminal and ridiculous. Melodramatic. Pointless. Northrop Rilsky had called in all the guests at Saturday's dinner party. He intended to question them one by one and then perhaps all together. Such formality was as absurd as it was inevitable. Some of them had come in the evening dress they were wearing when Gloria saw them for the last time on Saturday, October 15. Zorin was one of these—Zorin the sincere mourner, the romantic lover, bereft and shattered. Odile, too: she was wearing her gauzy parrot-red gown, probably less out of loyalty to the dead than out of vanity and to show Rilsky how eager she was to cooperate: "Look, Captain: I couldn't be more relaxed. I've nothing to hide." Pauline Gadeau was her usual self: in other words she was invisible, at least to Stephanie. Brian was as white in the face as on the days when he was going to have a fit; his eyes were puffier than ever. Larry barged into the room as if it was a newspaper office, and the Third World War had just been declared.

"Why do I have to be bothered with this stupid performance, I'd like to know? But isn't it too awful, Stephanie dear? One imagines everything's predictable nowadays, but no, there are always horrors lying in wait for us! And the police are as slow as snails! What does Northrop think he's up to, eh? Just wasting his time as usual, don't you agree? And ours as well!"

He didn't like to kiss her, so he just put his arms around her a bit more limply and cravenly than usual, tried to catch her eye, failed, sat down, stood up again, and then paced to and fro across the carpet like a caged lion, the image of a womanizer in a B movie.

"Well, I've heard Mr. Brian Watt, but Miss Hester Bellini's still missing. Never mind, we'll soon get hold of her; she's as good as found." (Rilsky, with an enigmatic but already triumphant grin.) "Meanwhile, suppose we continue with Mr. Pascal Allart? Will you come this way, sir?"

More waiting. Stephanie, who had a talent for pain as others have a gift for music or love, cultivated her skill with a modesty that turned it into cheerfulness and sometimes even impudence. With her short black hair and Chinese cheekbones she looked like an Asian nun. Her blue-green eyes shot a gleam of irony at everything she saw. Her royal blue jacket with its gold buttons added a note of military—or merely ultra-sophisticated—elegance to a black skirt revealing long legs and the rounded calves of a gymnast.

The blue light of autumn afternoons in Santa Varvara, and her reaction to the smell of the sea, made her look relaxed and smiling. She could have burst into song—given a rendering of Mozart's Haffner Symphony, for example. Pride chooses D major to convey complete detachment, freed of all sorrow. But singing would have been in-congruous in a room saturated by the fear of Saturday's guests. So Stephanie just went over and shut the window that had been opened wide on the garden, her gesture moved by pain, though none of the others suspected that. They set it down to professional zeal and morbid curiosity.

Sometimes in a dream the sleeper feels himself adapting to the shape of a strange bed, to the dimensions of a room he never saw till the previous evening, to the faces and manners of hosts unknown before, and to the secrets of a landscape stretching out under the moon, or the dawn, or even the midday sun. All these new things are diffused right through the dreamer, obliterating him through a kind of vast osmosis. In the same way Stephanie felt as if she herself were being canceled out by the Harrison house and by the ozone-scented darkness about to fall on people and things and amend their ugly ordinariness. But while both the Indian summer and the coziness of the old

English decor helped to make the self seem insubstantial and far away, the murder imposed its presence on every detail. Through the smooth mahogany labyrinth of the house, amid the odors of the lush autumn, Gloria's mutilated corpse seized hold of Stephanie, and the still invisible but mysteriously present scenes of carnage seemed to sully her and drag her down to the roots of degradation. What was happening externally here at this moment, in the drawing room and in Gloria's study now more or less taken over by Rilsky, was merely incidental.

"I'm sure it was Hester who did it. I saw her during the night—well, she came to my room after dinner. She went up to her studio afterward—the maid's room, in the attic. In other words, she and Mrs. Harrison were alone in that part of the house. You see what I'm driving at? No doubt about it. And then she took off in the car. She didn't open the door to me this morning when I rang the bell for my session with Mrs. Harrison—you know, the translation of the sonnets. I had to get in through the garden; the French windows were open. And then I saw her—well, the body—but not Hester. I call that strange, don't you?" (Brian was stretched out near Stephanie in a black velvet armchair. Having escaped from the captain's clutches at least for the moment, he was babbling away to the world in general.)

"It's Gloria's head that's missing, young man, not Hester's." (Odile had to try to be witty no matter what the circumstances.)

"I'm talking about the murderer—or rather the murderess! If that's not a lead I don't know what is! Good heavens, it's staring you in the face!" (Brian.)

"But I thought you liked her—Hester, I mean, this time!" (Odile, still overexcited.)

"I think we should leave Rilsky to get on with his job as he thinks best." (Zorin, sensibly.)

"I quite agree, Maître. But what a mess, and what a waste of time . . . when we're already in the middle of the horror that's Santa Varvara! I'd bet my bottom dollar that underneath this affair there's some political business that's way beyond the scope of friend

Northrop." (Larry, increasingly comfortable in the role of journal-
ist-cum-judge, a universal specialty in these times of crisis and what
the press calls "power vacuum.")

More waiting. The air turns russet, signaling a lingering twilight.
Everything smells of spice and roses and dust. Stephanie doesn't like
waiting; it sets her mind racing. Outside, a blackbird whistles irritat-
ingly amid the leaves. Stephanie's palms are damp with dread, her
eyes can no longer distinguish one person from another. The salon is
now a waiting room, and every countenance blurred as in a wan and
colorless dream.

◆ CHAPTER EIGHT ◆

While successive Santavarvaran regimes of all kinds did their best to skirt around the laws or adapt them to a new world order that was increasingly corrupt and hard to pin down, Rilsky was supposed, in very concrete and often horrible situations, to come down in the name of Truth on the side of Good against Evil. The paradox inherent in this intolerable situation ought to have depressed him and made him cynical. But at the age of fifty-seven, which included thirty years of faithful service in the police, he willingly, if secretly, admitted he had been tempted by each of the two options in turn but was glad to have lost no time in choosing his role. It was a role that kept him at a safe distance from the slippery slopes he found so distasteful. It was *just* a role, however, though based on his own natural inclinations and planned and developed deliberately. Everyone adopts attitudes, poses, masks, "looks" of all kinds in this world of pretense where "truth" dissolves into the confusion of remote-control images, where "integrity" is a claim that can be undermined in an instant by financial speculation or legal skulduggery. Rilsky didn't try to play the role of denouncer of role players. But from his father, conductor of the Philharmonic in Bourgas, the second most important city in Santa Varvara, and from his mother, a piano teacher, Rilsky, a music lover himself, had inherited a feeling for tempo, and perhaps for measure and moderation in general. At an early age, not having any particular talents, he found he had little liking for the world at large but a taste for solitude that was rare in a country where indiscriminate friendliness—called conviviality—is regarded as a natural virtue. So he studied law and then went into the police. He regarded crime as revolting and therefore fundamental, brutality as inevitable, and sham as something to be avoided at all costs. Despite his negative traits he did believe life had a purpose, its object not to serve mankind, as the old humanists maintained, but to arrive at a proper appraisal of it. He saw himself, with some justification, as a combination of humanist and aesthete, not deigning to feel at one with his fellowmen except when they joined him in appreciating a musical masterpiece. That occasional osmosis was perhaps the only thing that brought some happiness into Rilsky's rigidly ordered and strictly supervised life as a policeman. Nevertheless he'd coped gracefully with the horrors involved in his chosen profession, and despite the reservations of his superiors, who thought him too sophisticated for the job and even a bit pretentious, he'd earned enough of a reputation for good sense to make the normal progress up the ladder of promotion.

The care Rilsky took over his appearance made him look like a fop strayed among oafs. But it also served to keep others at arm's length: self-regard tends to intimidate the mob. And though some thought him square and made fun of his "obsessive elegance," at the end of the day a well-cut jacket and fashionable necktie are useful for holding off the hoi polloi. Rilsky's clothes were his way of showing respect for convention—which for him, given contemporary laxity, signified law and morality. And since most people had forgotten the meaning of the word *ethics*, Rilsky's mere presence served to remind them that the thing itself did exist after all and that they had actually encountered it.

As for music, being concerned with tempo and measure it helps to make feelings "keep time." Sublimity, grace, and all the other marvels that justify human existence—what are they but feeling that "keeps time," emotion observing the right tempo? Of course men and women can't go further than that, but it's enough. In fact it's quite amazing, when you come to think of it, that a few of them have managed to get so far. Geniuses like Bach and Vivaldi. Virtuosi too, like Paganini and Menuhin. Among others. Which is not to say that tempo cancels out crime or measure justifies murder. But it does mean there might be some measure, some moderation in society's attitude to criminals—that is, to everyone. Isn't that what's called civilization? Hence, as Rilsky sometimes observed when sharing his reflections with his friend Stephanie Delacour, the very special role of music: an educational role that functioned when you listened in the company of a few other people, select and sensitive ones if possible, at once well-defined and temperate—moderate, measured, like himself and Stephanie. Even when measure and moderation had to deal with nausea or disgust they could distill it into exquisite emotion, extract from it a certain kind of pleasure. The only kind that really deserves the name. Rilsky, a connoisseur of both music and nausea, was secretly a distinguished kind of Sartrean and proud of it, though no one even suspected such a thing in Santa Varvara, where existentialism had never caught on. Only Ms. Delacour, if she went to a concert with Rilsky on one of her all too brief visits, used sometimes to favor him with subtle allusions to his ideas and to his secret sympathy for a great philosopher whom he believed to be fundamentally misunderstood. When Stephanie did this Rilsky would take out a gray silk handkerchief and slowly polish his spectacles, allowing his eyes to be seen misting over at a pleasure at last sanctioned and a position vindicated.

Having made his position clear as far as clothes and demeanor were concerned, it only remained for him to try to act justly: to find whoever was responsible in a case of, say, murder, rape, or drug trafficking and then to convince his superiors, insofar as it was possible, that he'd got it right. That was as far as it went. He wasn't interested in tilting at Santavarvaran windmills, and his sense of reality sometimes made him give up on the idea of seeing a crime duly punished. Stephanie regarded this attitude as a cop-out, showing that Rilsky was shallow and weak, unaware of the true depths of evil and too lazy to make all the effort required to unmask it. But if Rilsky ever *was* shallow it was in appearance only, and only in certain circumstances: as when a decaying corpse or the body of a child who had been raped brought back the revulsion he'd felt as a child at the taste of the skin on boiled milk or the sight of the toilet bowl his father always forgot to flush. He thought he'd put such feelings behind him, but he hadn't. However, the real paradox with Rilsky was his desire to reconcile an uncompromising love of what's just and right ("in the musical sense of the term," he insisted to Stephanie) with the impossibility of applying such principles in a rackety society that had no use for them. Without being unduly tolerant of squalor, he was on the side of the victims. He stood as a true embodiment of justice at a time when no one else was capable of doing so; but he did his best to avoid provoking obstruction or malice in an establishment known to have become corrupt. He was a saint fallen among rogues yet able to live with their villainy: so long as he could remain straight, he didn't mind being taken for a fool. In short, the way he dealt with his cases was conclusive but not spectacular. He'd learned to do without the headlines that bring such gratification to so many, and in a way this situation was even a source of strength, for he got a certain sardonic satisfaction out of his own obscurity.

"Will you come with me, please, Mr. Allart?" (Rilsky had to repeat his invitation: Pascal, for all his swagger as a managing director used to conquering easy markets, was as tense as everyone else. He seemed to have been rather struck by Watt's revelations and was chuckling morbidly at the idea of a mistress being strangled by her maid.)

Naturally, *he* had nothing to fear! And he wanted to thank the captain now for being prepared, as he was sure he would be, as any reasonable man would be, to accept his alibi as quite beyond dispute. He and his wife, Odile, had left Gloria's place at around a quarter past midnight and driven to the seaside hotel where they were staying throughout their visit to Santa Varvara. The night porter at the Golden Sands would confirm they'd arrived there at about 1:30 on Sunday morning, and this ruled out any possibility that either of them could have been with Gloria, or even with her corpse, during the crucial period—even supposing they had any motive for harming their old friend, which the captain himself would readily agree was a completely ridiculous idea. As for Sunday, from ten o'clock onward Pascal and Odile had been caught up in a whirl of important business meetings with local industrialists all eager to make their visit as pleasant and profitable as possible. Odile didn't even have a moment to call Gloria up and thank her for the delightful party the previous evening; she'd have done so after the weekend if the recent tragic events hadn't supervened and thrown everything into disarray.

"I'm not an emotional person by nature, Captain, and the rough-and-tumble of business is enough to harden anyone, but I don't mind telling you this ghastly affair sends shivers down my spine. It's not only barbaric—that hardly needs saying—it's also incomprehensible. How could anyone even imagine such a thing?"

"You knew Mrs. Harrison pretty well." (Rilsky, his nose buried in his files.)

"Oh, you've heard about that, eh? So what? It's ancient history. And what does it prove anyway? On the contrary, all the more reason why I should still be fond of her. Maybe there was a tinge of bitterness. Maybe. But *that*! Can you see anyone normal doing *that*?" (Pascal threw an exaggeratedly horrified glance at Rilsky, who remained expressionless.)

"Jealousy . . ." (Rilsky, persistent, or perhaps cruel.)

"I don't know the meaning of the word. I love women the way other men love whisky, but the only thing I get worked up about is contracts. And, by the way, I do pretty well in that respect in Santa Varvara. Everyone's corrupt here, I'm told, but what's that to me? The Mafia aren't choosy about where they operate, east or west, north or south, and you don't need me to tell you there are plenty of crooks among the politicians in Europe. So I set my own conditions. I'm interested in their raw materials: the essential oils are first class! The refining processes are pretty crude here, but what body, what strength! We do some further refining, and the big French perfumeries are wild about the result. Not to mention the pharmaceuticals industry!" (Allart, very full of himself.)

"Let's get back to Gloria Harrison, shall we? Did you spend the night with your wife?" (Rilsky, still absorbed by his folders.)

"What do you think?" (Allart, refusing to be thrown. But it seemed to Rilsky he was a bit less sure of himself.)

"I imagine Mrs. Allart doesn't entirely approve of your having a soft spot for her friend Gloria." (Rilsky, as impartially as a weather forecaster.)

"All that's in the past." (Pascal, quite relaxed.)

"A past as recent as last Saturday's dinner party." (Rilsky, looking up from a short but interesting fax he'd just received from Popov.)

Popov knew the Golden Sands like the back of his hand. Especially the switchboard operator, a blonde with large hips and a small brain—just his type. And just the thing for finding out, at negligible cost and even with a certain amount of pleasure, all the little secrets of the Golden Sands clientele. It was one of most luxurious hotels on the coast, and some of its guests had plenty to hide: clandestine contacts, shady deals, dubious connections with government offices and local business barons, all eager to tap into an international network of easy profits, money laundering, drug dealing, and arms trafficking. Most of the files amassed through Nora's generosity—Nora was the switchboard operator—lay gathering dust on the shelves at police headquarters. Rilsky merely ran an expert eye over them, not sure whether to be sorry he couldn't use them (it was to no one's advantage to know the truth) or glad that he held such enormous though only potential power in his hands. (But that power had to do with morals and transcendence, both of which had as yet few supporters in Santa Varvara).

Rilsky was familiar with Popov's methods. They never varied. After a couple of whiskies and a glance around the bar at the regulars, whose gaunt faces and vacant eyes reflected addiction to cocaine rather than the asceticism of the saint or the sportsman, Popov would

hurry off to see his buxom informant. In return for some sexual satisfaction she would give him all the news. But when he mixed business
and pleasure he couldn't entirely trust his memory, so he was in the
habit, while Nora was completing her part of the bargain with a blow
job, of recording a coded version of what she'd told him on a dicta-
phone. He transcribed the tape when he got back home.

It was his last report that Rilsky was now reading. From this it
emerged that Allart had had phone calls from certain local perfume
manufacturers who had links with clandestine drug producers, and
he'd called them back early on Sunday morning to confirm a lunch
date. He'd also called up the car rental firm he always used and
asked for the latest mileage figure on the car he'd hired for his current visit. The car rental people referred him to the garage. Nora
also related, with some indignation, that Mrs. Allart had been out all
night "with Daniel, the maître d'; I don't know what he sees in
her—she's as flat as a board." Mr. Allart had tried to make a pass at
her, Nora, "but he didn't have any luck!" And perhaps not much
enthusiasm either, thought Popov, as he urged her on with her
account. Nora then told him how surprised room service had been
when Mr. Allart opened his door to take in the breakfast tray. He was
almost naked! Popov adjusted his own dress, closed his notebook,
and went to see what he could ferret out in the game room. Poor
Nora wasn't able to help him there: she couldn't even recite her mul-
tiplication tables. Yes, Pascal Allart had come in alone at about three
in the morning. He'd looked nervous, played badly, lost all his
money, and gone off again in a lousy temper. "End of report. Over
to you, sir."

Needless to say, Popov wasn't required to give an opinion, but
everything in his story seemed to suggest that Allart, crooked and
cowardly though he might be, was not involved in the beheading.
Even so, Popov, on the off chance, had checked out the times Nora had
given for the Allarts' nocturnal comings and goings. He'd visited the
garage, where they confirmed the curious fact that Mr. Allart had

phoned to ask what the mileage was on his car when the tank was last filled up. "I couldn't remember, Lieutenant! I don't know where we'd be if we had to write down the mileage on every car whenever we filled it up. Anyway, they'd rented theirs with unlimited mileage and had been driving all over the country for a week. The office could tell you what the figure was when they started. After that it's nobody's business but Allart's and his wife's." Exactly.

So, news traveled fast in Santa Varvara, and the crooks were hand in glove with one another. But that was beside the point. For Popov the point was his wife and children, needless to say. Rilsky couldn't quarrel with that. But both he and Popov liked to see a job well done. Even Nora understood this in her way, and Popov was grateful to her for helping him complete his report in a couple of hours. He faxed it to the boss's office right away. And now, in what used to be Gloria's study, the boss held the report in his hands, reading between the lines to find out all he'd wanted to know about the man sitting opposite him. Pascal Allart himself was unaware of this.

"It's nothing to do with you, Captain. Haven't you ever heard of the right to privacy? Okay, maybe it doesn't exist in Santa Varvara. But don't forget you're talking to a Frenchman." (Pascal, beginning to lose his cool.)

"Speaking of which, I understand Frenchwomen are very jealous." (Rilsky, roguishly.)

"Oh, I suppose that fool Brian fed you a lot of tittle-tattle about the dinner party? So what? As I said before, what does that prove?" (Pascal, really angry now.)

"So you were with Mrs. Allart until ten o'clock in the morning of Sunday the sixteenth?" (Rilsky, cool and sharp as a bunch of wallflowers.)

"I'd ordered breakfast at nine, and it was brought to the room half an hour late, as is usually the case in your country's most expensive hotels. I shudder to think what it must be like in the others." (Pascal, as if everything were quite normal.)

"I believe you opened the door and took in the tray yourself. So no one could check whether Mrs. Allart was in the room or not," (Rilsky, courtesy personified.)

"Do you think I bother my head about such trifles? Sometimes I get up and open the door to the maid or the waiter, and sometimes I stay in bed and let them bring the tray in. That doesn't prove anything. As for the members of staff who work for the police, I can see why I might disappoint them. I don't give them much to get their teeth into. Except tips, and heaven knows I'm generous enough in that respect!" (Pascal, apparently quite unconcerned.)

"What if I told you your wife made a scene when you got back to the Golden Sands? And left? And that you didn't see her again until the lunch engagement on Sunday with the big wheels of Santa Varvara's business community? A very pleasant occasion, I gather, and one that Odile Allart wouldn't have missed for anything." (Rilsky, pretending to be dumb.)

Pascal suddenly changed tack, adopting a man-to-man attitude copied from the movies.

"My friend—I may call you that, mayn't I?—you're well aware that modern couples, at least in my country, can live very independent lives and still remain quite attached to one another. Quite passionately attached, sometimes. Oh yes, I know; here it's either an idyll or a drama. But in France we go in for more subtle distinctions, you see, and have done for centuries. Nuances are a French specialty, you might say. So I mean a lot to Odile—you may be sure of that. But just the same she needs to demonstrate—to herself as well as to me—that she's a modern woman with a mind and a life of her own. So there you are." (Pascal, trying to conceal a vague uneasiness.)

"She could have gone back to the Harrison place while you were asleep in the hotel room. On your own, you say. Well, one swallow doesn't make a summer. I don't think any the less of you for it, my friend (if you insist). I'm a bachelor myself, but I can imagine what a relief it must be not to have to listen to the little woman for one night!" (Rilsky, quite at home in the man-to-man act.)

". . . ." (Pascal, hoping to leave it at that.)

". . . ." (Rilsky, trying to put him on the spot.)

"I did think of that possibility, you know. Not very seriously, though you can never be sure. But in the end I decided against it. Odile may be impulsive, but she's incapable of action. And as for killing anyone—! She wouldn't even be up to getting the car out and driving there and back—too lazy. That's one of her charms, if you get my meaning." (Pascal, fond and gallant.)

"But you took the trouble to check the mileage on the rental car before you came in for questioning." (Rilsky, matter-of-fact.)

"You think I suspect my wife? You can't help yourself, can you? But there's no reason why I *should* suspect her, as I've told you already." (Pascal, still putting on airs.)

"Unfortunately you couldn't remember what mileage had been on the meter after you'd driven back from the dinner party. You tried to get the figure from the garage, but the man there didn't know any more than you did." (Rilsky, still looking down at Popov's report.)

"Sheer paranoia—your profession, your country, and your city all reek of it! I'm beginning to get the hang of this place now! You and your garage man! It's incredible! I was just checking up in the ordinary way. Nothing to do with the murder!" (Pascal, inwardly wondering if the time hadn't come for him to call his lawyer.)

"You may be right. I'll keep you informed about how the case develops. Meanwhile I'd be obliged if you'd hold yourself at our disposal. That means you mustn't leave the country. So long, Mr. Allart." (Rilsky, affable.)

"You're barking up the wrong tree! But I have things to do in Santa Varvara, and regardless of what you want or don't want, here I am and here I stay!" (Pascal, just restraining himself from slamming the door.)

Rilsky always enjoyed his witnesses' discomfiture and allowed it to worsen until the victims flew right off the handle and revealed their lack of good manners or taste. This gave him a sense of superiority and power, not unmingled with pity. Such Olympian feelings were especially apt in this instance, for there was no objective reason for Mr. Allart to worry. Mrs. Allart had spent the night with the maître d' of the Golden Sands, a strapping fellow whose prowess was renowned among female tourists. Nonetheless, Mr. Allart did have some purely subjective reasons for crediting his wife with murderous tendencies: he found it more interesting to entertain that idea than to explain her absence in terms of the dreary adulteries practiced by them both. Such is life. But what was the connection between all this and the beheading of Gloria Harrison? Was there a connection at all? There was a kind of link when you really thought about it, but as well as being rather far-fetched, it was still far from clear even to Rilsky. The trouble was, there was no knowing whether the whole affair, like life, would turn out to be horribly vile or merely meaningless.

Rilsky took a swig of Schweppes Light, dusted off his charcoal gray pants, glanced at his reflection in Gloria's glassed-in bookshelves, found the reflection satisfactory, and had Larry Smirnoff brought in.

◆ CHAPTER NINE ◆

"I'm a racist," joked Northrop Rilsky, "and believe me I'm ashamed of it. But I can't help it. There's nothing I can do about it. Besides, the geneticists are in the process of proving that kind of feeling is innate."

And to stymie the curiosity of those who'd have liked to know more about the science in question, he went on:

"Some people are anti-Semitic; others hate Arabs or blacks. I personally loathe journalists. They're all priests—the modern equivalent of priests. They manipulate everything and understand nothing."

To do him justice he could do better than that. Society forces people to explain themselves, and he was good at doing so. He maintained, among other things, that journalists exercised a kind of absolute power. They influenced the politics and economics on which everything else depends. This phenomenon, said Rilsky, was peculiar to our civilization (if it still deserved that name). Religion had once been a supreme force, but it had always been to a certain degree occult, occult and above all moral, despite notorious distortions and exceptions, whereas the journalists of today triumphed openly, occupying every possible inch of space on radio, television, and even at dinner parties. As well as in the "book" sections of the supermarkets, where their effusions filled yards and yards of shelves. Rilsky claimed the human race hadn't yet recognized the arbitrary power wielded by the media, a sect that hadn't even the modesty to conceal itself. And it had good reason not to hide, for by definition it ranked highest in the order of visibility. Nor were the media subject to any higher authority, only to fluctuations in their power to please public opinion and pressure groups that themselves suffered from media contagion. In other words, journalists operated by exploiting people's basest instincts, including their small talent for truth and their great aptitude for crime. "Would you like me to give you some examples?" (Rilsky was mocking.) " 'Ladies and gentleman, we are speaking to you live from Rwanda. Several hundred thousand people dead. A plane carrying humanitarian aid landed this morning. So far only the journalists have disembarked. [Close-up of journalists.] This is John Smith, special correspondent of the CNN, speaking to you live from Rwanda on the eight o'clock news.' No comment. Isn't that enough for you? Listen to this, then: 'Ladies and gentlemen, we have just arrived at the scene of the crime. Only the press have been allowed inside the security area. There is no victim yet, still less any murderer. The murder is due to take place at any moment. The journalists are on the spot, ready and waiting. [Close-up of journalists.] This is Mary Smith, speaking to you live from Santa Varvara on the eight o'clock news.' Did you hear? I know you watched, but did you hear? We've achieved what is all for the best and what can only happen in the best of all possible worlds. Don't you see what's happening? I'll tell you: journalists are talking to journalists about journalists. And what are they telling one another? Everything, nothing, any old thing—it doesn't matter what so long as you can get an article out of it, or a pic, or a clip. They might almost say—in fact they must say—how horrible showbiz society is. That's a journalistic idea that journalists love, just as they love to be part of showbiz, just as showbiz disparages itself in passing and then passes on to even worse offenses. Yes, journalists are talking to journalists about journalists. Are we all journalists? Not yet, not all, we're not all as famous as we'd like to be. There'll always be some who succeed better than others. But that's our only dream: How to get in on it? How to occupy the TV screen even if only for a moment, or at least to get a few lines in the paper, in the best of all possible worlds, where messages talk about other messages and images transmit other images."

Rilsky, who never forgot his fundamental though skeptical humanism, was ready to admit that in certain circumstances news could be useful to democracy. And his antijournalist prejudice vanished completely in the presence of certain specimens—Stephanie Delacour, for example—and was replaced by a feeling inclining toward friendship. An exception that proved the rule and proved quite simply that links between individuals were the only genuine ones. But as recent scientific progress showed, they too were determined genetically.

Without even saying hello, as if he'd already had quite enough of Rilsky, the editor of the *Morning Star*, overwrought and moving like a sleepwalker, renewed—or rather continued—their eternal argument.

"I already know what you think about journalists, Northrop. Pure jealousy! You're just afraid of losing your own power. Because we're really in the same business, the cops and the media! It's true, it's true! Except that *we* have to use kid gloves. *And* we're often on the spot before the crime's committed. Whereas *you* always arrive too late and then claim to establish the Truth with a capital *T*. And on top of all that you want everything to be simple, for heaven's sake! 'This is the victim, that's the guilty party, ladies and gentlemen of the jury. Now it's up to you to give the verdict.' Don't make me laugh! You reached your verdict before the trial even started, so you can spend your time looking down your noses at the doubts and procrastinations of our wretched legal system. Not to speak of your aristocratic scorn for public opinion, You regard everyone else as incapable of objectivity—or, in other words, of reason. I refer of course to the kind of reason available to a senior police officer and to him alone. You'd like the truth to be cut and dried, established once and for all, with the criminal identified, the weapon found, and retribution meted out to the hand that dealt the blow and the mind or minds that were behind it all. But that's just the crude logic of the run-of-the-mill detective story, an ancient technique to justify the existence of elderly English spinsters who are really permanent teenagers living in a time warp, in a world just waiting to be boned and dismembered like a dead chicken, the skeleton of its antiquated passions sticking out plainly through a hypocritical substitute for real flesh. It's the press, let me tell you, Captain, that really investigates crimes, that carries out the only valid inquiries. Because the press represents society as a whole. Oh, I know it's too slow for you; the result isn't as enjoyable as a nicely roasted chicken attractively served. Eh, Captain? They're two different things: tracking down a complex truth in a way that challenges the whole of society and feasting in a lordly manner off quails cooked by somebody else!"

Larry Smirnoff reeled off the familiar rigmarole regardless of the fact that he was a witness and perhaps even a suspect in the case in question. His attitude not only reinforced Rilsky's "racism" against journalists; it also revived his aversion to the sort of macho men who pride themselves on being exceptionally shrewd and modern. As Rilsky had often noticed, these types also tend to fancy themselves experts in matters of sex.

"I'm afraid we're going to have to lower the tone of the discussion and talk about your movements, if you don't mind." (Although the change of direction was inevitable, Rilsky was reluctant to embark on this unsavory path and determined not to linger on it too long.)

"No problem at all, Captain! I've got a cast-iron alibi. Though perhaps that's not quite the word—the party in question was not at all impenetrable, if you see what I mean!" (Larry liked smutty jokes. Rilsky, disgusted, didn't pursue the matter.)

". . . ." (Rilsky.)

"Don't press me—I won't tell you who it was. But I did spend the night of Saturday to Sunday with this charming young person. I was with her until Sunday afternoon, if you really want to know. Anybody could have seen us having brunch together in the News Café." (Smirnoff liked bragging, too.)

As Popov had just given him a report compiled by one of their men on Smirnoff's movements, Rilsky already knew who'd been with the editor of the *Morning Star* in the News Café. She was a Frenchwoman, the special correspondent of *Events*, a Paris paper. This, while throw-

ing a rather unwelcome shadow on Ms. Delacour's image, didn't tar-
nish it enough for Rilsky to bracket her with the customary targets of
his prejudice. However, the subject was too distasteful for him to want
to dwell on it and point out the holes in Smirnoff's argument. You
could have brunch with somebody without necessarily having spent
the night with him or her. So, in the absence of confirmation by the
person concerned or the evidence of a third party, Smirnoff's alibi was
far from "cast-iron." But it wasn't totally implausible, either. Rilsky
was well aware of Ms. Delacour's weaknesses. It was this knowledge
that helped to explain his indulgent and protective attitude toward her.
So instead of harping on the night of Saturday to Sunday, he went on:

"So you haven't any alibi for the afternoon, after brunch. And it's
most probably during the afternoon that the beheading took place,
after the murder itself." (Rilsky couldn't resist this underhand blow.
Smirnoff was so arrogant he'd asked for it.)

"And why, may I ask, should I have committed such a senseless
act? Come on, Northrop, that's enough horsing around. I admit your
theory about there being more than one person involved is convinc-
ing. But now will you kindly have the patience to listen to me?"

Larry was in his element now, and enjoyed giving the captain a
foretaste of the front page article that would shortly appear over
his signature.

For some months Santavarvaran politics had been tainted by a number of real estate scandals. The party in power—and even members of
the president's entourage, if not the president himself, though up till
now this had been difficult to prove—had been expropriating and then
requisitioning certain plots of land. Subsequently, under cover of
bogus companies and with the collusion of the municipal authorities,
various risky and elaborate transactions were hatched. Tourism having become the country's most lucrative source of profit, the racketeers had set about building hotels and marinas, camping sites and
other similar facilities. Farewell salt marshes, bird sanctuaries, woods,
parks, and vineyards! And as if that wasn't enough, schools, hospitals,

and even private dwellings were to be razed to the ground. And liberal and ecological protest was meeting with less and less support.

The property speculators had recently turned their attention to the health sector, which was criticized as being too expensive, and responsible for the famous social services deficit. A number of psychiatric centers and clinics, unluckily all situated in an area being eyed by the tourist business, had been closed down, their inmates crammed into two already overcrowded hospitals on the outskirts of the capital, more or less on top of Santa Varvara's residential district. This gave rise to unrest among the staff, strikes by the managers, and a deterioration in patient care. But such understandable though suicidal reactions left the politicians unmoved, and as usual it was ordinary people who suffered. Several patients escaped, and the crime rate, which as Rilsky knew all too well was already soaring, started to rise faster still. The police, influenced by the government of which Rilsky seemed to be such a loyal servant, were far from eager to take the matter seriously. That might mean having to name those who were really responsible, and the culprits were uncomfortably close to people in high places. But wasn't this just what Rilsky had been hinting at when he said Gloria's murder was a collective and thus a fundamentally pathological act? Every murder is more or less that, but this particular one, because of its extraordinary brutality, obviously pointed to the most sordid depths of human insanity.

Larry Smirnoff's theory was clear and conclusive, a certainty rather than a hypothesis. As no one could possibly have wished the charming Gloria any harm, only somebody unhinged, a sex maniac or confirmed kleptomaniac—a few small articles were missing from the scene of the crime—could have stabbed her, a woman asleep in an unguarded house, to death. Not that there was any lack of policemen in Santa Varvara, but as elsewhere the public were always wondering why they were never there when they were needed.

But to get back to the facts. For a week people had been talking about a serial killer who might very well be responsible for the Harrison beheading. He'd raped and strangled all his victims, which proved he had an obsession with women's necks. Rilsky was well aware of the serial killer's existence, but he also knew that line of inquiry might lead to the real estate scandals. So, perhaps for that reason, he decided to ignore institutional and political maladies. Instead he concentrated on his own private form of psychology and on trying to destabilize the friends of the murder victim.

"Psychology has never been anything but a feeble attempt at avoiding politics. You know that as well as I do, don't you, Captain? After all, you do all you can to skirt around my theory. But sooner or later you'll have to admit I'm right. At least if you're honest enough to carry your investigation through to a conclusion." (Smirnoff, threatening.)

It wasn't Rilsky's job to be concerned with politics. He wasn't even sure whether professional politicians shouldn't be lumped together with journalists as an object of his contempt. Their fate had gradually become so dependent on their televisual skills that they now formed a subsection of the mass media and shared in their omnipotence. But Rilsky couldn't help being intrigued by Smirnoff's idea of a serial killer, escaped, perhaps, from a mental hospital and in cahoots with the racketeers. The papers never tired of recounting the misdeeds of their latest star, and the public were growing familiar with the psychopath's fetishes and trademarks. He never left any fingerprints. His victims were systematically raped (though so far it was hard to say what the women had in common, except that they were all attractive and in their forties). The murders all involved strangulation together with other injuries, particularly to the victim's neck, which was usually slashed with a sharp instrument. There was nothing about Mrs. Harrison's corpse to suggest she'd been raped, but the police were still awaiting reports on vaginal samples. As for the attack on the neck, this time it had been especially brutal. And extreme. Smirnoff might dismiss the psychological approach as useless, but the merest novice in that profession could have distinguished between the pathology of the serial killer the Santavarvarian papers were so keen on, with his fixation on necks and throats, and the pathology of the person who'd cut off Mrs. Harrison's head. Of course the possibility of another serial killer as yet unknown to the media couldn't be ruled out: a serial killer who also stole pictures and stabbed his victims. There might be even a third, so lacking in taste as to lop the heads off corpses already cold. As investigations now stood these were merely extravagant theories, though if they were ever confirmed they'd throw Santa Varvara into the most enormous panic, enough to arouse and even excuse the journalist's vengeful zeal. But Rilsky didn't want to be responsible for causing a national crisis. So for the moment he stuck to the details of the case and set about dealing with these by a process of elimination. He started with those that were the most minor and obvious.

"The stolen picture's a Picasso: *Woman with Collar.*" (Rilsky, getting down to brass tacks.)

"You don't say! I knew the older Harrisons had some nice things, but I'd never have thought they had anything like that! Mind you, I don't know anything about painting myself; we all have our limits, don't we, Captain? But I do know a picture like that must cost a packet. As a matter of fact I always thought Picasso's women looked as if they'd just emerged from a scuffle with a murderer. Those heads without bodies perched on their collars as if they were sitting on trays. The serial killer would have seen this one as the embodiment of his fantasies. All the more reason for lifting it."

"So now you're going in for psychology rather than politics?"

"If you like. But only as one more way of flushing out the real culprits. They're much more dangerous than the wretched psychopaths who are your usual customers."

"I don't have any customers, Larry. I'm quite happy just to listen to your evidence."

"I think I've told you everything."

"The case is only just beginning. And I'd be obliged if you—and your alibi—would refrain from leaving the country. I'll be seeing you!"

Rilsky, all politeness, saw Smirnoff out to the drawing room, more convinced than ever that journalists were the scum of the earth.

He listened quietly to Pauline Gadeau's deposition. It didn't tell him much he didn't know already. She scarcely qualified as a suspect as she'd left the dinner party long before it had ended in order to take Jerry out to her country place for the Halloween holiday. But Rilsky was obliged to question her, partly out of routine, partly in the hope of picking up a few revealing details about the victim and the people around her. Unfortunately the speech therapist hadn't much to say. She was very reserved, and her observations were all strictly professional. Jerry was her patient, so she naturally knew more about the deaf boy's difficulties—largely surmounted—than about any secret suffering his handicap might have caused his mother. Ms. Gadeau explained that as an experienced psychologist she'd been careful not to get too close to the mother so as to remain entirely at the disposal of the son. She was sure Rilsky understood the need for this precaution.

Her precise monotonous voice and drab appearance were starting to make him yawn. He'd been working hard since the morning and had had only a cup of coffee for lunch. It was now that he remembered one of Smirnoff's crude but not always completely irrelevant remarks: "Psychology . . . a feeble attempt at avoiding politics." Rilsky cut short Ms. Gadeau's scruples. She had no desire to linger either ("It's seven o'clock already, Captain. I live a long way away, and Jerry's waiting for me to give him his dinner"). He then ushered in Professor Zorin.

◆ CHAPTER TEN ◆

For more than a century St. Ambrose's Hospital had occupied an unsightly old building in the southern suburbs of the capital. The peeling facade, the wilted garden, the stale institutional smells mingling with whiffs of garbage cans, disinfectant, and boiled cabbage— all these only added to the desolation one expects to find in places allocated to the handicapped. Despite pleas from the leading lights of local psychiatry, Zorin included, and despite the growing number of its inmates, St. Ambrose's hadn't been redecorated for decades. There were some excellent specialists in Santa Varvara, expert in the biochemistry of the brain, skilled at using the few scanners the country possessed, unrivaled in the art of administering narcoleptic drugs (when there were any), producers of research published in the best periodicals and admired throughout the ever-expanding world of the cognitive sciences, but all this notwithstanding it had to be admitted that everyday practice at St. Ambrose's left much to be desired. And that was putting it mildly.

Inadequate medical supplies, incompetent management, over-crowding, and staff shortages accounted for the deplorable level of the care provided in the hospital and the increasing violence prevailing in personal relations there. Igor Zorin felt horribly ashamed about all this, even though he'd been quite successfully psychoanalyzed and practiced that art himself, as well as being St. Ambrose's consultant psychiatrist. This latter activity usually absolved him from undue qualms. He took comfort in the thought that at least in his own department of child psychiatry, which he ran with great efficiency and energy, professional standards were largely upheld, and its researches had won it an enviable international reputation.

That being so, Zorin wore a satisfied smile as at 12:40 A.M., on Sunday, October 16, he drove past St. Ambrose's grim walls. He'd just reluctantly quitted the delightful company of Gloria Harrison—in his view the most distinguished as well as the most attractive of women—and was on his way home to his official apartment on the second floor of the small and dilapidated mansion that housed the hospital executives. The porter, aroused from his slumbers, was surprised by Zorin's smile. The professor was something of an introvert, and his expression rarely showed any change as he steered his red Volvo through the hospital gates. But, after all, so much the better if the "children's professor," as he was called, could achieve some personal satisfaction, maybe some domestic happiness, just like everybody else.

What Zorin was really thinking about was the paper he was going to deliver the next morning at an international conference on autism. He was due to open the proceedings at nine o'clock in the hospital's main lecture room—not a very congenial meeting place, but the paper itself was going to be brilliant. As he automatically raised a hand to the porter by way of apology for waking him up, Zorin was going over the main parts of his speech in his mind, relishing the cogency of his arguments and reminding himself to tone down some of the more affected phrases before he went to bed. He sat up doing this until two in the morning. Zorin was such a perfectionist he tended to get submerged in detail.

And so, as expected, his contribution to the conference was outstanding, and he himself was warmly applauded—a rare occurrence at a conference, especially one on so hopeless and obscure a subject as autism. To put it simply, Professor Zorin was putting forward the theories of the English school which assumes autism is endemic to all human beings. It holds that each of us has a sensory trauma, a kind of black hole in the psyche made by some tremendous but forgotten event, either pleasant or painful. We try to plug the hole as best we can until we are able to desire our mother and kill our father (as poor old Freud maintained, referring of course only to boys). However—and this was Zorin's original contribution—a compensated autism could sometimes enter into our lives in various strange but positive forms. Thus certain children—and consequently certain adults too—have the gift of what's called absolute ear. If their cases are examined more closely, as the professor had done, these individuals are seen to fill in the famous "black hole" of their endemic autism (already established by the English school)—or in other words to counteract the effects of an overacute and highly painful sensitivity—by paying extraordinarily close attention to the world of sound. They cling to it, absorb it, and reproduce it faithfully, wrapping it around themselves like a protective bandage, a Band-Aid on their aural wound. Having once suffered violence from sounds, they now imitate and tame them. "As of course you know as well as I do, ladies and gentlemen, you perceive sounds by means of the right side of the brain. But people with absolute ear can't do that; it hurts them too much. All the sensory waves, everything that reaches them through the right side of the brain, completely overwhelm them. That's my theory, and I'm in the process of confirming it through MRI. So what happens to such people? Well, nothing, in most cases, and we hear no more about them. But others transfer their aural lives to the left side of their brains, the part specially adapted to the learning of language and logic. They can then perceive and create music as you and I do language. If you've been following me so far you'll have realized that people with absolute ear are the logicians of sound or, to put it another way, the software of the aural world. Let's leave geniuses out of it; they rarely if ever consult a specialist. The people I'm concerned with here are compensated autists who have become absolute ears. But their trick only works insofar as they achieve complete accuracy. And even then their exploits are a kind of caricature: they're imitators, not budding Mozarts. They reproduce; they don't create. At best their efforts meet only with laughter, and that demonstrates how far they are from the source they merely echo."

Professor Zorin illustrated the phenomenon of compensated autism by another example of artistic prowess, this time involving the plastic arts. One of his young patients, deaf from birth, had developed a strange ability to draw just like Picasso. He kept on producing bogus Picassos that only experts—and not always they!—could tell from the real thing. The young "forger" was quite unable to draw an apple or a tree "properly," like any "ordinary" child of his age.

Rilsky's preliminary inquiries confirmed that Zorin had been a great success at the conference on the Sunday morning after the murder, though the captain was not unduly impressed by the professor's triumph. Rilsky's prejudice against journalists was paralleled by a half-fascinated, half-aggressive exasperation with the soul doctors who claim to be experts on mental health. Zorin's self-assured prattle had taken him back to the previous winter, one of those luminous white winters that alternate with Santa Varvara's sweltering summers and for a few months make the country look like the setting of a fairy tale. Sergeant Paolo Voli, of the section dealing with sex crimes, had just been murdered, and Rilsky went to the funeral mass. The black-clad widow, the dead man's three daughters, the incense, someone fainting, the priest's sermon: "God rest his soul, for he did not hesitate to come to the aid of the lost soul of another and to risk his own life to ensure the safety of all. . . ." Amen.

Rilsky wasn't an enemy of religion—he recognized its civilizing influence—but beneath a conventional exterior he used to seethe with secret rage as he listened to the mawkish homages the establishment offered his men on such occasions. This time, however, it wasn't the priest who called down Rilsky's mental thunderbolts. Seated in the front row was the official psychiatrist whom the Ministry of Health sent from time to time to keep the police up to date on the psychology of murderers. After Voli was killed this man had come to explain the killer's "case." As if the cops hadn't understood his "case," and the "cases" of all the other killers, from experience. And as if any explanation could lessen the irreparable loss of death. The psychiatrist solemnly suggested that a thorough knowledge of mental truth, or "psychic verity," such as he himself pursued but of which Sergeant Voli had unfortunately been ignorant, might have saved the worthy policeman's life. For brave as he undoubtedly was, he was just a little neglectful when it came to psychiatry's most recent discoveries. Rilsky, much as he delighted in the absurd, could scarcely contain himself. What this scientific toady's explanation boiled down to was that the murderer, being a pervert, was structurally unable to tell right from wrong. He was also incapable of feeling and compensated for his "psychological deficit" by paroxysms of exultation in which love and death were inextricably mingled. What nonsensical rigmarole! And a fat lot of good it would have done Voli to know about it! All the knowledge in the world about black holes wouldn't have helped when the rapist and pedophile came face to face with the sergeant and shot him as he tried to talk him round. ("Come along, now—calm down. Just let the kid go and hand over the gun, eh?"—along with the other stupid things one burbles at times like that). At the end of the day, and despite their proclaimed (or hidden) intention of making everybody alike, what the sciences of the soul really did was clear the murderers of guilt. And what about the victim, pray, Mr. Psychiatrist? Is his or her soul the same as the murderer's? Can it tell right from wrong? Does it feel? Where is *its* black hole? The psychiatric experts never asked themselves such questions. And that day at Voli's funeral, with the widow and the three little girls weeping and even Popov taking a crumpled tissue out of the pocket of his jeans, Rilsky felt like punching the ministry's soul specialist on the nose. You idiotic old fogy with your dryasdust books—I'd soon show you the difference between your rubbishy theories and the life of a cop!

Rilsky was feeling the aggressive, even vulgar impulses usually attributed to Popov. No one ever suspected the captain might hide such urges beneath his distinguished exterior. In such moments—and it must be admitted they happened often—he understood the deeply rooted reasons why he put up with the insufferable Popov and took a perverse pleasure in their close but inadmissible similarity.

And now here was Zorin producing the same old stuff about holes and deficits, yammering on about psychical life—that of a forger, this time—and forgetting all about the victim! Gloria Harrison's devoted admirer emerged as a mere chaser of souls, and all he was interested in was the Picasso picture. Was this the professional bias of a psychiatrist? Or the sign of a platonic lover?

"Which brings us back to our subject, my dear Rilsky. [The professor had just given the captain a brief account of his movements. Rilsky, though allergic to pedants, listened carefully. Post-Freudian psychoanalysis was on the way to becoming his second hobby, after the violin: You had to deal as best you could with the ravings of all these interchangeable officials.] Would you believe it, the gifted forger I spoke of in my paper is none other than Jerry Novak, son of the dear departed. [Here at last the child psychiatrist's voice betrayed real sorrow. To Rilsky he even sounded close to tears.] The other evening, when I was talking to my unforgettable friend in her study, a few minutes before the other guests arrived, I was able to admire again that wonderful imitation of *Woman with Collar*—the original was painted in 1937, if I'm not mistaken—hung there by a mother who really took an interest in her son's talents."

Zorin turned around to point at the picture in question facing Gloria's desk. He blinked in surprise at the dark green square that stood out against the paler green background. Then he swung back toward Rilsky.

"Stolen, Professor! The only thing that was taken. Well, the most significant thing as far as we know at present. But needless to say our investigation's only just beginning." (Rilsky, pleased with Zorin's expression of mingled satisfaction and astonishment.)

Julia Kristeva

"But good heavens! This is amazing! It must mean that that night, at the very moment when I was writing, or rather revising, my theory about *Woman with Collar*, someone—the murderer, if I understand you correctly—had exactly . . ."

". . . exactly the same idea!"

"You're insulting me, Captain! Or else you're joking, which would be in very bad taste under the circumstances. There's all the difference in the world between scientific analysis and cynical theft."

"As I don't need to tell you, Professor, the human race has invented many different ways of appropriating—of entering into possession of—other's people property."

"Your insinuation is so ridiculous I prefer not to answer it. With your permission I'll regard it as merely the undue zeal of an amateur psychiatrist. Rather amusing, isn't it—and perhaps proof, for anyone who might be inclined to doubt it, of our usefulness to society—to see that our profession's so popular with the police? Anyhow, your—how shall I put it?—your coarse humor, or your humorous coarseness, at least puts me in the clear. For if I actually was engaged in intellectually 'stealing' Jerry Novak's picture, with the sole object of vindicating my own farfetched ideas (that's what you're driving at, isn't it?), then I couldn't have stolen it in reality. And therefore I can't be suspected of attacking the painter's mother. Be that as it may, I presume you don't believe what all the rest of them have probably told you: namely, that I might have killed her because she rejected my advances? But what else might have entered your typical sleuth's mind? Why, for example, shouldn't I have killed the mother just to get my hands on the picture? In order to study it at leisure and relate it to the circumstances surrounding it, in the interests of my scientific career? Professor Zorin and Mr. Hyde . . . Professor Zorin and Dr. Jekyll . . . But no! In your own way you're too subtle to imagine anything like that. You don't think I'm a pathological case, do you? I'm not a split personality—that's obvious. Thank you very much for that at least, Captain Rilsky!"

Despite his long experience of human nature Rilsky was always surprised and even shocked at how clearly the free associations of psychoanalysts (even more than those of most people) revealed their murderous impulses and their contempt for others. Men and women ask nothing better than to talk; all you have to do is let them run on. And that is as true of psychoanalysts as of all the rest, if not more so.

"But to return to the picture, Captain—I'm as familiar with every patch of color in it as I am with Jerry himself. [Zorin was jubilant, as if the murder, plus the theft, validated his humble researches even more than the ovation he'd received at the conference.] The purplish red line all around the edge, with the wide egg-yolk yellow band outside that. The two dark green olive branches standing up, at once graceful and threatening, like claws or fangs! The broken triangles to left and right separating the unstable equilibrium of the shoulders and repeating the same olive-green tone shading toward gray-blue. The speckled mother-of-pearl of the breasts, flesh-tinted, like those of a wicked fairy. And in the upper part of the masterpiece, the hat. An enormous orange snail, broadening out over the head and made of straw woven into a spiral. And the straight hair, the same straw yellow with some more watery streaks. Oh, all those yellows, Captain! There's nothing like them for depicting tamed passion, flesh at peace! And here there's the velvet of the sun, the tang of saffron, the impudence of daffodils, the bluntness of marigolds, dusty mimosa and lively wallflower—all crowned by a supernatural orange, the warmth of the sun itself smiling at you in the hat. The face, in the middle: one eye looking straight out, the other askance; one black imperial nose and another in terra cotta, the color of dried blood, like the lips. You remember those Egyptian profiles of beautiful goddesses—or gods, I'm not sure which—with long skulls and huge eyes, that you see in the pyramids and on sarcophagi, representing the divinity of writing? And the yellows there, sometimes soft and smooth and sometimes piercing, giving off not the stench of a corpse but the drowsy odor of unguents. 'A woman,' according to the caption. Perhaps. A palette of

scents and tiny sounds. The power of sight shorn off but starting to
move. [Zorin, carried away and dreaming aloud. "Nothing like painting and death for turning men into poets," thought Rilsky.] The
whole thing completed by a squared-off neck, as if the head was
being served up on a tray. . . ."

"A severed head."

"If you like. It occurred to me too. Pure coincidence!"

"Do you think so?"

"What else? And those gray shoulders set above two pink breasts
that might just as well have been an X-ray of lungs, the white stripes
suggesting the ribs. I've made a close study of the original—in a
reproduction, of course. Do you know it?"

"I'm not sure. Maybe. Between ourselves, all Picasso's women
look more or less the same to me."

"Wrong again, Captain—terribly wrong! This is a portrait of
Mademoiselle Marie-Thérèse Walter. All her charm, all her delicacy,
all her freshness is in the cut and thrust of the brush—if you'll forgive
the expression! Entirely different from the sham happiness of Olga,
or those grim portraits of Dora Maar, Jacqueline and Françoise Gilot!
Oh no, Jerry made the right choice. It was his mother the young
forger was painting—the violence. His too of course, but hers to
begin with, do you follow me? Not forgetting Gloria's girlish side:
vulnerable, rather naive. You didn't know her yourself? What a pity!
Really, what an irreparable loss! You know, affection will always get
better results than the most efficient prosthesis, not to mention the
poet's pointless mirth, if you see what I mean, Captain. The love that
existed between them—what greater success could anyone have to
show for a life? And Jerry found his own way of containing that love
by reproducing it a thousand and one times, stroke by stroke, via
Picasso. It was simultaneously his way of defending himself against
that love and his way of celebrating it. Much to the disadvantage of
Novak senior, a very minor painter despite his recent notoriety. Of
course Jerry's paintings haven't really got anything to do with

Picasso; no expert eye could miss the oedipal message under the surface, could it? And Gloria showed she realized this when she chose *Woman with Collar*, out of all the rest of her son's false Picassos, to hang up facing her desk. She loved all shades of yellow too: ocher, ivory, ecru . . ."

Once more Zorin's voice held a hint of tears. He was quite ready to expatiate indefinitely on painting, but that wasn't really what Rilsky was interested in.

What was Rilsky likely to get out of Zorin, then? Nothing more that day. But his evidence, narcissistic as it was, was far from useless. The relation between affection and violence; compensated autism; the Cubist mummy—all these might help in drawing up a profile of the murderer. Or murderers. The jigsaw was beginning to fit together in Rilsky's mind.

CHAPTER ELEVEN

The strange things you feel when time stops, as if cut off by murder. And yet murder brings us together to wind time backward. Remember what you were doing between midnight on Saturday, October 15, and the evening of Sunday the sixteenth! Try as hard as you can, ladies and gentleman, to recover lost time. And good luck to you!

I'm still waiting, lying on a pine deckchair on the wisteria-clad terrace. The captain is playing with me. He thinks he's playing on my nerves. If he only knew!

I can feel the roughness of the kelp-colored canvas hard against my skin. The light resin-scented wood isn't at all reminiscent of a coffin. My slumped body makes me look like a dog slinking close to the ground. I merge into the air quivering just above the gravel, into the low and taciturn leaves of the orange trees.

I can feel my breasts, full curves clammy in an outfit of a blue too hot for an even hotter afternoon. Like a pair of plump bream full of algae and plankton, poor drowsy wretches dreaming of stealthy hands and cool lips. But today, full though they are, they hesitate, tense and anxious despite their torpor. If I were a fish I'd leap into the first wave, flee nets, hooks, and harpoons, and hide away in the sand. But I'm not a fish, and I'm afraid of the waves, sharp as blades paralyzing muscles with pain. Waiting arouses madness, and Gloria's corpse keeps washing back over me.

"He's deliberately leaving me to cool my heels, don't you think?" (Odile, swirling the draperies of her evening gown over the terrace, would like me to keep her company.)

I pretend I'm not really there, and it's true. I'm in my mouth, the parched little bowl of my mouth. My tongue abhors a vacuum. It presses its damp warm surface against my teeth, lingering on the sharpest canine, a rounded molar, the smooth contours of the gums. It flinches away from a scratch still bleeding a little inside my upper lip. I'm possessed by the familiar but magnificent roof of my mouth, a lonely cave, a higher counterpart of my sex, which after all I visit less easily and less often. Is it absurd or monstrous to indulge in such intimacies in a body fused with opacity both within and without, other people's as well as my own? But there's a tiny margin left for peace and distress, an almost nonexistent region where I take refuge when menaced by murder, or more especially indifference.

"I've nothing to say that Pascal hasn't told him already. We're above suspicion; we were at the Golden Sands. [She stands opposite my deckchair, leaning against the gnarled stem of the wisteria and trying to get my attention.] He ought to have interviewed us together; married couples shouldn't be separated at a time like this."

". . . ." (I pause for a while before speaking, to show her I too am harassed and exhausted.)

"At least they should take the women first. You ought to complain too, my dear: he isn't treating you with the consideration you're entitled to in your position. Not to mention that you and he are supposed to be friends. When things go wrong it's supposed to be women and children first, isn't it?" (She has no intention of leaving me in peace.)

Sensation is an ordeal because it isn't thought. Thought modifies things, distances them, gives them a name. But when I feel, I'm *in* the object, or in my body as object. So much in them in fact that to me they're no longer objects or things, because I can't stand far enough away from them to think about them. I love that frontier; I revel in compromises and betrayals; sensation is my own special form of possession. It's the secret garden I withdraw to when a police captain is about to question me; when life disintegrates into an arbitrary zapping of images; and when each of us is a potential killer, as the wor-

thy Rilsky insinuates, or at least an accomplice of the unconscious
murderer, the serial killer who'll get us all in the end.

Is this typical female regression, childishness, a retreat from the
lucidity of thought? "Be silent, wretch, and remember it was pleasure that brought you forth out of nothingness!" But long before
pleasure, in the very heart of it and long after it, what is experienced
cannot be said: it just ripens and withers—a fruit, *fruitio*. I feel its
delights just as much as I do the dangers now oozing from the roof of
my mouth, from my breasts, from the pine deckchairs, and from
Gloria's wisterias, mauve veins standing out against a house that
takes pleasure as others die, while the erstwhile guests grow more
and more uncomfortable and each human atom, hunched in his or her
genuine antique chair, broods on the small secret dramas, the pathetic
acts of perfidy, the trivial sorrows that might and ought to have made
him or her a murderer. It will soon be dark, and everyone will feel
increasingly suspect, irrevocably guilty, or at least like an accessory.
How could it be otherwise if one's the least bit sensitive, amid the din
of transistors, the bawling of loudspeakers, and the silence of steam-
rollered consciences?

"All I hope is that she died quickly. You do die at once if you're
stabbed through the heart, don't you? And I think I've read somewhere that you don't feel any pain." (Odile beams at me optimistically.
That naive grin is a habit of hers. It doesn't mean anything.)

"She was probably strangled before she was stabbed. There wasn't
much blood." (I adopt a technical tone to call her bluff.)

"Have you interviewed the forensic expert? Did he tell you that?
But she hasn't got a head—how could they tell she'd been strangled?
And there weren't any fingerprints, were there? I mean the sort of
marks that are usually left on the neck? [Odile can't leave it alone.
Jealous and goggle-eyed, she gloats at the thought of a crime of passion.] Strangled! Good heavens! That's all we needed! As if it wasn't
bad enough that the poor dear had her head cut off. Strangled! No, it's
too much, I shan't be able to bear it . . . Pascal! [She starts to go.] Can

you imagine? Is that the captain calling me? Coming, Captain—at
your service. Strangled? Well, I *must* say!"

Well, well. A little too eager to be true, that Mrs. Allart—too excited,
too interested in the fingerprints on her best friend's neck. She envied
Gloria's attractiveness with deep, patriarchal resentment. A woman as
dim-witted as that is capable of anything. She must have thought herself safe from suspicion because the body was found without a head.
But if you accept the theory that the victim was strangled before being
decapitated, it's only logical to look for the strangler first. I was
wrong to think Odile was indulging in fantasies. You need a special
talent for that, or at least the basic ability. And has she got that ability?
It's by no means certain. She's more the active type: Mrs. Allart,
expert at acting out. But she's panicking already, the poor tedious
featherbrain. My favorite brand. The ideal disguise for a monster.
What a treat in store for Rilsky: he likes to think crime is the result of
illiteracy, consumerism, and the decline of thought in every shape and
form, including the most privileged.

I'm not making fun of him. When all's said and done I agree with
him in my own obscure and disillusioned way. When thoughts become no more than worthy petitions that everyone can and must sign,
when the signatures are interchangeable because a clear conscience is
universal and what's universal is a nonthought on the part of universal indifference, then the sensations I experience on the scene of a
crime disturb me greatly. But that's putting it too mildly. Quite simply, I feel. I'm possessed by elusive sensation. Think what you like
about it. Those who live by thought may have noticed that our arguments are growing weaker; they're shrinking into codes, standards,
conventions, illustrations, images. Everyone either produces or con-
sumes them, and they're of no interest to anyone. And so, away from
the sort of consciousnesses that are broken down into clips, my sensual pleasure is my private treasure trove, my own microresistance
and absurd paradise. I admit this is a somewhat diabolical resource,

for disorder of all the senses drinks at the same spring: passions, pathological states, sound and fury of all kinds. When someone merely pretends to think, when thought is a sham, then it's crime that cries out the at last inescapable truth. Crime explodes like a rocket in the night of feeling.

What do you think? I'm just waiting. And while I wait I cling to my tepid, narrow frontier, and I compromise, make do with the flesh of objects and beings, my own to begin with, and move from side to side, from one plane to another. As a stranger, a foreigner. "The power of God keeps me safe, / Despite the ancient dragon, / Despite the gaping chasm of death, / And despite all terrors. / Let the world rage, let the world be shattered— / I remain and sing." I love Bach's motets, but it's the powerlessness of God that keeps me safe, and I can't sing. I experience things, I name them, I betray them, I start over again, I'm faithful to nothing except my own sensations, though all I do through them is betray myself. And as I try to avoid both murder and a good conscience, both the delinquents and the cops swarming over this charming house as they swarm over everything else, I examine my own possessions. I do so to prepare myself for the task of working as a detective under the watchful eye of Rilsky, who's at present pretending he's got me down as a suspect.

Waiting makes your thoughts turn back and return to the rudimentary state they should never have left behind: the state of the just-segmented embryo of a dream, scarcely visible but standing in for the world of here and now. A vision valid only for tonight or for always? Congealed since Gloria's death? Or there all the time, waiting until something happens to develop the negative and make the hazy image emerge more clearly?

"*You* look tired now, Stephanie dear. But this is just a formality. Still, you never can tell." (Northrop, friendly, teasing me.)

"You always know what really matters, Captain." (Stephanie, knowing the detective's deceptively naive questions had made all his previous interviewees give themselves away, striking chords in which he, the music lover, would later be able to hear the truth.

Must pull myself together. Find the thread of time again, the thread of what was said. Gloria. How can one think about anything else? Anyone else? Allusions, hints, all the more or less malicious words exchanged about her. It was the same even with Rilsky. We've known one another a long time, and he likes to take advantage of my trips to Santa Varvara to "exchange witticisms," as he puts it. A game that only succeeds at the expense of a third party. And that third party was often Gloria.

Like abstinence, its opposite, the devotion that goes with a woman's passion adds to her capacity for pleasure. "Total invest-ment—without it a woman isn't really complete," the erudite Northrop used to joke, echoing some French duke or other. For despite Gloria's dislike of autobiography her affair with Michael Fish couldn't remain a secret in the narrow world of Santa Varvara society. "I don't like to exhibit myself, but I won't hide myself either." (Gloria.) So the whole thing was obvious, especially as Michael Fish by no means shunned publicity. "Ruin isn't enough for her." (Michael.) According to him, Gloria's senses were quickly kin-dled. "Madame How-Many-Times?" (So he called her.) An unlim-ited number, she might have answered, but she never said anything. Motherhood had completed her because it had wounded her. In this sense she was now the perfect lover. But only for herself. Taking or being taken, master or slave, man or woman, nothing mattered; she was like a flower. Unconscious of the dual danger it made her part-ner feel. Sated without being satisfied, Gloria gave her lover the impression he was merely a laborer in the matter of sex, never the master. And by taking the initiative when his imagination ran out, she also made him feel it was a male rather than a female he was deal-ing with. Then Michael either let himself go or got into a rage. Feigned violence and genuine brutality. For her part, Gloria loftily exposed herself to it all and asked for more. She never stopped because of the pain; that was always bearable. Only if she happened to open her eyes, and those green orbs encountered her lover's distorted face.

"If Madame wants to know what I think, I believe men are frightened when a woman feels pleasure." (Hester.) "I can understand him: with you he's in danger of turning into a homosexual." (Odile.) Gloria couldn't understand either of them. She was becoming intoxicated with her own body, awakened at last after years of misunderstanding and privation. Now nothing in the world would have made her dismantle that suddenly imperious sensibility. There's a myth about the woman who's frigid. And another about the woman who dreams of a romantic idyll. Neither had anything to do with Gloria. Like a plant open to the dew, to butterflies, bees, and even hornets, she overflowed with pleasure, with pure indecency. It was as if she had neither body nor organs, only avid flesh with sex in skin, breasts, mouth, and anus: the flesh of the whole world, of nothing, flesh itself.

A woman who enjoys sex has made up her mind to die. I wondered if Gloria knew this, and how I, Stephanie, had to be able to guess it for her. And what was the connection between this and the forgotten dream that had come back to me just now on the terrace and left me with a dread I couldn't throw off? Even now, as I was just about to be interrogated by Rilsky.

Hardly had I lit a cigarette to try to jolt myself out of the nebulous state of mind into which Gloria's murder had thrown me and into enough brightness to deal with the captain's little tricks, than Popov's car appeared on the road that ran along the river. It drove through the gates, lights flashing, and came to a halt in the garden. Then the lieutenant burst triumphantly into what had been the victim's study. He had just arrested Hester Bellini.

◆ CHAPTER TWELVE ◆

Hester wasn't very proud of herself when at about three in the morning during the night of Saturday to Sunday she left the guest room temporarily occupied by Brian Watt and went back to her attic studio in the right wing. Not that she'd expected anything to come from her affair with the sickly, pompous student. But until then she'd always been able to make him come. And she'd almost convinced herself that she was the only woman in the world who could bring off this exploit. Which after all was so important to a man that it gave a woman a certain amount of power.

The previous evening she'd cleared the dinner table, served the coffee and liqueurs, and tidied up the kitchen a bit. She'd finish the job off in the morning (Madame never asked her to work on Sunday, but Hester didn't like letting things slide over from one week to another). So it was about one-thirty when she joined the young man in his room. She'd found him already aroused, as usual, but very nervous. Neither her large breasts, nor her skillful tonguings, nor even the scabrous stories complete with homosexual references that she kept in reserve for difficult cases produced the lasting erection they both needed. Pouring with sweat in the long Indian summer night, tired and irritable after several unsuccessful attempts, they were both almost falling asleep when Hester sensibly decided to leave and go up to her own bed. She'd had enough of Brian, the dinner party, Madame's guests, Madame herself, and everything to do with her. Only a stiff brandy would wipe out the whole boring scene. Gradually, as she sipped, she almost decided to drop Watt. But she couldn't quite make up her mind.

The student was a mine of information, and Hester hoped, through him, to uncover a number of things that still remained obscure about the past and present of Mr. Fish. Not content with getting Madame into his clutches and becoming the official lover of a lady infinitely his superior, that upstart nobody had for some months now been leading her a dog's life. Hester, worried at first and then increasingly scandalized, had finally resolved to act. Hence Brian Watt and the information he might supply.

"To tell you the truth, Captain, it's very boring being a maid. And for a modern girl it's humiliating too. Having to answer the bell, for example. Or to stand up straight and starchy to the left of the guests, handing round the *sole meunière* to people who haven't the faintest idea what's going on and have obviously never used a fish knife and fork in their lives. But then unemployment's even worse in Santa Varvara than everywhere else. And Mrs. Harris was so beautiful and distinguished! And so unlucky too, what with little Jerry and that husband of hers—a painter, and not much of a catch. Then he has to go and die and leave her a widow, a young woman still with a sick child to look after . . ." In short, Gloria was so unlucky that Hester felt herself being raised above her menial job and summoned toward a more noble and dramatic vocation. The truth was, Gloria Harrison needed Hester Bellini, conceited though that claim might seem to the people Madame regarded as her friends. But they could see only the mistress's charms. They despised . . . no, they didn't even notice the maid!

They didn't know what went on between the two women in secret: the languorous pleasure with which Gloria submitted to Hester's ministrations; the softness of the skin on Gloria's back, arms, belly, and thighs, which she let Hester massage at length when she was tired out by her typewriter and Jerry. That is, nearly every day. Then there were the brief, anxious, but—Hester was sure—amorous glances Gloria sometimes cast at her before taking a bath or going to bed. The same slanting eyes as those of the little female cousin in her native village who'd made love to Hester when she was fifteen, during the grape harvest. Gloria's eyes had the same vague look, but more stealthy and even more apprehensive.

Brandy cleanses body and mind and makes you able to face trying to sleep. Hester left the darkened kitchen and her reveries and went out into the garden. It was then that she caught sight of Michael Fish. The French windows of the bedroom adjoining the study on the ground floor were wide open, and the master's car was clearly lit up. He'd evidently just arrived. He hadn't been there a little while earlier, when Hester had left Brian's room. Wasn't Fish supposed to be in London? No planes landed in Santa Varvara after midnight. And usually both Mrs. Harrison and Mr. Fish took a taxi to go to or from the airport. So had Fish stayed in town? But if so why all the production about having to leave in a hurry for London?

Hester crossed the part of the terrace that was in shadow and slipped into what had been the nursery, just next to the parents' room. It was more or less unused these days. Jerry slept mostly in a larger room on the second floor, next to his father's studio. The rarely opened door creaked. Footsteps sounded on the pavement outside. Hester, terrified, crouched against the wall.

◆ CHAPTER THIRTEEN ◆

Face to face with Rilsky, Hester was unable to describe what had happened. It was obvious she didn't want to. Moreover, as the captain could tell, she'd had such a shock her mind must have gone blank. So there was little or nothing to reproduce.

To Hester it had seemed like the everlasting domestic row she'd been overhearing for months. Michael Fish came home in a bad temper, probably drunk, wild-eyed and gesticulating vaguely, upsetting plates and glasses and laying into Madame on the slightest pretext.

"Wasn't it shameful, perhaps even suicidal, to knuckle under to such a man? Because she really did let him do as he liked in bed. You can take my word for it, Captain; a maid's bound to know about that sort of thing. Of course it was understandable, in a way. For years she'd been suffering in silence with young Jerry. And then when this guy turned up she thought her luck had changed. But did she have to go overboard the way she did? And with someone like that? Very dubious, very shifty indeed, that's all I have to say. Although . . . there's plenty more that *could* be said. You've only to ask Brian; you'll be astonished. He was only after her money, the family fortune, and her pictures. Greedy and wicked, that's him. And he thought all he had to do to get what he wanted was marry her. But Madame wasn't having it. Anything—and I know what I'm talking about—anything but that! I think she wanted to leave everything to her son; she adored him, anyone will tell you that. And it was only natural: what would become of the boy if she died and he was left without any money? She'd thought of all that, Madame had. And now it's happened. But it was bound to; I'm only surprised it didn't happen before. I say this because despite appearances that woman's life was a nightmare. And if you ask me there was no other way it could end, when you really think about it.

"But that wasn't how Mr. Fish saw it. He wanted everything, and he wanted it now. There was a big fight the day before he was supposed to go to London. But during Saturday night—or was it early Sunday morning?—I found out he hadn't gone abroad at all. He'd left the house sure enough, he'd left Madame—blackmail, if you ask me—but he came back to twist the knife in the wound. She implored him, poor thing: she didn't want to lose him. 'My poor Hester' (she talked to me like that because she was pretty sure I must have overheard all their quarrels), 'my poor Hester,' she said, 'for a woman, being alone is worse than being ill-treated.' Well, I don't agree with that, Captain, and you've seen with your own eyes the proof that she was wrong to give in to him like that. Yours truly wouldn't let a man treat her that way, I can tell you. But she was so beautiful, so fragile, what could you expect? But she made me angry. I couldn't say anything of course, but she knew I didn't approve! She really did make me see red, lowering herself like that!

"She must have had a bit too much to drink that night, and perhaps she was only half conscious. She often took pills before she went to bed, sometimes more than she should have done; I could tell from the way she looked in the morning. I think they ended up making love, on the big bed on the other side of that wall. It was always the same after they'd had a scene. The sounds of flesh on flesh, panting, groans, sheets, puffing and blowing, cries . . . I was almost drunk myself and hardly dared to breathe in case I gave myself away. I may even have dropped off.

"It was almost daylight when I heard a noise outside. Mr. Fish was stuffing pictures into the trunk of the car, then he got in and took off.

"I don't know how long I stayed there, huddled up on the nursery floor. No sound from Madame. Had she gone back to sleep? Had she been in the car? Had she gone off with Mr. Fish without my realizing it, dazed as I was? I thought that must be it. I couldn't move for fear of drawing attention to myself and perhaps causing embarrassment. But in the end I got scared of the silence. So I went in. And saw her. Dead."

"Are you quite sure of that, Miss Bellini?" (Rilsky, speaking very slowly.)

"No doubt about it, Captain. You saw it yourself: that purple face, those blue lips. Poor Madame, how she must have suffered!"

"Do you think so?"

"Of course I think so! Stretched out on the bed as if she'd been suffocated in her sleep, but her face all twisted with pain. And red marks around the ears; they stood out very clearly against that fair skin, didn't they? I can't have been the only one who noticed them!"

Rilsky wasn't about to contradict her. She was the only witness (so far) to have noticed the retroauricular petechiae characteristic of strangulation. And to have seen the victim before her head was cut off.

"*He* strangled her; I don't see who else it could have been. [The maid had collected herself again and was giving free rein to her fury.] He's a brute, I tell you, a beast pretending to be a man. To be a gentleman, into the bargain! Brian had told me he was a crook, a racketeer, but Madame wouldn't believe me. He knocked her around just for fun, if you can imagine that. He was prosecuted for assault by his ex-wife, or some other woman—I can't remember which but everyone's heard about it. Brian knew right away and he told me, just between the two us, you understand."

She'd suddenly become aggressive and more precise. Was she accusing Michael Fish so as to divert suspicion from herself? Detectives had contacted all the London galleries in an attempt to find the missing art dealer, but in vain: he hadn't set foot in any of them for eight months. A search warrant had been issued, and a warrant for his arrest would soon follow. But what about Hester Bellini herself?

"You don't like Mr. Fish, do you? And yet you didn't inform us when you discovered the murder. When you saw the body you just ran away . . . taking the silver spoons with you. [Popov, impatient, pretending not to see the wrathful looks Rilsky was giving him. Then, lowering his voice and addressing his colleague,] "The sort of woman who's no good to anyone and ready to do murder because of it."

The hunted turtle retreats into its shell. She can't express it, she can't even think it, it descended on her like fate. Some strange alchemy has changed her hatred of Fish into fury against Gloria. Most people mourn for the victims of misfortune when they're people they've loved, but some people (and they're often women) loathe them just *because* they once loved them. Madame ought not to have entertained so vile a passion; it only made things easy for a killer equally base. Another Gloria had taken the former one's place, inhabiting a randy body that asked for the ignoble death finally inflicted on it. Hester didn't know that other Gloria and didn't want to know her. The other Gloria had continually hurt her feelings and offended her sense of sexual superiority. She whom everyone took for a surly spinster, vaguely nymphomaniac and anxious to comply with the latest dictates of bad taste, in reality aspired only to the most diaphanous and chaste admiration; there was a wistful madonna under that degrading uniform. So Hester Bellini couldn't stand the other Gloria at any price. What luck to be rid of her, to have *got* rid of her—to escape, go far away, never have to endure such subjugation again, ever, with anyone, to live alone, live out the rest of her life in a style that was modest but possible, possible if she took a few valuables, why not, you were always being trampled on in this sort of job, doing much more work than you're paid for and being treated as a nobody! A "housekeeper"? You must be joking! At someone's beck and call twenty-four hours a day! That was the truth of the matter. Well, never again; she would never be had again! Not her! Not Hester Bellini!

Popov had had an intuition, and Hester had been arrested not far from her native village in the mountains, a hundred or so miles from Santa Varvara. She'd stuck to her plan and stolen Gloria's black Austin Metro, together with the silverware Popov had mentioned, and set out for home. Then, in a more lucid moment, she'd turned back and left the car by a hut and, sobbing and distraught, set out on foot along a mountain trail. A night went by before the local police, notified by Popov and intrigued by the deserted Austin Metro, managed to track down the fugitive. At about 4:30 in the afternoon of Tuesday, October 18, they delivered her to the police station in St. Mary's. the village where she was born. She hadn't offered any resistance. She was still wearing her black maid's uniform; it—and her little white apron too, of course—had been torn by the brambles. Her blond curls were plastered down, dusty and damp with sweat, over her predatory face.

"She's leading us up the garden path, boss. She could be the strangler herself. That story about the lover running amok doesn't hold water, not without any proof. And the idea of the devoted skivvy taking off without warning, well, that's very weird! [Popov wasn't too sure of all he was saying, but he was chortling with satisfaction at having got hold of a likely murderess and made what he considered a crucial contribution to a case that wasn't getting anywhere.] If you ask me, she strangled the victim with her own hands!"

"What a horrible idea! [Rilsky, sincere, imagining Popov imagining Hester in the process of strangling Gloria.] Do you think Miss Bellini could have killed Mrs. Harrison in the noble cause of class warfare?"

"Why not? There was no one there to hear the victim shrieking, let alone the sounds of her being suffocated. The weedy student was already out cold thanks to Miss Bellini's ministrations. He was under her thumb anyway, and she thought she could count on him to keep quiet even if he had heard something. But our young vamp here overestimated her power over him. Some power, by the way, seeing he's not really interested in nooky! The boy's not normal: that stands out a mile! Luckily he put us on her trail, though I'm sure I'd have worked it out for myself anyhow. Because we mustn't forget she'd got a motive: revenge. In these days, as you know, slaves don't know their place any more." (Popov, blushing at having uttered such an opinion.)

"You understand the witness perfectly, Lieutenant, as is very natural. Just the same, Popov my lad, I'm inclined to believe her. We may have the beginning of the tragedy here, or at any rate the physical cause of death. I could be wrong of course, but still . . . Needless to say, I'd like to see everything you've been able to get on Fish. I've always thought—and we've both seen it from experience—that the love of money is the least attractive of all the passions. It's uglier than sexual perversion, as I've told you often. But I can see you don't agree with me—"

"Yes, I do, sir, I assure you. As always. But this Hester's a real monster, and I'm an expert on that subject. Whereas needless to say I don't know anything about money." (Popov, annoyed at having given Rilsky the opportunity to hold forth.)

"No, no, don't protest: I know you, and I'm well aware you don't agree with me at all. But still, if you agree with me in the main . . . on the whole . . . as best you can . . . Well then, don't worry—we'll work it out, as usual! So where was I? Money and sex, wasn't it? That's all society's interested in. But to get back to Fish: I need your help with this unfortunately not very rare bird. But despite what you were taught at school, man isn't just a social animal. Hatred, madness—mere social scourges, they'd have us believe! But no, it's even worse than that! It's genetic, they say, or transcendental, take your choice! . . . Now, about this Hester of yours . . . After all, why shouldn't she be on our list? She's no genius, though, not by a long shot. And no saint either, with her pretense of being a brazen man-eater! But she overdoes it; women always overdo it when they try to rebel, or liberate themselves, or whatever. Plus most people are compulsive liars, and everyone's subject to the death wish. So don't let Hester Bellini leave town, if you please, and go on checking up on her habits and movements and the people she sees. But don't forget the guillotine, my boy! After all, we *have* got a severed head to deal with! Or rather we haven't got it! Incredible, isn't it? Maximum virtuosity in perpetrating maximum brutality. If you weren't here it would make me throw up! And we still haven't got anything on the knife, much less on the decapitation, not to mention a few other details. But have we got to the heart of the matter? What *is* the heart of the matter? Death or hatred? Death, hatred, or madness? That is the question. We still have a long way to go, needless to say."

Popov had to admit Hester Bellini hadn't mentioned either blood or a knife and that the last time she saw Mrs. Harrison her mistress was still, so to speak, all there.

CHAPTER FOURTEEN

A few days had gone by and the case was "taking its course," to use Rilsky's time-honored expression, amid general unease. Stephanie decided to stick to the more rational aspects of the affair, those most likely to supply material for the article she'd come to this confounded place to write before Gloria Harrison was incomprehensibly slain. So she followed the trails Smirnoff had suggested and found out all she could about psychiatric hospitals, expropriations, real-estate scandals, and corruption in high places. Larry was right: the trails led back to very high places indeed, ultimately to the president himself. Smirnoff, the Solomon of the *Morning Star*, had just made his own discoveries public, and he'd deliberately linked them to Gloria's murder. According to the front page of his paper that morning, Friday, October 21, everything suggested that the person chiefly responsible for the whole sorry business was the serial killer. When the maid last saw her mistress the lady wasn't dead but merely unconscious. Michael Fish couldn't possibly have stolen a forged Picasso. Only a psychopath would get any satisfaction from such an absurd theft and on top of that committed such barbarous cruelties. But if the murderer was a patient who'd escaped from St. Ambrose's Hospital, the lamentable state of which was due to expropriations and other real-estate scandals, then the true perpetrator of the crime was corruption, in other words the government, and hence the president himself.

"You see, Stephanie, in this murder we have a story, a history with a small *h*, that looks like the end of History itself. The terminus, the *exitus*, or, if you prefer, a murder that has already taken place. Everything seems to be over because death has struck. But no, everything is only just beginning, and all the more insidiously, cheerfully, and crazily in proportion to the awfulness of the crime. And you won't deny it *was* abominable. That's what makes murders, and detective stories, interesting, isn't it? The main thing, the essence of the matter, has happened, but it turns out that wasn't really the essence after all: the death may have been filmed but other versions are possible. And that's where everything—the case and so the novel as well—has to start all over again. So we conclude that the end of the history wasn't the End of History. Is there such a thing? Intellectual snobs—you know who they are as well as I do—are always talking about the End of History these days. But they've got it wrong yet again. There *is* no End of History, as is proved by this case of ours: it claims to have an end too, when really everything's only beginning. Violent death, knife, decapitation: it's all there, it's the absolute limit. You'd think it was impossible to go any further. But no. It *is* possible! Death isn't the end, death leads a human, and even a social, life. Death is a socialite. And we mustn't forget that it's thanks to death that our own histories, the genuine ones, get off the ground at all. And everyone joins in, and by adding one tale to another we get a whole network of causes, a multiple logic, a polyphony. And if you ask me, *that*'ll be the absolute limit, the culminating point, not Gloria's wretched murder. When everyone's had his or her say we'll have a much clearer view of the ins and outs of individuals and of society. Of Society with a capital *S*, which will be X-rayed by means of all these new little histories and reveal its hideous truth. Don't think I've gone off the rails: the real guilty parties will be unmasked, those who line their pockets at the expense of the unworldly, who exploit them, who try to make them think there's such a thing as the End of History . . ."

How pompous he was once he got on his hobbyhorse! But Stephanie thought Larry might be right for once. Everything had already happened. But they still had to find out what, who, when, and why. Isn't that why we make up stories in the past tense? They happen in the pre-

sent; the past tense shapes though it also distorts them. One story will
be the true one. But we won't always know which one it is. But be that
as it may, Larry's "social" investigation had made Stephanie's task
much easier. Though she hoped she'd be able to carry it further herself.

Rilsky had invited her to dinner. He didn't say much about the murder. So much the better. They'd have a little rest, listen to Menuhin
playing one or two masterpieces; they both needed a respite from
words. She enjoyed the policeman's silence. The atmosphere was
relaxed: both liked listening to the void; both were afraid of making
mistakes. Despite Rilsky's habit of acting the elderly troubadour, she
felt she'd like to trust him. Without giving up on her own inquiries but
without getting in his way either. For the moment.

Gloria's murder was turning into the "Harrison affair," and all
Santa Varvara was busy with the subject. It—or rather the "inside
story"—was the only subject of conversation. Everyone had a theory,
a certainty, an inner conviction, a secret to add to what was still a very
hazy picture. Especially, it goes without saying, the women. Including,
surprisingly enough, the woman who lived in the apartment next door
to Stephanie. She was one of those women who bring out their knitting on suburban trains. Pink knitting and pink T-shirt. Stephanie had
noticed her—how could she not?—for the neighbor had started smiling at her over her spectacles. Nice brown eyes, the knitting bobbing
up and down in time to breasts braless under the T-shirt as the train
carried both women home. Stephanie back from her inquiries into the
real-estate scandals, and the neighbor back from who knew where.

"You're living in Bob's place, aren't you? Hi!"

"That's right. Hi!"

"I knew her well."

"Oh?"

"His sister, Gloria. Did you?"

"Yes, in a way. Slightly,"

"Be careful; he's still lurking around, that serial killer. I'm sure it's
him. And there was that case a few blocks from our place, at number

seventy-six; I knew the blonde who lived there on the fifth floor. We both went to the same hairdresser. At number eighty-four. All the victims have been fair. He stole a picture from her place too, so it must be the same man. Shall I tell you how he gets past the doorman? He goes through the basement, where they keep the washing machines; you must know that by now, you've been living here for a couple of weeks. Then he goes up by the service stairs. So this woman didn't think anything was wrong, she thought it was the doorman when he rang the bell. Anyhow, that's what I think. What do you say?"

"It's possible."

"It's certain! I don't go down to the basement any more. If you have any washing to do I can tell you where there's a laundromat."

". . . ."

"Don't you get bored staying in Santa Varvara? I'm going for a bicycle ride this afternoon with some girlfriends. Cycling's fashionable here. It's environment-friendly. Why don't you come along? We can talk about all this murder business. And it's good for the figure too."

"Afraid I can't make it this afternoon. Very kind of you, though. Another time. Keep in touch."

Cycling was definitely not Stephanie's sport. What an idea, sitting astride a kind of prosthesis supposed to increase your physical agility! It was the same thing with cars: stratagems invented by apes who were clever and industrious but had lost the cat's natural litheness and the horse's muscular intelligence. Can you see a cat riding a bike or a horse at the wheel of a car? But Stephanie's feelings on this subject were inconvenient sometimes, especially abroad, where you're supposed to get around on your own using the local modes of locomotion. She was quite willing to admit that if you were a journalist or a detective it was a major handicap. She never drove a car unless she had to. She usually traveled in taxis, trains, and planes. As for looking after her figure, an hour or so every day at the pool took care of that. The cool shock of the water moving swiftly through the skin and disappearing in motion, movement of arms and legs, then in back, neck, nape, and all the other muscles. All your surface merging with the air and the lapping water: an interchange of liquids and currents. Stephanie planned to go to the pool the next day, alone. She was missing her usual swim. But no, cycling was out.

The pink breasts had put away their pink knitting. The train had just arrived at the station nearest to where they lived. Oh to get back to the opaque comfort of the laser cube; to hide; to disappear.

". . . a very passionate woman. Passionate about her son, passionate about men. I'll tell you something. I met her recently—we often bumped into each other like that—in the New Café. Rather standoffish, she was, but still . . . I said to her . . . She said to me . . ."

With the help of such encounters, accidental or inevitable, Stephanie's investigation was making progress. Adding note after note, without really going out of her way, she was building up a file of her own on the Gloria case. As detective work it was necessarily irrelevant: what could they add up to, details like this, trivialities about a woman's life recounted by a knitter, whether pink, blue, or green? Never mind, it was up to Rilsky to be efficient, though that wasn't the poor fellow's strong point. But since it amused him . . . ! Meanwhile Stephanie plugged away at a vague and uncertain reconstruction of the victim's life and character.

Passion, the knitter had said. But that destructive passion, endured in secret like tuberculosis, had made Gloria seem proud, almost happy. Except for Odile, in whom she occasionally confided, and Stephanie, who imagined in silence, no one guessed that Gloria was really a mask worn over a wound. In Santa Varvara people regarded her as a cerebral type, cold and full of her own success, an arrogant go-getter. At first this had isolated the young mother and encouraged her natural aloofness. No woman—in other words, no one at all—had anything to say to the wealthy heiress obsessed with her translations and her avant-garde painter.

True, when Jerry was born some ladies rallied around: visits, presents, questions. "How are you?" "How is he?" "Is everything all
right?" "It seems there's a problem?" "Is he really normal?" "Someone said he's hemiplegic, psychotic, autistic, narcissistic, insane?"
Avid friendships throve on shared anxieties. Gloria didn't like this at
all; in fact she hated it. The result was they dropped her. The pseudo-
considerate pseudopals just disappeared for good. After that she did-
n't notice the passage of time. What year was it? She was never sure.
She knew what time of day it was and which day of the week. But the
year? Time was measured as "before" or "after" Jerry. Not that his
arrival was comparable to the traumatic birth of Jesus: that had
marked the beginning of a calendar, a new age apparently there for
good despite certain well-known attempts at sabotage. No, for Gloria
it was just that time had stopped, or rather been weighted down by the
demands of affection and things to do. Meanwhile events had taken
place, fashions had come and gone, women had brushed History aside
and then been brushed aside by History. But Gloria had scarcely
noticed all this, shielded as she was by her withdrawal from the world
and the disappearance of her friends.

The distance between them and her had turned to detestation
when local attitudes changed, when exaggerated admiration of
professional women was superseded by the old affectation of gal-
lantry toward the fair sex. Former feminists—Simone de Beauvoir
groupies and ardent petitioners on behalf of Angela Davis—weary
after so much unrewarded effort, started to rehabilitate, both in their
writings and their lives, the scented charms of the boudoir and the
honeyed poison of adulterous affairs. These "new libertines"—the
supermarkets soon found a brand name for them—didn't mind risk-
ing ridicule and went in for confession. But they didn't really go
further than admitting a little weakness of theirs, known in modern
parlance as "desire": "desire" for an unavowable lover who nonetheless was avowed. So feminist pens began to produce hordes of
lovers, with their train of unnecessary adorations, proud escapes,

anguished partings, and pointless though unconditional reconciliations. To these were added hard sex and stiff upper lips and lastly the words of the gentlemen themselves, apparently madly in love with mistresses madly in love with them. What authenticity! What courage! What sin!

The foundations of a society obsessed with show were heard to tremble. The new world order itself was shaken by the new revelation. Instead of the "old mole" of communism, once expected to eat away the roots of capitalism, desire—and feminine desire at that!—now threatened to subvert not only decadent Europe (everyone knew nothing would ever really happen *there* anymore) but also the status quo in Santa Varvara itself and even the barbarity of the human race as a whole. No less!

For of course the ladies' fictional lovers turned out to be strangers, foreigners, workers even—in any case socially and linguistically inferior to the storytellers themselves, though very desirable, quite irresistible. Or else they were youthful and as-yet-unrecognized geniuses, whom the ladies' know-how and greater experience were able to raise to their rightful places. The sign of the eternal feminine! The motherly virtue that makes itself small in order—it's the only way—to wield real influence and power. The press raved about it. Larry Smirnoff himself deserted his usual political column to publish several articles in the *Morning Star Literary Supplement*—the woman who edited it describe the articles as "truly revolutionary"—praising the courage of the women, young and not so young, who dared to defy conformism and speak of their own *desire*. At last! What a relief!

Titillated thus, lethargic Santa Varvara turned further and further away from poor Gloria's invisible tragedy. To her preoccupied mind the farce of ordinary life, as reflected in conversation or print, seemed merely naive and silly. "Minimalist," was her verdict. "Too repressed!" was the diagnosis made of *her* in the backlash of the new wave, if ever it deigned to notice her or her foibles at all. But that happened less and less often. So Gloria plunged ever deeper into her tasks: as the fiercely devoted female on whom Jerry had to depend or as the translator of some amusing book that the local press had failed to notice in the original language. Philip Roth's *The Breast* had been offered her at the very same time as she'd been asked to do Shakespeare's sonnets. She regarded the latter as an enormous honor, the chance of a lifetime, an opportunity to escape completely from ordinary time. The prospect cheered her up enormously. "But it will be a tremendous task as well as an honor! I'll have to stretch the Santavarvaran language to its limits and beyond, make the sentences do acrobatics and knock the heads of metaphors together. But I mustn't go too far; people think new turns of phrase are mistakes when they read them in their own language."

Gloria naturally sought her publisher's advice. Equally naturally, he made it clear he couldn't care less. Like everyone else, he'd been won over by the ladies' falsely true confessions, the flattered purrings of the gentlemen, and the sycophancy that both sexes flaunted in what a few stick-in-the-muds still thought important: the world of books. "My dear child, we don't sell books nowadays! [He patted her on the shoulder as if to brush off some crumbs.] We don't sell novels or poems! We sell secrets, sex, life!" The gesture with which he meant to convey solicitude was rejected by Gloria with a dutiful smile. She then returned to her translations of the sonnets, neglecting the tantalizing but uncertain biographical elements that generations of historians have tried to decipher and concentrating instead on their verbal magic and her own attempts to import it into Santavarvaran.

Thus, without her even noticing, the gulf between Gloria and the society surrounding her grew deeper and deeper. But Stephanie Delacour wasn't a journalist for nothing, and since she could also be a detective when she felt like it, she started to enter into the scenario.

◆ CHAPTER FIFTEEN ◆

Gloria came to seem so near it was overwhelming. A bad sign for a detective. What about objectivity? Better give up, go for a swim, forget. Recuperate with some gin and some Mozart in the laser cube up above the river. Sleep and then send the article off to Paris rather than let yourself be suffocated (ouch!) by that delightful but inhibiting friend. No doubt about it, it was impossible to love such a woman.

Time expands when instead of being saturated with action it's left to take its natural course. A day grows into a season or a year: dawn stretches out and merges with the long coolness of spring; the strengthening daylight fills broad months of summer; the peace of late afternoon loiters toward sunset like a pale reluctant autumn; and night burrows endless wintry anguishes beneath the trivialities of day.

Waiting merges certain dreams together, summons dreams-in-waiting to the surface. But one—is it always the same?—will not declare itself one way or the other: do these scenes belong to the dark that has reigned since Gloria's death, or have they been there always? But today, at last, Stephanie has pinned it down. For you're not your "self" when you're dreaming: another "self" wakens beneath the closed eyelids. Dreaming, I am another; dreaming, I speak of her. "I" is just one view of all the "shes" assembled in my dreams.

As for Stephanie, she's lying in a bed that might be a triple coffin. Her mother sleeps peacefully beside her; the scent of milk and honey, the foamy softness of her breasts—she's smelled and felt, the parent of an infant still blind. A little way off, separated from Stephanie by the insuperable body of the mother, a man with the face of an invalid, the man of sorrow pleading for mercy in the face of an invisible threat. The threat isn't part of the dream; the dream obliterates it. Or rather the dream itself disappears; the dreamer has operated the remote control.

The next channel's showing a second-rate film that the dreamer doesn't remember. She presses the remote control: the same film again. She wakes. But the man's face is still there. Is it her father, who was killed in the hospital, the Goya-esque victim of men changed into wolves? How long ago? But the nightmare keeps recurring, more or less unchanged, and accompanied by the same sense of guilt. The father's guilt or the daughter's? The dream shifts to another channel.

This time the man is different. A bearded warrior in anguish, with imploring eyes. His contorted face is turned away from the two women; his head lies on his left shoulder, from which a stream of blood flows, soaking the mattress. Stretches of reddish ocher; Caravaggian pathos.

Switching channels again but still dreaming, Stephanie remembers: the averted face she couldn't see before she now looks down on from above, as if she were leaning over the horrified, gory head. Artemisia. The dreamer isn't Stephanie: it's Artemisia Gentileschi, painting Judith cutting Holofernes's throat.

Stephanie's dream and Artemisia's picture: virtual images contaminating one another. Two women attack the supine body of the Assyrian general: the blasé-looking servant and a ferocious Judith wearing a loose brocade gown. The splayed legs of the man are swathed in smooth crimson velvet. This sets off the confused conflict raging among the six arms, committing a kind of endless rape around the victim's head. The servant is using all her strength to hold him down, while Judith's violent onslaught propels her to the far side of the picture. Her right hand plunges a sword into the man's bare throat; her left hand holds his head down to receive the blow. The face of the murderess shows no horror. Only her body betrays aversion, by the way it stiffly avoids the spouting blood. Her concentrated expression is that of a mathematician, a biologist, or a surgeon, relishing her success even as she goes about her work. Is hers the victory of absolute knowledge? Of the people of Israel? Or of woman over man?

No feminist of the palmy days failed to study this picture, applauding Artemisia's talents and Judith's prowess. Not forgetting the scandal, early in the seventeenth century, when Artemisia was allegedly raped by a painter called Agostini Tassi who worked in her father's studio. Sued rather belatedly by Artemisia's father, Tassi was sent to prison, but later the young people were said to have been reconciled. A very mysterious business, involving master and pupil, father and daughter, rapist and victim. But who violated whom? Was Artemisia a whore, a plaything, or a genius? Probably all at once, and anyway what does it matter? What matters is that she painted as no other woman has done before or since and that she didn't paint just any old thing but a man being raped—beheaded by herself, Artemisia the female genius! Unless this whole cruel spectacle was produced by Stephanie, our dreamer?

Stephanie, who thinks her dream is absurd, like many of her other dreams, probably most of them. Why, she herself has never been raped. None of her lovers has even ill used her, and her father was gentleness personified, a saint; there was no question of any conflict or jealousy. On the other hand, one never knows what unlikely places a daughter's passion for her father may be hiding in, and vice versa. Witness the way her own hands kept perspiring while Captain Rilsky deliberately kept her waiting, that day when he was staging the interminable questioning of the dinner-party guests. And all the time the dust-laden air of twilight, fusty with the smell of decaying roses, filled her throat with vague disgust, and she was haunted by this dream but unable to recapture it. Now it was revealing itself at last in the laser cube, in fiery cascades of blood-red and gold.

No, sex had never been rape for Stephanie, whatever her feminist friends might claim in the name of humanity or femininity. In fact that was why she'd had to stop seeing them. It was never rape. Never. On the contrary, it was secret intoxication, smooth as velvet. A heart filled with blood in the body of a nun. Flowers open to the sky in a Georgia O'Keeffe painting. Scents made tangible in the pages of Colette. Stephanie could recognize in other people's work the nameless pleasure that men gave *her*. And that she liked to keep hidden and apart.

No doubt by chance, her greatest experiences of passion had taken place on islands: Corsica, Corfu, Martinique, the Ile de Ré. Pleasure without bounds and without future. They both knew that. He, because he had his own life and there was no question of disturbing it. She, because he'd touched her in the inaccessible place women generally call their "heart." The invisible spot where the uterus is linked as by an umbilical cord to the blackness of the mind. A soil propitious to slavery unless great pride is there to prevent it. Stephanie had made herself proud. Women know how to sham, but *he* knew her as she really was and never tired of her. She could only refer to the man in question as *he* out of loyalty to a memory of which only sun-baked light remained. Like a landscape with so many points of view one recalls it as merely a shadow.

The lush greenery of Corfu, the dark red roses and fragrant clematis smothering the brick walls of the monastery; the shower from the west, blowing blue clusters of flowers and salt mauve air in through the open window. His mouth on her breasts, and on her eyes, caught in the amaranths. Or again, lying on her back in a rose-colored creek in Corsica, or by the oyster beds on the Ile de Ré, with a scent of citronella and lavender. He fulfilling her wholly: sand, salt, and sperm all one. Or again: a thin orange cloud like a fox's muzzle over Fort-de-France, clusters of red alpinias and the lewd skins of anthuriums on her lips as he slowly grew inside her. No, I didn't tell him I'd kept the child. What would have been the point? Our situation was quite clear, but I wanted an incarnation of happiness. I didn't need him, or the long term, or a plan, or vistas of the future, or love, or worries, or security in my old age, or any of the things women imagine when they want a child. I just wanted to make present, outside myself, what throbbed inside me when he inhabited me beneath the mauve clematis, on sheets of salty sand, or in the light of the cloud like a fox's muzzle. It's something that can't be shared. He never knew anything about it. I could have been a happy single mother, or an unhappy one: a mother is a mother, happy or unhappy. When you're pregnant you don't think about the chores, the sore throats, the meningitis and dyslexia and polio. You try not to think about them; you think about something else. And that's because something else is at last possible.

He'll never have known anything about it, and anyway there wasn't anything to know. Although medicine was always advancing and could usually predict if not anticipate the future, the latter *could* still present itself in the form of malformation, especially when you weren't expecting it. Awful things could happen, though they weren't inevitable. If something did go wrong it wasn't always immediate. But it was always tragic. Though without the medical profession things might have been even worse. When she was seven months pregnant, Stephanie was found to be suffering from toxoplasmosis. Toxo what? Toxin, poison. Strong possibility that the brain would be affected. A therapeutic abortion. The terrible pain of a forced delivery, a delivery of nothing. Corfu, Corsica, Martinique, the Ile de Ré all emptied out into bowls in the clinic or preserved for use in biotechnology, she'd never know which, and what did it matter? So Stephanie had had more than her share of decapitation.

Afterward it took all her pride and workaholism to enable her to recover from such butchery. The struggle lasted a year. At least. Only Bob Harrison may have suspected something. Bob and *he* were close friends. Of course no one said anything. She tried to avoid meeting the man. In fact, there had been a sort of rape. Stephanie's dream had something to do with Artemisia's painting. So did the story that haunted her, possessed her, but that no one or practically no one else knew about. But who was it that had been raped? Stephanie herself? She still suffered because her body had given birth to nothing, been butchered for nothing, just as people who've lost an arm or a leg still feel pain in the phantom limb. Was it *him*, doubly raped through not having known and not having had a stillborn child, dead and not born, not dead and not born, the ultimate negation, the canceling-out of both *him* and the child. The father, the Father, her own father?

"But what connection *is* there with Dad? Is the beheaded Assyrian general Dad, *him*, or me? And who's wielding the knife? Artemisia, Judith, or me? Me again! A good thing Gloria didn't invite *him* to the fateful dinner party on Saturday the fifteenth: that really would have blurred the picture." (Stephanie, forcing herself to think: nothing drives a bad dream away more effectively than a little bout of reflection.)

If a dream is exhausting, put a stop to it! There's more than one decapitated woman in the picture galleries of our lives, but I know some whose desires are so strong they turn reality upside down and then paint it as skillfully as if they were Artemisia. And that's not an easy role to play; far from it!

Stephanie had had enough of old masters and drifted off to sleep, feeling that for once she understood Northrop Rilsky, who said painting was too slow an art. Ah yes, very true, my dear Northrop, and I'd go even further: painting is not only slow, it's immobile, anachronistic, outside time, pure time incarnate, especially in dreams. Let's dream on!

CHAPTER SIXTEEN

Michael Fish made one mistake. He took Jerry's picture down off the wall.

When he felt Gloria go limp, not breathing or moving, he realized her heart had stopped. Was that really what he'd intended? At first sight, not really. He'd wanted to frighten her, yes, but that didn't mean . . . Still, why not? He was supposed to be in London, after all, and even if that weren't the case no one would ever suspect the ideal lover of having murdered his mistress. She had just agreed to something he'd been trying to get her to agree to practically for months: to leave him half her estate when she died. Even after all his efforts, it was a pleasant surprise. And a nice packet of money. But he'd been expecting it, and of course that could be seen as a motive. But the bequest was only half the estate. That wasn't necessarily enough of a motive for murder. Admittedly he'd been very excited by Gloria's capitulation, announced out of the blue while they were making love, she eager as ever and even more ardent after a violent quarrel. But Gloria was used to such quarrels. Perhaps he'd been a bit rougher than usual. Quite possibly. In such circumstances one doesn't always know one's own strength. "Unconscious, perhaps even preconscious murder," Zorin might diagnose. But he wouldn't diagnose anything this time, because no one would ask his opinion. Gloria was the only person who nagged at the professor to give his precious opinions, in and out of season. Mostly about Jerry but also about everything else. And now Gloria was no more. But there was still the meeting, very compromising for Fish, that the deceased (Michael had to admit that's what she was) had had with her lawyer that Saturday morning. And a persistent Rilsky might well cite what happened at that interview as sufficient reason for M. Fish to get rid of G. Harrison. But no one was supposed to know about the will, least of all Michael, because he was in London, as he would never tire of repeating to anyone who asked him. If that wasn't an alibi, he didn't know what was.

Still, no harm in taking a few precautions. Wipe off the fingerprints, for instance. Impossible to get rid of all of them, but after all he did live here, didn't he? It was only natural for there to be some traces of his presence. Make a vague attempt at camouflaging what had happened: by stealing Jerry's Picasso, among other things. No one could imagine an expert on modern art pilfering a fake Picasso. They'd assume the thief must be some ignorant amateur.

But as well as that to him insignificant object he did take a few conveniently small and by now much admired canvases by Stan Novak. They were really worth something by this time, thanks to him, Michael Fish. Gloria was the first to admit it, despite her stupid insistence on acting like a mother hen and wanting to keep everything for her son's hypothetical future, instead of letting herself go and being a real woman. He stowed away as much as he could in the trunk of the Audi and made sure all the lights were switched off. Hester was usually exhausted after a dinner party and didn't get up till quite late the day after. And young Brian, for all his intellectual and social talents, which by the way often came in quite useful, was too delicate to keep late hours. So Michael Fish drove off with his mind at rest. All he needed to do was stay away for a while: wasn't he always on the move between London, Lima, and New York? "We were going through a bad patch, Gloria and I, and I wanted to make myself scarce for a bit . . ." Then one day he'd phone or send a wire: "How terrible! I've just seen it in the paper! I can't believe it! I'm coming home as fast as I can . . ." A disaster, a period of mourning, and then it would all be forgotten.

He crossed the frontier at about noon on Sunday, and from Santa Varvara, where he had a lot of friends who could be relied on, he took the first plane to Latin America. The authorities in Santa Varvara were not all that scrupulous, but for certain rackets the international networks were much more profitable. And for some years a loyal set of businessmen had turned a blind eye to Fish's comings and goings and let him enter and leave the country under false names. So he had no problems moving his various wares to and fro.

The art dealer was tall, strong, and lean. He had the craggy face of a sailor and an Adam's apple that bobbed up and down every time he swallowed. Black eyelashes contrasted with brows bleached by the sun. Cropped hair, the husky voice of a smoker fond of whiskey, bright eyes that seemed to give back all the world's simplicity. All these made him look like a provincial philanderer, a look that attracts some women because it suggests reassuring inferiority. Wily, greedy, hyperactive but slow, he was so self-indulgent he might have put on weight as he approached fifty if it hadn't been for his height and a couple of games of tennis every day. He'd always been stronger physically than mentally. It had been clear since his childhood that he was maladjusted, but this aspect of his personality was useful when it came to dreaming up risky and dubious deals, which he was able to carry off through a natural ruthlessness and a flair for detecting its absence in others. His activities included asset stripping and money laundering, and he was suspected of Mafia connections. But from all these doings the leading Santavarvarians of all parties modestly averted their eyes, not wishing to hamper the country's economic recovery. Women were not his chief interest, but he was good at using them to help him win the game of speculation. To him it was a kind of Russian roulette: the excitement of winning in order to lose and losing in order to win gave you the brief but intense certainty that you were above the common herd, superhuman. Often, after losing heavily, he'd get back on his feet again through new friendships and sudden changes of direction. He spent some time exporting wine, paper, and perfume. It was this last that put him in touch with the more elegant circles of fashion and art. And then, while not giving up his previous lines, he started, through Gloria, to operate as an art dealer. He really enjoyed himself then, playing the part of a distinguished entrepreneur. Unfortunately the greed that encouraged risk taking led also to rashness and didn't rule out bad taste.

It was Smirnoff's column in the *Morning Star* that informed him a warrant was out for his arrest: Captain Rilsky had included him among the suspects. So Fish gave up the idea of acting the repentant lover and tearful widower and decided to stay in Cali, where he was relatively safe thanks to the goodwill of his Medellín friends.

It was there, basking in the false sense of security the second-rate are so apt to fall into, especially when they're gamblers who've already eluded several traps, that Michael Fish decided to unload the fake Picasso. Who'd notice in Colombia? The purchaser, as reckless and impatient as the vendor, sold it on at once, without stopping to ask himself inconvenient questions, in a Middle Eastern emirate where he was in the habit of turning crooked deals. But the emir, who'd had his fingers burned once too often, had recently sought the advice of the Americans. As soon as he'd finished interviewing Zorin, Rilsky asked Interpol to track down *Woman with Collar*. At that time the U.S. organization in charge of hunting down forgers was more efficient and more highly respected by art lovers and the big banks than the Medellín cartel. So the U.S. agents soon got the better of the cocaine thugs, and in late November Fish was arrested. By then, under the name of Peter Moor, he was running an import-export business as a cover for laundering the money he made from drug trafficking.

Rilsky couldn't resist the pleasure of arranging a confrontation among Fish, Hester Bellini, and Watt. He took great trouble over what to wear on the day fixed for the encounter, and from a carefully selected wardrobe worthy of the Hollywood actors of his youth, he chose a black alpaca suit with a bold gray stripe. A white shirt completed the ensemble, making him look as formal as if he were just leaving for a night at the opera. This incongruous elegance concealed the effort of will Rilsky had to make to control his almost youthful excitement. "Good manners are of the utmost importance! One must behave properly," he used to tell Stephanie modestly. And she'd agree. It was for such subtle reasons that the two of them got on so well together. All that remained of Rilsky's natural sensitivity was something resembling a little drowned rabbit. Not even that: an empty burrow hidden under Humphrey Bogart's jacket. But from this refuge Rilsky was better able to appraise the situation: the man sitting opposite him was capable of killing. Not boldly. Coldly. Fish didn't have the hidden warmth that makes some ordinary rogues attractive. He was just a godless brute without a conscience. One of those mediocrities that shrink from nothing. A typical popular idol. A sort of hero of our times.

"Accidents will happen! She'd taken her pills and was all muzzy. So there you are! And afterward you panic; it's only human. Why should I be different from everybody else? Okay, so I took the pictures. But if it hadn't been for me those daubs wouldn't have been worth a cent. Taking them wasn't a crime, was it?" (Fish hadn't shaved for several days. He was thin and exhausted. This time he seemed to have hit bottom.)

"I gather you were due to inherit the victim's fortune if she died? [Rilsky wasn't mean enough to mention Jerry's picture, though it was through the false Picasso that he'd tracked Fish down.] So you're the main beneficiary of the murder."

"I only get half! The other half goes to the son and the brother, Jerry and Bob. And you haven't arrested *them*! That's the first thing. Secondly, I didn't know anything about Gloria's will. I only just heard about it from you. Anyhow, my lawyers says the lousy thing was dated Monday, whereas the death—or rather the accident—occurred on Saturday night." (Fish was struggling to get his head above water.)

"He's lying, Captain. He did know: I heard Madame talking to him about the lawyer." (Hester's curls were as crisp as ever now, her voice as shrill, and she yelled as if everyone else were deaf.)

"What *is* all this? Just listen to her! She followed her beloved mistress around like a shadow, her ear always glued to some door, her eye peering through every keyhole! Always ferreting through people's sheets and underwear, and in the can too, weren't you? [Fish in all his glory.] She's mixing everything up, Captain. She's talking about a fight I had with Gloria when one of us must have mentioned the lawyer, the will, and so on. But that was ancient history—and I left the house three days before this other thing happened."

"But *I* hadn't left, sir, and I heard it all from the nursery on the ground floor, when you came back in the middle of the night to frighten Madame, as usual. Maybe it isn't polite to listen at doors, but it can be useful sometimes." (Hester, suddenly recovering the memory she'd lost the day she was arrested. Even if she was lying, thought Rilsky, her recollections were plausible enough.)

You can understand just by listening to their voices. You don't need to see their faces or work out the meaning of their words. Constriction of the female vocal cords gives a harsh dry sound that pierces your eardrums: melancholy using hate to ward off weeping. In the male, relaxed nasal tones low down in the throat, stretching toward the sphincter and excrement. As for Brian Watt, his voice had two registers: one that was shrill and controlled, the utterance of the obsessional, and the other guttural, moist, elusive. Rilsky, looking at him, had a strange impulse to go and open the windows. Watt's appearance was that of a typical researcher. He looked as impassive and reassuring as a computer: a tidily arranged stomach with lots of drawers and labels and files in which to organize and store everything that's been swallowed. " 'Better a laugh to write of than a tear, / For it is laughter that becomes man best.' Who wrote that, Mr. Watt?" "You must be joking, Mrs. Harrison! It's Rabelais, of course." "Right. Now something more difficult. 'A wise man will not lock the chamber of forgiveness; for to forgive is fine victory in war.' " "Difficult? But that's a quote from Dante, Madame—obviously!" "Now for the dessert: 'In Xanadu did Kubla

Khan / A stately pleasure dome decree: / Where Alph, the sacred river, ran / Through caverns measureless to man / Down to a sunless sea.' " "Coleridge!" "And for coffee: 'Ya pomnyu chudnoye mgnovenye: Peredo mnoy yavilas ty . . . Kak geniy chistoy krasoty.' " "That must be Pushkin!" "And lastly: 'He must teach himself that the basest of all things is to be afraid; and, teaching himself that, forget it forever.' " "Child's play! Faulkner!" Watt knew all the answers, even to riddles much more difficult than those that Gloria plied him with to lessen the boredom of her dinners. But as Rilsky listened to Watt's voice, he heard the other music. It was false: too low, discordant, out of tune, persecuted. The overorganized stomach revealed itself to Rilsky's ear as no more than a trash can full of musty and repellent rubbish.

Of all the guests at the last dinner party, Brian Watt seemed the most affected by the murder. He'd lost everything. As a computer he'd been really useful to Gloria; now the computer was out of order. As a lover needing to be jump-started, he'd lost the good offices of Hester. She'd abandoned all pretense of being a modern young woman—even if rather an uncouth one—and now gave free rein to her primitive peasant reflexes. A sickly youth like Brian brought a house bad luck: that was her present verdict. His job as a go-between was over. He'd sold his services—on the side, and sometimes for dubious ends—to Bob, to Gloria, and to Michael Fish. But that was a thing of the past. Old ritual was succeeded by rout; organization by chaos: he'd had a series of fits, accompanied by a permanent sense of persecution. He was nervous, irritable, and quarrelsome; always on the lookout for enemies, plotters, a conspiracy against him. Someone had it in for him—for his honor and his life. But who was that someone? Women, for a start: all of them. Self-seeking domineering creatures ruled by some vague cosmic force. Gloria's corpse and Hester's know-how were disguises worn by witches. Then the menace seemed to come from Michael Fish: the chief culprit, murderer of the elegant Mrs. Harrison, a disgraced master dragging his manservant down with him. "A classic case: paranoia always turns out to be rooted in homosexuality": that's what

Professor Zorin would have said if he'd known. But he didn't know; he was involved in another investigation and so had nothing to say on this one.

"Everyone knew you were just after her dough! And that she always gave in to you in the end! You could get anything out of her, even her life!" (Brian hurled both his vocal registers in Fish's face, with such fury the art dealer stared at him speechless. You tend to be struck dumb when you're confronted by madness, and wonder whether it's you or the other person who's gone round the bend.)

Brian had plenty of reason to panic. Police inquiries were in the process of proving he'd colluded in Fish's Colombian activities. The Santa Varvara Mafia, dealing in arms, drugs, and works of art, was permanently in cahoots with the Medellín cartel, and Brian acted as errand boy between the two sides. With his computer skills and knowledge of foreign languages and because of or despite his obsequiousness, he'd made himself indispensable to everybody. His sincere grief at Gloria's death and the fact that he was innocent of her murder were of no help to him: in due course he was sent to jail for two years for complicity in illegal trading in arms and narcotics. (The Santavarvaran courts didn't seem too worried about the works of art.) "But given the links between the Mafia and the government, we can expect to see Watt's sentence whittled away through appeals and remissions," Larry Smirnoff predicted. His theory was plausible enough. Even Rilsky, for all his prejudice against journalists, had to agree with him.

Michael Fish confessed to the murder—or rather to what he called an "accident"—but definitely not to the stabbing or the decapitation. Even Hester didn't blame him for that horrible performance.

"Tell me, Captain: I'm quite ready to accept some responsibility, but what about the severed head and the knife? That *is* what happened, isn't it? My lawyer told me about it: someone else got up to some tricks too, didn't they? Some pretty odd tricks, eh?" (Fish was counting on the "extenuating circumstances" of the mutilation to shorten his sentence. Then he planned to resume his lucrative activities in Bogotá.)

"Yes, I can believe a knife *was* involved, Captain. Because I noticed Madame's dress was torn . . . the bodice. The head was still there when I saw her, though; I can't deny that. But now I remember the knife being there too. [Hester had got Madame's lover where she wanted him and didn't intend to let go.] What a brute: enough to drive you out of your mind!"

"Just listen to you! You were keen enough to be driven out of your mind in my room, whenever the mistress was out of the way! What other lies are you going to make up? I suppose I can count myself lucky you didn't see me go off with her head under my arm, wrapped up in the Picasso! But don't think you can say whatever you like because I'm in a tight corner. Just calm down, honey!" (Fish was perking up again.)

"A bit of whitewash here, a bit of whitewash there, and now he reckons he's as pure as the driven snow! And he's not far wrong, the bastard!" Larry was exulting to Stephanie: the "Harrison affair" proved he'd been right all along, by exposing to broad daylight the corruption rife in contemporary society. "If you can call that a society!" he added.

Meanwhile Rilsky slowly folded up the *Morning Star* and then listened for the umpteenth time to Paganini's *Campanella*, played of course by Yehudi Menuhin. Nothing like the plucking of a pitiless violin for drowning out the croaking of reporters.

Apart from that, if Fish really had strangled Gloria, then someone else must have been responsible for the beheading and perhaps the stabbing too. So the theory of a serial killer now came into its own. Rilsky had already accepted it, anyway.

◆ CHAPTER SEVENTEEN ◆

"Someone once said if there weren't any doctors there wouldn't be any patients. What do you think, Professor?"

Zorin peered over his spectacles and then fixed on me a gaze of vague but merciless commiseration. I realized I oughtn't to have started the interview with so blatant a challenge. After all, I wasn't really interested in psychiatrists and their patients. What concerned me were the political facts in this ghastly country, where corruption denied the people even their elementary rights to health, including mental health, and to safety, especially that of women and children. Bribery, embezzlement, and sleaze in general had ended up letting loose a serial killer—perhaps several—who according to the present state of police inquiries was the person most likely to have perpetrated Gloria's beheading. The serial killer or killers, as Larry had supposed, could be traced back to St. Ambrose's Hospital, so I'd made up my mind to explore this trail myself and get to the bottom of things.

I can't stand hospitals: I loathe illness—mental illness in particular. Still, I had to remember I was writing not for myself but for a Paris paper whose readers still regard madness as the ultimate rebellion against conformity. True, psychoanalysis was out and antipsychiatry in, but—as my editor had told me on the phone the previous evening— "Madness is always topical, darling. So whether it's the serial killer who did it or not, let's have a few pounds of *Clockwork Oranges*. A ream or two of copy: I'll buy it just as it comes. And in your usual style, please; don't let anyone off lightly. We need a surefire thing to keep up the supply of horror and sex, and madness just fits the bill. But no pussyfooting around, eh? *Events* doesn't mind stepping on *anybody's* toes!"

The "clockwork orange" theory was right. Every single family was dying to hear about its serial killer. The pink knitter had come over to me in the elevator and whispered, "I haven't met him yet, but I have come across a corpse. I swear it! It sounds incredible but it's true! I was coming home from a bicycle ride. Pity you didn't come along! It was getting late, almost dusk, and I was tired and a bit drowsy, dreaming, really, instead of looking where I was going. And then all of a sudden I turned a corner and saw someone lying in the road. I thought they'd been taken ill, or fainted, or tripped over; it does happen. I rang my bell. But it was too late; I ran into the body and fell off my bike. It was a corpse. A blonde, as you'll have guessed, with her throat cut. Covered in blood. Horrible! I ought to have called the police, but, would you believe it, I couldn't! I hadn't got the nerve, and I hadn't got the strength. I hope you don't blame me. For not doing my duty as a citizen and all that. I know—I'd be the first to say I did wrong. That night was the worst. 'Don't worry,' my husband said. 'If there was blood on her throat it was too late anyway. Besides, law and order can manage without you; some other passerby will have told the cops. And how do we know the serial killer wasn't still there all the time, watching you? You were quite right to run away. Don't go out too often for a while.' My husband was being sensible for once. Do *you* think I should have called the police? I can't stop worrying about it! My nerves are in shreds. Anyhow, you take care! Don't open the door to anyone!"

She saw me to the door of Bob's loft and then, unable to tear herself away, stood whispering warm hopes and fears into my ear. I promised with a wink and a smile to be careful and then quickly double-locked myself in.

But that evening, as I was driving out of the garage, my rented car, going around the dimly lit corner to enter level two, struck some strange long object. I couldn't avoid it, so I accelerated over it. But

Julia Kristeva

unlike my pink neighbor, I was myself again, morally, after a couple of
seconds. My heart thumping in the darkness, I walked back to see what
I'd hit. It was a rolled-up carpet. It might have had a corpse inside, but
that wasn't very likely. It wasn't big enough. But this demonstration of
public-spiritedness struck me as quite enough: I wasn't going to stop
to untie a suspect package left in a deserted parking lot. Serial killers
are too fond of places like that.

Popov, on the other hand, was more than eager to track down the
psychopath. Embarrassed by the eagerness with which earlier on he'd
accused Hester Bellini and just to show that a police officer wasn't
going to be taken in by what some crazy student said, Popov had concentrated ever since on Brian Watt's testimony. He was now going
through it with a fine-tooth comb for the umpteenth time.

" 'The French windows,' 'from the outside' . . . That's funny, boss,
very funny. Why should he mention such a detail except to try to clear
himself? But he knows very well he was *inside* Mrs. Harrison's study.
[Rilsky's silence didn't indicate much approval of this argument.
Popov tried another.] But that's not all. What about those heads of
moldy oranges? Do they sound normal to you? And an 'alien, intimidating presence' . . . I bet it was intimidating! Especially if Watt was
its accomplice, had been for a long time perhaps! But *whose* presence,
may I ask?"

"That's the whole point, needless to say!" (Rilsky, taken aback by
his lieutenant's lack of imagination. But alas, that was nothing new,
and Popov could be very efficient if given something concrete to do.
As he soon would be.)

"Right, but we've got several solutions to choose from. If the
'presence' in question was noticed on Monday the seventeenth at nine
in the morning, as the suspect Watt claims, it might indeed be that of
a prowler like the serial killer. But not, you'll agree, *our* serial killer,
because the lab report gives the time of the wounding, or the cutting,
or whatever, as late Sunday afternoon. [Both Popov and his boss are
silent for a few seconds. Then Popov goes on.] If you'll be good

enough to give me a bit more of your valuable time, and if, as I think, Watt is leading us up the garden path, we might say that the 'presence' of the famous moldy head occurred during Sunday night. [Rilsky: "We might . . ."] Please let me go on. Disappointed after his unsuccessful roll in the hay with the maid, the student can't sleep, grows agitated, and finally gets up and goes to look for his mistress. The trouble is, on the terrace he comes across a head not unknown to him. But whose? A 'moldy head': *that* could be the head of his ladylove! That's why he accuses Hester Bellini right away. I can see you're not very convinced, sir, but who else's do you think it could be, that 'moldy head' that Brian Watt sees as 'alien' and 'intimidating'? There's only one answer: some acquaintance he's ashamed of. That's what I think. The serial killer is some nut Watt knows very well, but our precious intellectual isn't at all proud of mixing with such people. Now we've got a whole lot of nuts loose in Santa Varvara who've escaped from St. Ambrose's, and that supports my theory: Mrs. Harrison's killer is the escapee from St. Ambrose's who knows Brian Watt. They may have met in some loonies' clinic, or a high-brow club, or at a dealer's place. Something of that sort; we'll have to see." (Popov, usually afraid of overtaxing his brain and now suddenly, out of vanity, letting himself go on all cylinders, suddenly stopped, exhausted.)

"Right, my friend! You look into it, eh? Go over to the hospital, interview everyone, examine the files; you know the drill. To work!" (Rilsky, though he wore a melancholy smile, was delighted to get rid of his lieutenant.)

But to be fair it was Rilsky's account of Popov's arguments that finally persuaded me, despite my lethargy, to pay a visit to St. Ambrose's myself. "They're all guilty, boss, if you ask me," the lieutenant had said. "The politicians *and* the psychiatrists: the politicians because they cut the funding of public institutions and dispossess the poor, and the shrinks because they have too many ideas! What a situation! You can't imagine what it's like till you've seen what those lunatics have to put up with. It doesn't surprise me they escape if they can. Anyone would do the same in their place. But the shrinks: you can have them, if you'll forgive the expression! All they could come up with was—what did that professor say?—Would you pass me my notes, please? . . . Oh yes . . . "Trust to the subject's desire." ' 'What do you mean by that?' I asked him humbly. Let the subject loose to do as he likes: that's what it means, boss! Let him go and demonstrate his desire in the context of society! If he should feel like sticking a knife in society or fucking minors and women who are asleep and could do without it, why not, while the famous subject is about it! Right, I know it's not *my* problem, but whose *is* it then? The journalists'? Don't make me laugh! Anyhow, no sweat, that aspect of the affair doesn't concern the department. I've carried out my investigations from our own point of view: that's to say, correctly, as usual. No clues relating to Watt for the moment, but never mind, I'll get him sooner or later. But I've got two other leads that are worth following up, boss. One is a fellow who's been let out because they think he can manage on his own, apparently: a sex maniac and ex-con, you get the picture. The other's an inmate who just took off of his own accord, a confirmed rapist, the junkie-killer type. I'm in the middle of tracing his family and friends and the places where he may be hiding out."

While Popov was dutifully carrying out his routine I decided it might be worthwhile seeing what the inmates of St. Ambrose were like. I also wanted to find out how modern science could get the famous "desire of the subject" so wrong. As for my own desire to know, Zorin, as an old acquaintance of Gloria's, was the obvious target.

The professor himself met me at the main entrance and then led me through the archway into the hospital's main yard. The place was fizzing with therapeutic activity: dancing, music, basketball, and Ping-Pong vied with one another in what I supposed was a recreational session. Young bodies—rather clumsy ones, it seemed to me—shouted out to each other as they engaged in their various exercises, exchanging words that sounded confused but were apparently not aggressive.

As we went along, a few of the youngsters, both boys and girls, clung to me as if they wanted to kiss me or as if hoping for caresses yearned after for years. Others just cast dull looks at the natty intruder. I felt as if something had gone wrong with distances: some of the boys and girls were too close; others too far away. I found it hard to breathe, partly because of the unseasonable heat, partly because of the acrid hospital smell. I realized I'd become so used to the gray canopy of rainy days in Paris that I'd identified with it. Now, with the sky of Santa Varvara stretched out blue and blazing above and pinning me down in this dingy quadrangle, it was if I'd been expelled from space altogether. As if I was nowhere. Summer was an enormous desert where you had plenty of time but no place amid the elliptic wanderings of the sun and the insane.

Which of them could have been the presumed serial killers, Tyson Y. and Jason X.? Neither of those was still here: both had gone over the wall. Of course Larry's serial killer argument depended on whether Popov's investigations confirmed his theory about escapes from St. Ambrose's. I couldn't imagine any of these pale creatures, now edging away from or caressing me, having enough manual skill to cut off Gloria's head.

Zorin, though he too had started out by feeling pity, eventually opted for irony, a much more practical attitude for the head of a child psychiatry department.

"Oh, you Paris intellectuals! You're very good at splitting hairs. But whoever heard of taking Artaud seriously? Because it's his ravings you're quoting at me. Okay: all the youngsters—even the young psychiatrists . . . need I say more?—are drunk on his diatribes. It was an epoch-making time, as well as a belle époque—my generation's heyday. But it's over now. Nobody, nobody in the world reads that sort of thing nowadays. [For the moment Zorin had forgotten the subtleties of the expert on autism, the connoisseur of modern art. He spoke very slowly and deliberately. Was he being sarcastic or didactic? As a matter of fact, the professor believed a careful delivery was conducive to the authenticity you needed in order to get in touch with someone else's unconscious.] If you expect me to admit psychiatry is to blame for madness, and even responsible for the murder, via a serial killer, of our unforgettable Gloria—no, no, a thousand times no! [At this point his voice became so slow it betrayed no feeling whatsoever about the deceased.] I tell you this with all the cool appropriate to my calling, if you'll pardon the expression."

Zorin admitted that some of his colleagues might feel a certain sympathy for extremist practices of antipsychiatric origin. It wasn't impossible, he thought, that some of them might have been willing to "integrate" or "reintegrate" prematurely some individuals still requiring "heavy" treatment. Such errors were naturally unthinkable in his own department, child psychiatry, where the treatment of every patient was followed through consistently, thanks to the joint efforts of biochemistry and the cognitive sciences. But he couldn't answer for what went on in other units, so lax had standards become in Santa Varvara, as in the world in general.

One of the two suspects—Jason X.—was quite unknown to Zorin. It was usual for the departments dealing with adults to accept ex-prisoners who had apparently reformed or more or less served out their sentences. After a short period of observation and education, these worthies often recovered their taste for life—so why not for death as well? Treatment wasn't always all it might be, what with staff shortages, overcrowding, and inadequate management. Moreover, long years of clinical experience suggest that a sadistic pervert is bound to reoffend: a pervert remains a pervert to the end of the chapter. Perversion is untreatable. It persists even after a long and thorough psychoanalysis, although the professor had had some private cases where considerable progress had been made. But Jason; Jason hadn't been analyzed. He'd received only biochemical treatment, and that, as we now saw, had been sadly inadequate. The police were sure it was he who'd been spreading terror through the better-off districts of Santa Varvara, raping and strangling women.

As for Tyson Y., that was another kettle of fish. He wasn't really one of Zorin's patients. No, the professor had never taken a close interest in that kind of pathology. But this person—a teenager at the time, for the case dated from several years ago—*had* passed through his department. Until the case was closed Zorin preferred, for reasons of professional etiquette, not to reveal the surnames of his patients. Tyson was a tall red-haired lad, slightly stooped, with a white skin and freckles, who blushed like a girl and used drugs freely. He acted as if possessed when he needed a fix or had mixed his dope unwisely, readily wielding knives and switchblades and other sharp instruments. His mother was a blonde, like the victims, and, needless to say, depressed. Father unknown, as usual. A case of psychosis obscured by drug addiction: Zorin more or less agreed with that diagnosis. Obscured, perhaps, but Tyson Y.'s psychosis was far from stabilized, for at the slightest irregularity in his medication the subject started acting out. This was all the more dangerous because he looked so mild, cherubic, and androgynous that his victims had no misgivings. While he was still in the child psychiatry department of the hospital he'd been kept under close observation, but when he was put among the adults; well, what could you expect? Some of Zorin's colleagues couldn't tell the difference between the various kinds of pathology and acted accordingly. And so Tyson ran off, as everyone now knew, even the police.

"I can imagine him bending over Gloria's handsome bosom. Or rather I can *see* the two of them, her with her auburn hair and magnificent green eyes and this man who must be . . . what? Twenty-five? Older? I know only the teenager, the delicate demon who when he was eighteen looked as if he was only ten, ten very disturbing and indefinable years old. Do you know Mark Twain's *The Prince and the Pauper?* I read it as a child and have only a dim memory of it now. But ever since the murder it's haunted me. Just as it did when I was a kid. Perhaps it's because the twinlike similarity between the two characters reminds me of Tyson Y.'s frightening ambiguity. A face that wouldn't be out of place in an English church choir. But with the psyche of an assassin. I wake up drenched in sweat, I shriek through Gloria's throat. Forgive me for being so romantic. [But if his words were romantic, his voice was not. The slow delivery reaching out for the unconscious made it sound staid and solemn.] You'll think I find easy consolation in an overliterary explanation. One all too appropriate to Gloria herself. You'll think what I've been saying is quite horrible . . . [He started speaking more quickly now, as if suddenly realizing what he was saying. A sign of lucidity, and of delicacy too. Had he really loved her then, his Gloria? Might he have been the only man who really loved her? It couldn't have been much, probably—a love made up of literary quotations and clinical observations—but as good as most. An affection that now keeps a vain but awkward scientist awake at night.] After all, the police still don't have any proof . . ."

I crossed the yard of St. Ambrose's again, brushed against once more by some of the inmates, encountering micalike stares from others, and breathing in the nauseating smell of cabbage and overcooked pasta characteristic of all health service institutions. Tyson Y. had prowled among them, and among them now there prowled a future Jason X: a Prince of Wales crossed with Poor Tom, a young page with a milk-white skin and a sadist's heart, poisoned by a harassed mother, medical error, and all the deprivations that may be inflicted by the Establishment: by a negligent educational system, rising inflation, an underfunded national health service, suburban violence, and a general decline in civic consciousness! Now I had the subject—a highly political one—of my article for *Events* in Paris.

"As for your question, Stephanie dear, I made up my mind on the subject a long time ago. With or without doctors, the way things are going there will be more and more patients." (By way of farewell Zorin sent a compassionate look over his spectacles.)

I didn't press the matter. St. Ambrose's hadn't taught me anything I didn't know already. What was more laughable, or more disturbing, was Zorin's suggestion that Jason X. or Tyson Y. might or might not have stabbed and beheaded Gloria. It was possible but unlikely. Probable and not really impossible. Not impossible and highly probable. Or else highly improbable. And so on. Only one thing was certain: the professor had really loved Gloria. In his own way. Between English choirs, Mark Twain, Antonin Artaud, *Woman with Collar*, and his own rose-tinted fantasies. He loved her still. He'd carefully constructed a mosaic of feelings, opinions, affects, and poses so as to be able to go on, hold out, as head of the child psychiatry department. That would take some doing! It was his own form of madness, forged amid a world of morons and delinquents.

Now I could count only on Rilsky, or rather Popov, to find the missing link between psychosis, obscured or otherwise, perversion, treatable or otherwise, and the serial killer. Great! Gloria had all the luck!

CHAPTER EIGHTEEN

And so, while some dreamed and others declaimed, Rilsky was hard at work. He'd have liked, as often during complicated cases, to talk to Stephanie about it, to know what she thought. For he believed she had the feminine—and foreign—intuition that can spot the trifling details capable of changing the whole face of an investigation. But this time Ms. Delacour, won over by the simplistic theories of Larry Smirnoff, was concentrating almost entirely on the question of corruption—an all-consuming task indeed in Santa Varvara, and one that left her no time for the Harrison affair. Rilsky sensed that his old friend was reticent and preoccupied: she wouldn't even go to concerts with him, whereas usually she didn't need asking twice. Rilsky was all the more perplexed because Bob Harrison had come back sooner than expected from his trip to Southeast Asia, and he and Stephanie were now sharing the great light-filled cube overlooking the river. Of course there was plenty of room for two in that luxurious apartment, and anyway Bob was inundated with the problems arising from his sister's death: the will, the lawsuit, and above all his nephew, Jerry, though in the last task he was helped by the still-devoted speech therapist, Ms. Gadeau. So Bob and Stephanie practically never met, and Rilsky couldn't see who, apart from the editor of the *Morning Star*, could be so monopolizing Ms. Delacour as to make her avoid *him* so obviously. But never mind: the captain could always rely on the faithful Popov, who often came up with sound advice. There was also old Doc. Rilsky had to admit his contributions were often very bright.

The police surgeon had worked hard on Gloria's corpse, which had already had more than its share of attention. The autopsy was only a continuation of one of those sinister assaults our societies occasionally make on some of their citizens, though the real motives of such attacks are never uncovered. If you added it all up, it amounted to persecution. There couldn't be much left of Gloria Harrison by now: of the curves that fit so snugly into her ivory satin gown; of the lovely body that when it was discovered—the effects of rigor mortis were already beginning to wear off—recalled some famous beauty decapitated by time. But now the echoes of Dione, Aphrodite, and—why not?—the Winged Victory of Samothrace that had earlier been awakened in Stephanie (though she had either a morbid imagination or a sardonic approach to death) had died away, obliterated by the macabre archaeology of the forensic surgeon. However, the aesthetic damage was not as outrageous as it might have been: Gloria, as a true atheist, had lodged a will with her lawyer just before the tragedy, arranging for her body to be cremated. The cremation had already taken place. And all the citizens of Santa Varvara, including the most devout, had accepted that wise decision. Or else they chose not to think about it.

In the autopsy report, written in the historic (some might call it the gnomic) present, Gloria still possessed all her organs—except her brain—though in a more or less damaged condition. All of us, the most famous as well as the most obscure, will be similarly recorded, in what can only be called the "organic present," in the eternity of computers and data banks. As long as they undergo an autopsy, our mortal envelopes, together with our organs, may be sure of enjoying that indestructible present.

"Do you want to go over the file again? I mean—if I can be of any help . . . Well, as I've said before, Northrop, there's a bruise on the left lung, caused by the pressure of gastric liquid on the lung tissue. A typical smell of putrefaction. Because, needless to say—to use your favorite phrase—the yellow substance is part of the contents of the stomach. The subject inhaled these, so to speak, as a result of the strangulation that brought about her sudden death." (The police surgeon. He seemed less sure of himself than the technical phraseology implied.)

"What's the problem, then?" (Rilsky, sensitive as a psychologist to what other people said, and similarly neutral.)

"I've told you that before too, but I'll say it again: the coronary arteries have shrunk and the left ventricle is not dilated, so it's not a real case of cardiac arrest. And on top of that there's the slight bruise on the lung, some petechial hemorrhages in the heart and lungs, and a large amount of alcohol, Rohypnol, and Elavil in the stomach."

"Did you say Rohypnol and Elavil?" (Rilsky, absently.)

"You read my report, didn't you?" (The doc, irritated.)

"What bothers me is that her family doctor had never prescribed any antidepressants. We didn't find any trace of Elavil in the medicine cabinet, and there was only the bottle of Rohypnol on her bedside table." (Rilsky, slightly worried.)

"Oh well, that's your problem, my friend! [The doc, aggressive at first, then relenting.] What does that signify? Let me remind you that the lady in question, like any well-enough-known patient in that part of Santa Varvara, could easily get any drug she liked from the girl at the local pharmacy. (The doc, making no bones about it.)

"True enough. The manageress at the Progress Pharmacy nearby thinks she remembers Jerry's speech therapist buying some Elavil for Mrs. Harrison recently. How much of that sort of stuff did you find?" (The captain, being practical again.)

"Four times the normal dose. Enough to knock out whoever was experimenting with it, without any help from champagne or sleeping pills. She could have flushed the box down the john. Unless one of her many night visitors filched it, together with other unconsidered trifles such as some jewelry, a watch, a knife, and then tidied up after him- or herself so as not to leave any clues. How would I know? It's just one little piece in your jigsaw. There are plenty of bigger ones."

"*Our* jigsaw."

"If you like! So what do you conclude?" (The doc, strictly professional.)

"Nothing, for the moment. What about you?" (Rilsky, sober and phlegmatic.)

"As you can see from the report! The case looks very much like one of narcotic poisoning. But it's difficult to say what was the actual cause of death. Without the head or the neck we can't say for sure she was strangled. Marks on the throat would have helped there—helped *us*, I mean." (The doc, embarrassed because he couldn't be more precise.)

"Poisoning or strangulation, then? I'd be quite willing to accept both. [Rilsky, the dialectical philosopher.] Mrs. Harrison had taken a mixture of barbiturates and antidepressants, washed down with plenty of champagne. Hence she was in a comatose state, and added to that there was the psychological intervention by Mr. Fish."

"*Psychological* intervention? Both the vaginal and the anal samples showed traces of sperm. Mr. Fish's sperm. I checked with his medical records. In circumstances like these you'll agree confidentiality has to go out the window. Besides, we *are* in Santa Varvara." (The doc, normally a stickler for professional ethics.)

"Thank you. As I was saying, a comatose state caused also in part by a physical intervention that might have been accompanied by rough treatment. Pressure on the throat or abdomen could have caused stimulation of the parasympathetic system, swiftly followed by cardiac arrest. The asphyxiation process must have been slow, if we accept the testimony of the housekeeper, Hester Bellini. She said she noticed a lot of reddening of the skin behind the ears, as well as partial cyanosis of the face. The suspect Fish doesn't deny this is possible. It must be said that all the evidence is against him. I'm not forgetting your toxicological data don't rule out strangulation, but they do make it less certain as the cause of death. They don't make the suspect any less responsible for what he *did* do, but they bring in additional factors. Do you accept this way of putting it, Doc?" (Rilsky, careful to get his text right.)

"To tell you the truth, it's impossible to rule out completely the theory of sudden death through inhibition: sudden cardiac arrest resulting from fear, or assault, or any of the various psychological factors that can cause pneumogastric stimulation . . . Right! And then there's the knife. Haven't you found it yet?" (The doc, not sorry it's his turn to catch Rilsky out in incompetence.)

"We've just arrested the serial killer—or rather one of the serial killers: there are probably several of them, either escaped from St. Ambrose's or released too soon. What's the difference? The monster confesses to everything, only too delighted to be in the media spotlight. He wore gloves and claims he threw the knife he used to stab his wretched victims into the sea." (Rilsky, not so confident as his recitation would suggest.)

"Shall I go on? We have a choice between Jason X., the hardened habitual offender, and Tyson Y., a nut like something out of *A Clockwork Orange*." (Popov, who by dint of his inquiries at St. Ambrose's had acquired what he took to be the current vocabulary for classifying suspects. He now joined in the conversation to demonstrate the part *he* was playing in the case. An essential part, needless to say.)

"Popov's nabbed Tyson. But we may need both of them." (Rilsky, enigmatic, interrupting the lieutenant, but indulgently,)

"As you've known from the beginning, the pericardic bruise wasn't very big, and there wasn't much blood. It follows that the stabbing must have occurred some time after death." (The doc, positive.)

"The blood in the heart coagulates an hour after death. [Rilsky, very knowledgeable.] Fish could very well have used the knife before he took off."

"In that case he'd have had to hang around for an hour, while he took down and wrapped up his loot. But after all, why not? He's not very bright, but he may be a . . ." (The doc, straying on to the captain's territory.)

"... a sadist? Yes indeed. Second-rate but sadistic Or if you prefer, a second-rate sadist. Let's leave that for the moment. What else?" (Rilsky, pragmatic again.)

"The discolorations. And the fibroplasia on the two wounds: first on the breast and then on the neck. The cutting, as if by a razor, of the cervical structures, the hyoid bone, and the thyroid cartilages. The discolorations on the back are older, and there are others, not so clear, on the belly and the chest: the corpse was turned over. Moreover, the evolution of the mononuclear cells on the chest is different from that of the cells on the neck: those on the chest date from about twelve hours earlier."

"The conclusion must be that someone wielded the dagger (let's call it that; in any case, one of the weapons used in the crime) at about six or seven o'clock on Sunday morning, probably after Hester left: she doesn't mention either a knife or blood in her first statement. The serial killer, attracted by the comings and goings around the house, may have come to try his luck. Then, furious and frustrated at finding a dead body instead of the live flesh he expected—unless we're dealing with a necrophiliac, but he's not one of those because according to your data he didn't rape the victim—he struck. In a fit of rage. Let's say he left his dagger in the body; then someone else would have had to take it out. Or let's say he took it out himself and got rid of it later somewhere or other. But in any case, I don't see him retrieving the weapon and then turning the body over. Why should he do that? In order to cut off the head? Definitely not. If I've followed you properly, the beheading took place several hours after the blow to the heart, which brings us to the Sunday afternoon. Now okay, the serial killer may be crazy, but not so crazy as to wait twelve hours to complete his handiwork. So we need a second criminal to cut off the head and make it disappear." (Rilsky, rather pleased with his powers of deduction. "You ought to write detective stories," Stephanie often joked. "But I'm afraid they might be rather unsophisticated, at least for my taste.")

"A third if you include Fish." (The doc, impatient.)

"Correct. A third assailant, which gives us a second serial killer. You only die twice—or three times, I forget which. We've read that before somewhere, haven't we? " (Rilsky, putting himself in the other person's place and afraid of boring him.)

"It's the train that whistles three times, Captain. You're mixing up your sources." (The doc, distantly.)

"The one doesn't exclude the other, my friend. But let's keep all this to ourselves, if you don't mind. Whether there's one madman or two, what does that prove? The disastrous state of the health service? The scale of the real-estate scandals? The gangrene of corruption? For our victim it's too late. And as serial killer number one admits everything, that'll be quite enough to satisfy everyone. To 'pacify public opinion,' as the journalists say. No?" (Rilsky, cynical.)

"As you like. But it's all rather hazy, isn't it?" (The doc, keenly, looking askance across the table.)

"I suppose so. But we'll let the *Morning Star* sort it all out, and leave the journalists to bitch to their heart's content. Just think! If we were to tell the whole truth they'd lose their cushy jobs! Let's be kind and not put them out of work." (Rilsky, racism at half-mast, but only in the hope of solving the case more easily.)

The Harrison affair had by now come to symbolize life in Santa Varvara. It no longer concerned Gloria as much as it did "the situation." The press all over the world was talking about it; Larry was rubbing his hands. His article in the *Morning Star* had been translated in full in *Events*, in Paris, and printed right next to the one by Stephanie Delacour, "our special correspondent" in Santa Varvara. A scoop!

Stephanie herself had concocted a background article dealing only with political corruption and the violation of human rights. Something held her back from getting involved any further in Gloria's murder. As usual Rilsky had both fudged and finished his investigation. Stephanie might have helped him and challenged his overly simple explanation.

She could have taken an interest in the serial killer, looked for the missing head, and let him see the files she'd built up about Gloria's life on the basis of trivial details that might eventually prove significant. But that was asking too much of herself. She couldn't do everything. Gloria always *had* done everything; maybe that was why people had disliked her, had got fed up with her, hadn't shrunk from getting rid of her (Rilsky hinted that several people had contributed to her death), had wanted to teach her a lesson once and for all. A woman alone, taking herself seriously! She had no sense of humor, that was Gloria's trouble, and that was the main reason for the envy and exasperation she inevitably aroused.

"And here am I running her down posthumously! Attacking her like all the rest. *With* all the rest."

And what conclusion did the inquiry come to? No conclusion at all. After a while the whole thing would probably seem as absurd as it was horrible. Why? Because although it was undoubtedly sad, it was performed by puppets. It was the story of a set of sad puppets. It wasn't *values* that had become nonexistent, as old Northrop solemnly complained, polishing his pebble glasses and lamenting the hopelessness of present prospects. No, it was *people*: their lives, tragic though they used to be, full of anguish and potentially criminal, were now dwindling into so many virtual images.

So where were we? Having passed from one theory to another, from probabilities to uncertainties, public opinion had come to the conclusion that Gloria had got what she asked for, as Odile Allart would have said. She'd been stoned for a start, even if she was only half dead when her sadistic lover added the final, fatal coup de grâce. And he was a brute and a crook, whom the role of murderer fit like a glove. But seeing him named as the guilty party didn't fulfill all the promise inherent in the scenario. For that—to produce the maximum horror—at least one psychopath was necessary, if not two. But since madness was not legally responsible for its acts, the guilt had to be accepted, and diluted, by society as a whole. Or at least by the most corruptible part of it, its soft underbelly, the small fraction that by some strange coincidence held the reins of power, as the *Morning Star*'s editor rightly observed.

The sense of impenetrability and déjà vu that had overwhelmed Stephanie when she arrived in Santa Varvara had gradually intensified. But by now what had seemed unreal had become unstable too. Like images, crimes had to be virtual, because people themselves were virtual or in the process of becoming so. Young Jerry, fascinated by Picasso's cubist women, had seen more clearly than the adults: faces crushed; identities mocked; shots and angles that attacked or receded; changing points of view; states of mind all in a whirl—where were the reference points of yesteryear? Out of all these possible jigsaw puzzles Rilsky, true to his own aesthetic humanism, had chosen the most spectacular and least harmful. He'd retained the character of the tragic, ill-used mother; he'd taken his revenge on the vulgar lover by casting him as a not-very-bright mafioso; and, diluting Larry Smirnoff's theory, he had reduced the idea of society's responsibility by attributing the most atrocious elements of the crime—the stabbing and the beheading—to the serial killer.

The serial killer or killers: that was the key to the whole thing. Perhaps. But Stephanie sensed that Rilsky wasn't telling the whole truth. Nothing new about that. But this time he was holding back more than usual. Yet wasn't it natural, really? Why should the captain, even if he was an existentialist aesthete, be able to escape the power of the semblance, the false—no, the virtual—that was Santa Varvara? In order to preserve the surreal possibility of music? In the name of the secret worship of some deep emotion that's intrinsically stable and incommunicable but that one may deflect, divert slightly, betray a little so as to observe it indirectly, to give it, and oneself with it, a better chance of survival?

Come off it! Her father had warned her: "Young lady, you have a tendency to project your own obsessions onto the mysteries of other people." It was no use: Stephanie could laugh at Rilsky as much as she

POSSESSIONS

liked, but in fact she took him too seriously. She must be careful. Why should Northrop have a more solid existence than other people, than Gloria, for example? He was only an official, a cubist construction, a virtual image, a ghost—quite a distinguished one, certainly, but what difference did that make in this world of phantom brutes?

"Our special correspondent" was wandering from the point. Those were mere psychological—perhaps even metaphysical—suppositions, nothing to do with the chance and necessity that, as everyone knows, are at the root of all crimes. *Basta!* Stephanie gave up. Never mind about her career as a detective. She'd see about that some other time. Later on; never: who could say? It was time to leave Bob and his luxury loft, the harsh light and these opaque and intrusive people. To sleep on her own. To get back to her own way of sleeping, let her bones tame loneliness, calm down, savor the warm silence in which dreams take shape. Especially as, for the moment, her colleagues on the paper in Paris were leaving her in perfect peace.

She'd sent them her article, they were pleased with it, that would do. Enough of Santa Varvara. For the moment.

I'm going home.

♦ CHAPTER NINETEEN ♦

I like being back in France. No more opacities, dramas, or mysteries. Everything obvious, transparent, in the open. Clarity in the language and in the unsullied sky. Each tree by the side of the road makes a courtly bow. Here intrigues are always sexual and therefore violent, but when terror is frankly erotic it fades away. The fields are divided up into regular rectangles: the ancient geometry of the Romans, the Gauls, and other self-assured but affable landowners. I'm well aware that there's France and France and that not all the French are as transparent as they'd like to appear. But when you're just back from Santa Varvara you can't help being impressed. There's not an inch of the landscape that doesn't reflect the fact that, here, being is immediate and logical. These slender elms, these clipped gardens, these carefully drained marshes provide a background for people who *are* because they *think*. But action gets swallowed up in all this, and though argument never ceases, it dwindles into irony and seduction.

Lots of people are in love with Italy, and I'm one of them: a wealth of beauty, a thrill and surprise that last until they become their own serene image. Others yearn for Spain: haughty in its unreason, mystic but nonchalant. But for me, France is the ultimate refuge.

I once knew someone whose zest for life was restored when he laid his hand in the hollow made by millions of pilgrims in the stone at Santiago de Compostela. Time incarnate in that human-shaped cavity reconciled him with the present—and with eternity. Twenty-five thousand years earlier Cro-Magnon man pressed his left palm against the wall of a rock shelter near Marseilles and then outlined his hand with black paint. There are two hundred and forty such hands in a cave at Gargas, in the foothills of the Pyrenees. Our species was seeking shelter but already had enough pride in itself to leave its mark on time. Time that comes right down to us.

In the same way I house my body in the logical landscape of France, take shelter in the smooth, smiling, comfortable streets of Paris, rub shoulders with its ordinary folk: reserved, cynical, impenetrably private, but, on the whole, civilized. They built Notre-Dame and the Louvre, conquered Europe and the greater part of the rest of the world, and then came home because they prefer a pleasure in accord with reality. But because they also prefer pleasure *to* reality, they go on thinking they're masters of the world, or at least a great power still. The world—irritated, condescending, fascinated—seems prepared to go along with them. To go along with us. Often reluctantly, but still, they're ready to keep it up for the moment. Here human violence has given way to love of laughter, and a quiet accumulation of pleasures lets them think destiny means keeping your cool. So detective stories are nonexistent in France, or else they get bogged down in mumbo jumbo. And so I forget the death that reigns in Santa Varvara.

The trouble is that after you've produced so much elegance— Chartres, Versailles, Descartes, Sade—there's not much left to do. Except two great, contrasting temptations: Terror or Museums. Robespierre or the Obelisk. The Rights of Man via the guillotine (perhaps even the guillotine without the Rights of Man) or the Louvre. We reached this point a couple of centuries ago, but the alternatives are still the same. By nature I prefer the Louvre; I don't understand people who regard museum culture as dead. These days France is probably good for nothing else but collecting its past, its antique furniture, its seventeenth- and eighteenth-century paintings, its champagnes, its perfumes, its foie gras. Welcome to the pyramid, to the mummy club! The future lies before you like a long Egyptian daydream. Maybe that's better than the painful topicality of the Holocaust, Sarajevo, or

Julia Kristeva

Rwanda—phew, that was a narrow squeak!—but when may we expect to see the exodus from Egypt?

I can hear just as well as you can the arguments of those who scorn museums. As if anything could be more urgent than to marvel at those who, since time began, have ceased to worry about time in order to celebrate beauty. Especially as today, Egypt or no, beauty's no longer in fashion. To be sure of that, all you need do is visit a museum of modern art.

Anyhow, I love the Louvre, and even if the country as a whole is being transformed into a more or less well-organized Louvre—except for the suburbs: there have to be exceptions to prove the rule—I enjoy nothing better than a glass of Perrier on the terrace of the Café de Marly late on a summer afternoon. The splendor and elegance of the Grand Siècle have no trouble coexisting with Pei's pointed void. The cosmopolitan T-shirted crowd, which couldn't care less about Bernini, or his equestrian statue of Louis XIV, or the Place du Carrousel growing pinker and pinker in the sunset, seems, in a rudimentary way, refreshingly universal. Without a future, perhaps, but not terrifying either. When they attain the detachment of satisfied lovers, "the lineaments of gratified desire," human beings of all kinds are like museum pieces: unique, immemorial, and charged with memory. Like the Café de Marly itself. France is out of time. But I won't go to the Café de Marly today. Today I'm a homebody, and I won't go outside my own neighborhood.

My Santiago de Compostela is the rue du Cherche-Midi. Let me tell you about it. First there's the naïveté and mystery of the name, which may refer to an ancient street that "sought the south." The sober middle-class facades conceal a thrifty but comfortable luxury. The shops disdain the big brand names: boutiques selling handmade dresses, sweaters, and shoes lead me to the pleasant aromas of a country bakery. There's a delicious smell of bread under the chestnut trees in the Luxembourg Gardens. The drowsy amber of the

POSSESSIONS

limes, the bees buzzing slowly toward the sculpted queens, remind
me *I*'m not looking for anything. It's all there in front of me, and it
isn't anything special. In an everyday setting, everything—stones,
plants, food—is ripened by the carefree care that creates an environ-
ment. Generations have left a trace of their prudent pleasures here.
The resulting charm is the Riviera of the memory. Something past is
recovered and need be sought no further. And this makes me forget
the murder in Santa Varvara.

In Italy I'm in the theater; in Spain I'm at some ceremony; but in
France I'm at home. Everything here is domesticated, in the mild,
patient meaning of the word. Between the infant greenness of the
nearby park and the ocean of Montparnasse—the human tide of the
commuter network; the new high-speed trains with their promise
of the sea—my own street is a small trough of peace. It tames the
ocean and turns it into comfort, discreet though seemingly inaccessible. Nothing in common with a refuge for sailors eager to forget
storms among the tame conventions of a "home." On the contrary,
there's style here: disturbing, continually sought after, and setting its
practitioners apart. But it has none of the isolating effect of fashion;
it's a memory living in accordance with a code, a type, a manner. The
French are rooted in style as other nationalities are rooted in earth or
blood. A salesgirl on the rue du Cherche-Midi, with the despotic yet
charming face of a queen in Chartres Cathedral, greets you with
flowery phrases. As if she'd just been performing a minuet at Versailles and was transposing her dancing into her tone of voice and the
convolutions of her grammar. Simplicity is a complex business and is
careful to show it. Not for nothing is Paris a magnet for migrants,
though they moan and groan about not being invited into people's
homes! But they all want that, and how are the French to cope with so
many foreigners? The trick lies in encouraging foreigners to keep
themselves to themselves, in dispensing consoling clichés, and in
making them understand they're different. And that though they may
live in Paris they'll always be outside it.

When logic's at home in the streets, the oceans, the railroad stations, there's no more depth: impossibility is on the surface. And what's concealed by so many appearances? Other appearances equally accessible, people think. Mystery disappears into different levels of logic, peaceful apartment buildings. Are the French superficial? They last. Of course I've traveled around the world enough to see us from the outside too (I say "us" because I have French nationality): stylish, stylized, wary. I may also say—as people say abroad—that we have no soul, don't know how to be intimate. Foreigners get attached, get angry, love, threaten. The French go in for role-playing, watch themselves, watch other people, stand firm in their impregnable retreats. Let's hope it's nice and comfortable *chez nous*! It had better be!

A window open in one of those smooth white facades lets through the strains of the second movement, *largo ma non troppo*, of Bach's Concerto in D-minor for Two Violins and Orchestra. One violin is shrill and sharp; the other vulnerable, vague. A great sweep of meanings that instead of unpacking themselves in words commune with themselves: a reticence setting human language at naught. Music simultaneously captures meaning and avoids it. But the mysterious present becomes even more disturbing when it borrows the voice of the violins, attaining the absolute through the harmonic genius of Bach.

Stephanie wasn't expert enough to recognize Yehudi Menuhin as the first violin, though perhaps that fine but exuberant vibrato, that precision changing to pleading . . . Rilsky would have recognized him right away. Rilsky again!

Take it easy! We're in Paris now. And the rue du Cherche-Midi leads to the bar of the Lutétia Hotel.

◆ CHAPTER TWENTY ◆

Odile Allart had decided she knew enough about beauty products and men to do more than just accompany her husband on business trips and to lunches and cocktail parties: she wanted to be a partner. Assistant managing director of Allart Perfumes sounded rather good and corresponded exactly to her abilities and her real activities. Pascal, despite a few understandable masculine reservations, was obliged to admit that his wife, as well as possessing both common sense and nerve, was more than a match for him when it came to diplomacy. If to these virtues you added the capital she'd brought into the business after her aunt died, increasing the company's assets by 40 percent— on condition that Madame Odile Allart-Lavoissière was made a managing director—the unexpected restructuring at the head of the group was on the whole a good thing. Odile loved meetings and public relations; even Pascal agreed that she not only bloomed in her new role but also produced excellent results. Especially when negotiating a hitherto uncertain deal over a late-afternoon drink.

In her hound's-tooth suit, elegantly cinched at the waist with a red leather belt, and with matching red purse and loafers, Odile looked both chic and efficient as she sat at the bar of the Lutétia over a gin and tonic. She'd already looked at her watch a couple of times when the barman came over and told her she was wanted on the phone. She'd been expecting it: the man from Davidoff Perfumes had been very demanding in the discussions they'd had so far, and his exaggerated politeness now as he excused his absence on the grounds that his mother-in-law had had to go into hospital only showed how lukewarm his own famous company was about doing business with Allart Perfumes. Still, Odile managed to arrange another appointment for the following week and went back to her dark green armchair resolved to indulge in a half hour of real relaxation. This despite the humiliations bound to go with the position of female businessman, which of course confers equally reliable privileges. Odile didn't waste much time on such bittersweet thoughts or on contemplating the bubbles in her glass. For Odile had a roving eye. The eye that belongs to women of an ardent but unsatisfied nature and that never gazes inward but leaps forward as if to carry the whole body with it—and the soul too.

Stephanie, hidden away in the darkest corner of the bar, couldn't escape those searchlights for long. It was the time of day when a white lady leaves faces featureless and the most disparate thoughts join together to create a world of surprises. Ms. Delacour, a connoisseur of surprises, even sinister ones, was enjoying the effects of a white lady. She'd have given anything to avoid exchanging them for a prolix and predictable tête-à-tête with Odile Allart. But how could she get out of it?

"Stephanie, how lovely to see you again after all those horrors in Santa Varvara! Congratulations on your article! Very clever. Pascal and I don't read the papers anymore: that'd be the last straw! We just glance at the headlines. But they tell you everything; there isn't any news these days! As for the commentaries, it's a well-known fact that once anyone sets up as a journalist they lose all sense of responsibility or shame. But we really enjoy *your* articles . . . [Here she slowed down, and a brief but meaningful glance conveyed that thanks would be tedious and unnecessary.] So you like this place too, do you? Nice and restful, isn't it? But I've never seen you here before. Of course I haven't been coming here long myself. But now I've made up my mind: the Lutétia bar is my place. You can breathe freely here, can't you? In a manner of speaking, of course: some people will go on smoking, and the management doesn't like to offend old customers.

But these days—don't you agree?—only neurotics and people in the third world still smoke. You may say that halves the number of smokers in exclusive places like this: we only have to put up with the neurotics. But there seem to be plenty of those!" (Odile, to release some of the tension of having been stood up, whirled her left hand around to drive away the cigarette smoke.)

What are people after when they talk to you? An audience, so they can go on talking as if that audience didn't exist. Or rather as if the public—you and I—were only there to provide the approval they need in order to talk and that they can never provide for themselves. Not enough of it, at any rate. Tell me that what I'm saying really is what I'm saying, and tell me it's okay. I'm not asking you to say what you think of what I say; don't even imagine I'm asking you to say anything at all. I'm merely asking the impossible: that you should bear witness to my being, and to my being okay. I speak to you, you listen, therefore I am. Listen to me in order that I may exist. After ten years of journalism, interviewing, and reporting, Stephanie had come to understand this, the secret that underlies all dialogue. And so she didn't expect any real exchange, let alone any concern for her own thoughts or feelings. Most people just plunged into her disenchanted attention and shamelessly imposed themselves on her: their family, their past, their present, their psychology, ideology, politics, metaphysics, and everything else. For a quarter of an hour now, Odile Allart's free associations had been lapping, without leaving any trace, against the pleasant shores of the white lady to which Stephanie had consigned the late afternoon. Everything was there: the spectacular rise of the new managing director, the company's success in France and abroad, Pascal's resentment of his wife's dominant role, and her recent tactic of letting him get the upper hand occasionally so as to save both their marriage and their business. "You can't imagine how much an intelligent married woman is forced to compromise, my dear!" Wrong. Stephanie could imagine it very well, though in fact she neither needed nor wished to imagine anything whatsoever about Odile as she sat there that day with her white lady in the Lutétia bar.

Except insofar as drinking was apt to make her philosophize. After all, self-regard—in a woman, and in the French in general—may reflect modesty rather than vanity. Not venturing to think, feel, or love in terms of others, of future generations or the human race as a whole, they limit themselves to their own small egos. Women and Frenchmen (with a few notable exceptions) lack the megalomania of people like, for example, the Russians and Germans, who tend to regard themselves as the whole of humanity. Women and Frenchmen are interested only in their own places in the world. This could seem arrogant, but it's really a kind of humility, or at most a small defect. Of course you could look it differently: ruling out mere naïveté, isn't it very difficult to express humility and limitation? But anyhow this probably didn't apply to Odile Allart. She was just a chatterbox and a show-off, though her attitude did have a certain charm. Stephanie looked back at her mockingly, but to no effect. Eyes that try to carry off body and soul don't see much of what's in front of them.

Odile was talking about her grief. "You're the only one who can understand how I feel! As I've often told you, Gloria and I had been friends since we were at school together at Beau Rivage in Switzerland. We were inseparable then and even afterward, when I was in France and she was in Santa Varvara, with the political problems there you're all too well aware of. For I haven't forgotten, Stephanie dear, that part of your own life was spent there. I don't mean to be disagreeable of course; I mention it out of pure fellow feeling. Because I'm absolutely inconsolable. Inconsolable! The more so as I find the whole thing quite incomprehensible, whatever experts like your friend Larry Smirnoff, and Captain Rilsky, and you yourself may say. Forgive me, my dear: I don't understand it, and I can't reconcile myself to it, and I never shall!"

Odile had another gin and tonic to intensify her grief by dredging up old memories, as is so often the case with the bereaved. So

Stephanie was treated to an account of the distinguished though individual education provided at Beau Rivage, including skiing expeditions complete with sun-tanned and susceptible instructors. Then Odile described Gloria's visit to France.

"Just think of the vacations she spent with my family, the Lavoissières, in Brittany, and the success—so-called—she had there. And not only on the beach. She looked wonderful in a bathing suit, and you'll have noticed, as I did, that she still looked as good just before she died . . . Was murdered, I mean. People still admired her then as if she was some kind of statue. And—don't think I'm being catty . . . we both hate bitchy women, don't we?—her body was far from her main attraction. Anyway, I must admit she was a great hit even with my own family, though the Lavoissières are *very* difficult to please! But Gloria was very sexy, wasn't she? Mother got her number right away. "Your friend's very discreet," she said. "Try to follow her example." I won't say anything about her critics, although—you know me!—I know what *they* used to say. Still, I was proud of Gloria, I was very fond of her, and I wanted to introduce her to my friends at the yacht club. What fun we had at the regattas! With the Gadeau family too! Do you know Pauline? No, I'm forgetting: she wasn't there that year; she was having her nervous breakdown. She didn't meet Gloria in Brittany; I introduced them some years later, when Jerry turned out to be handicapped. No, it wasn't the Gadeau family, it was the Meyer brother and sister. Gloria and I were both in love with Simon, the brother; we nearly quarreled over him. He was a good-looking boy who obviously had a future. Isn't it funny I should remember him now? It was he who introduced me to Davidoff Perfumes, whose rep I was supposed to be meeting here just now. But in this business people are always canceling, as you know; I don't need to tell you it doesn't mean anything. So where was I? Oh yes, Gloria and Pauline got to know one another much later on. Haven't I told you about it? Well, the Gadeaus, the parents of Pauline Gadeau, Jerry's speech therapist, had a place next door to ours at Camaret-sur-Mer. So Pauline's a childhood friend of mine. She's had an awful life, but thank goodness everything has settled down now, and she is, or rather was, very helpful to Gloria."

Stephanie was beginning to think it was time to leave. But she still had an hour to kill before she was due to have dinner with friends in the Third Arrondissement, and in the meantime it wasn't worthwhile going home. She ordered another white lady, ate a few cashews, and leaned back against the green plush.

"Anyhow, you met Pauline Gadeau at Gloria's ill-fated dinner party. [Odile went on bringing forth her unbroken flow of words, a sort of ectoplasm that's the real body of some women.] You know who I mean? She's the kind of woman you don't notice at first, but she's a really valuable person, I assure you. Though she looks much older— *much* older!—than she is. In fact she's about the same age as we are. You must be younger than Gloria and me, actually, but that's beside the point. Anyhow, here we are at the end of May, so it's more than a year and a half since it all happened. I still can't believe poor Gloria's dead. Sometimes I find myself reaching for the phone to call her. Have you been back there since? We have. Allart's is doing well, thank God— and thanks to me too, if you don't mind my saying so. But everyone admits we have the Santa Varvara market in the palm of our hand. But where was I? Oh yes, in Brittany. You know it, of course . . ."

◆ CHAPTER TWENTY-ONE ◆

In Brittany there's usually a breeze to make warm weather bearable, but that year the heat wave monopolizing the headlines affected the northwest coast as badly as everywhere else. A fierce sun draped fog over the deserted beaches: the vacationers had taken refuge behind closed shutters. The gray haze hovering over the lifeless sand made it seem like a graveyard. Pauline didn't feel like going anywhere. Nor did she want to study for a second try at her medical exams in September: there was still almost a month left for that, and she'd take care of it later, after the vacation. Besides, she was quite good at anatomy: it was only by a stroke of bad luck that she'd failed the oral in June. So she'd take a little nap and then start getting ready for dinner: make the mayonnaise, choose a pretty top to wear to go dancing at the Pergola. But the first thing to do was to sleep; what else could you do in this heat? A liverish, dreamless sleep, a maze of sensations and words, mouth open and throat parched. A clam, half-opening its shell and shriveling up at low tide. But is it really dead as long as its shell still unites stone and sky in a rough outside and a glistening rainbow within?

Pauline decides to nap a while longer. Aimeric insists on going for a swim: you need something to cool you down on a sweltering day like this. August 15: the Feast of the Assumption, a public holiday. It's more comfortable in the water than indoors. Aimeric's fifteen. Pauline, seven years older, usually does whatever he wants. She acted the little mother to him from the time he was born. Ms. Gadeau, very busy in her laboratory, was always congratulating herself on the fact.

Julia Kristeva

"I can't help laughing when they say little girls are traumatized by the birth of a baby brother. Just look at Pauline! Aimeric's arrival did her nothing but good. Isn't that right, Pauline?" At fifteen, Aimeric's already a young man, and his big sister no longer mothers him. They go sailing together at the yacht club at Camaret-sur-Mer; the boy's even started dropping in at the Pergola in the evening. Pauline thinks he's great. Attractive too. But far from laughing when strangers take them for a couple, she gets annoyed or upset. They're very much alike, apparently. "Your brother's a masculine version of you!" says Odile: she always complicates everything.

Aimeric's very keen on the natural sciences and is going to study medicine, like his sister. They'll both specialize in surgery: open-heart operations and organ grafts. Pauline already has a case of surgical instruments, and Aimeric likes to explore this magic casket and have Pauline explain how she's learning to use its contents. "She's as cool as a cucumber and precision personified; what more could you ask for in a surgeon?" (Ms. Gadeau couldn't help bragging to Madame Lavoissière, especially as Odile obviously had none of Pauline's talents.) Meanwhile Aimeric and Pauline were always together, even in the water—especially in the water. Two bodies separate but together. The salt waves of the Atlantic tighten their very skins. You're never more compact, more cut off from the world than in the depths of the ocean, heading for the open sea, the shore receding, your muscles first warming up then freezing, then warming up again with the effort you're making. It's good to feel alone, alone with one another. In the sunlight of our twin solitudes, steeped in it, clasped together, the space between us abolished, swallowed up. One sea, one heart.

Aimeric isn't back for dinner. Never mind, it's only fish—hake—and was meant to be eaten cold anyway. Lots of visitors from Paris gather at the yacht club in the early evening, and Aimeric must have stopped by there. By ten o'clock she starts to call up friends: a pretense of calm over growing anxiety. No one had seen Aimeric that day:

what with the heat and then a storm blowing up at the turn of the tide, his pals had dozed, chatted, read, and stayed at home.

It was the worst Assumption Day ever. Ever since ascending into heaven became a question of technology, an air display had been held every August 15 in Brittany in honor of the Virgin Mary, patron saint of pilots. The local airport fretted the threatening clouds with aerial acrobatics, a ballet performed by gliders of all kinds, followed by a sumptuous firework display. Pauline, who usually made fun of this feeble imitation of the Virgin's cosmic flight, immortalized once and for all by Titian in the Church of the Frari in Venice, now stood staring out into the bay opposite the house, growing ever paler and more silent. While her father phoned around to all the neighboring police stations and her mother stifled her sobs up in the bedroom, Pauline peered at the horizon, where a band of light hung between sea and sky, dull and limp as a dead fish.

Aimeric's body was found the following afternoon, washed up by the swell some five miles to the south. Pauline hadn't opened her lips. And she remained silent after the funeral. She didn't speak for months. At the funeral service she looked so thin as to seem almost transparent in her white cotton dress, her red-blotched face savagely exposed by scraped-back fair hair. She was like one of those shellfish, battered to pieces by time and the waves, that lie strewn over the beach, harsh and accusing. You can't tell whether they used to be mauve, white, or iridescent, but they challenge both the decomposition of seaweed and the brief brightness of dawn with their own crazy permanence. The permanence of death distilled into a husk.

None of their group of friends saw Pauline for years. She gave up studying medicine, became anorexic, and made several suicide attempts, slashing her wrists and even her throat. But she was saved just in time. The news filtered through to Camaret-sur-Mer. Odile had heard such gestures often came to nothing: "My dear Stephanie, if you really want to kill yourself there's only one answer: barbiturates. Provided of course you take the right amount. But Pauline was a tough nut really, despite all that mystical pretense of being consumed with grief for her male twin. She survived, didn't she? True, she's still got the scars on her wrists, and even on her neck, apparently, but she always wears high collars like an old maid, and you must have noticed those gloves? . . . I thought journalists were supposed to be observant, but don't bother to explain, I know she's not your type. Whose type can she be, poor thing, after a couple of years in a mental hospital and all those antidepressants, electroshock treatments, and the rest? It's a wonder she's still alive. Well, it was hard to credit it, but she made a new life for herself. And do you know how?

"She changed languages. A bereavement lasts only two years, according to old Freud—yes, yes, a friend of Pascal's told me so, he reads that sort of thing, he's an authority. Perhaps three years in severe cases. It was too late for her to take up medicine again. By the time she felt she could learn something again she was getting on for thirty. At that age, and delicate as she was now despite all the treatment she'd had, it wasn't likely she'd be able to face anatomy labs again or compete with ordinary young medics, rebellious young fellows and cheeky with it, I can tell you. And our Pauline's completely undeveloped sexually; it's obvious, isn't it? But she had an inspiration. She took up Santavarvaran and speech therapy: that was her way of being reborn and making contact with childhood again. It seems she got the idea when she was undergoing psychotherapy. Speaking for myself, I don't believe in all that psycho-what-you-may-call-it, just mumbo-jumbo, I call it, and old-fashioned now too. I'm too down to earth for that kind of thing, but I must admit it really worked with Pauline. Anyhow, it would be hard to think of a better solution, don't you agree?"

Stephanie was prepared to admit someone could be born anew in another language. Not only were her own voice and thoughts quite different in the two languages she inhabited, but it seemed to her that even her breasts, back, belly, thighs, and hands also changed when she passed from French to Santavarvaran. A kind of death followed by resurrection with which she trained herself to experiment every time she crossed the frontier, forgetting a deceased Stephanie on one side and bringing a new one to life again on the other. At first the migrant seemed to be sleepwalking. Her life was that of a dazed Frankenstein's monster: she did everything but was touched by nothing, and was regarded as unusually gifted. This impression, though false, worked: she fit in, as they say, and was accepted in terms of the new code, which came to be her own element. So much so that the mask became the flesh itself, a living person who saw the first Stephanie from a distance, from a height, like a skin sloughed off by a snake. The new language entered into Stephanie through the mind or the soul—in any case, from above. Professor Zorin says it enters an individual through the upper layers of the cortex, working its way downward until it affects his or her senses, organs, and sex. "You confirm my theory, Ms. Delacour: it isn't perception that stimulates language, but the reverse: language causes perception. You know the model I suggest: I call it *top down*, a snappy modern expression that fits the case exactly. Everything comes to us from above: in the beginning was the Word, as they used to say once upon a time."

Stephanie didn't know the model, as a matter of fact, but she was willing to admit a new language does precede a new body—so long as Zorin's *top down* model was complemented by another, equally necessary, that could be described as *bottom up*. This was slow, lazy, and sensual: a rising movement with the tingle of smells, the flutter of sounds, a few hints of color, all boiled up together. Then the mixture cleared and chose words; to put it another way, invented words or, more modestly, overhauled their old meanings. Until Stephanie reached the second stage in this alchemy she was still sleepwalking through the first stage: that of the *top down*.

Was Pauline a sleepwalker too, or had she managed to be born again?

Julia Kristeva

Some bereavements leave their victims with a choice: ossify or change. Go mad or adopt a new language. Death as a corpse or death with life grafted on to it. Pauline's intelligence and self-control were just as extraordinary as her passion for Aimeric. She had the strength to choose a graft: a foreign language and exile. But it's a dire kind of surgery that cuts off your roots and imposes an artificial insemination. In one in five cases this results in a successful pregnancy, and linguistic manipulation produces an embryo, just as genetic manipulation may do. So the previously suicidal Pauline found a new life as a caregiver. A caregiver who never went anywhere without her case of surgical instruments or her gloves.

"I'm just back from Santa Varvara, you know. Pascal couldn't come with me, but I don't really mind: our trip was an absolute triumph! [Odile was rounding off her Breton excursion by singing her own praises again.] I love Santa Varvara: it's the ideal place for anyone with a bit of enterprise. Apart, of course, from that horrible business! Poor Gloria! [Convention required a gesture toward the victim if not the friend.] But as I said to Pascal, the legal decision was very sensible, don't you agree? Bob inherits from his sister and is Jerry's guardian until he comes of age—and perhaps after that, depending on how the boy turns out. Of course, Bob's asked Pauline to take charge of Jerry meanwhile, with the court's approval, naturally. Gloria herself couldn't have wished for a better arrangement, if you can imagine a mother being asked to choose her own successor after she's dead!"

It was already long past the time of her dinner engagement; Stephanie had to call her friends and say she'd unfortunately been held up: a professional emergency. She'd join them later for coffee. Meanwhile the bar had emptied, and its shadowy recesses seemed sinister compared with the flashiness of the lounge, where a solitary American couple went on bawling clichés at each other as if through a storm on Lake Michigan. It occurred to Stephanie that there was nothing like contrasts of light and sound for presaging dramatic events. Uneasiness seemed to tauten the halogen-lit red upholstery; waiters seemed to avert their eyes, embarrassed by so much loudness, human and stylistic. As Stephanie's taxi made its way up the rue d'Assas, it struck her for the first time that this austere corridor, cutting boldly through an otherwise gracefully proportioned neighborhood, was very disturbing. As she was being driven along she wanted to forget Paris, not see anything around her, concentrate on sorting out the meaning of Odile's strange revelations.

What if Pauline had gone mad on that August 15 when Aimeric was drowned, the day of the air show and the Feast of the Assumption? What if she were a diabolical and dual figment of the imagination, with her two brains, left and right, *top down* and *bottom up*, or however Zorin chose to put it? What if the Good Samaritan, haunted by an incurable nightmare, was only biding her time until the loss of a brother might be forgotten in the possession of a son?

Thinking about it later, Stephanie couldn't really tell why or how she came to suspect Pauline. She had no logical reason for doing so, just rather rash conclusions jumped to by a journalist's mind excited by alcohol and perhaps led astray by a tinge of misogyny. ("Delacour's a bit of a woman hater, isn't she?" her female colleagues on *Events* used to whisper, seeing her prefer her own company to theirs.) But this view of things stubbornly persisted, as our fantasies tend to do when we're unaware of them and they don't obscure other people completely.

Yet the main discovery had still to be made. The motive Stephanie had vaguely descried seemed plausible enough, though rather oversubtle from the psychological point of view. But Rilsky would be able to understand it if you caught him after a concert and provided him with a few explanations. Proof was required too, but that might well be possible if you were on the spot. And no doubt some new scandal could be found in Santa Varvara that called for another visit from "our special correspondent."

Stephanie couldn't see how you could be anything but a journal-ist. These days, to cope with all the crime everywhere, you had to be a journalist if you wanted to be free—and to have your wits about you too, if possible, after three white ladies. Or four. She couldn't remember.

・ CHAPTER TWENTY-TWO ・

If you're lucky enough to have a project in mind, most of the things that happen around you are relevant and fall into place as if destined to do so. Your whole life turns into a kind of beehive where every cell instead of staying stupid and empty is filled with the honey of events that confirm either your good luck or fate in general. Unless perseverance itself is destiny.

The offices of *Events*, newly repainted white, fashionably partitioned, and fitted out with shiny desks, fax machines, Internet access, e-mail, and every kind of computer, were vaguely reminiscent of an operating theater. One of those spotless ultramodern cells that represent our age's high-tech attempt to confront death. "*Events* means death nowadays," Professor Zorin maintained. Stephanie couldn't tell whether he was making fun of her paper or summarizing his own professional conclusions. "Fortunately not everyone knows this, because those who do are often the most dangerous. What's to be done? Not much, except to try to analyze them. As a matter of fact, the better ones are already on the analyst's couch. This means fewer criminals but more scoundrels, and sometimes a few human beings too. Tolerant people, I mean, who know how to listen. You think I'm asking too little? You have higher hopes? No, all I look for is a bit of tolerance."

Even so he'd have his work cut out in both Paris and Santa Varvara. Meanwhile, since death alone counts as an event these days—the professor was right—one might as well—setting his subtleties aside—plaster death across the front page or the screen, preferably at mealtimes. If possible disinfected, bandaged, and served up with a dash of goodwill and humanitarianism, with the compliments of the cameramen, not to mention some witticisms from the reporters. In appearance as in its essential function, the newspaper office had thus become a link in the chain subcontracting death. This made it possible for the crime industry itself, whether linked to business, politics, or the Mafia, to install itself at the center of public—i.e., universal—attention and make every section of the audience appear, to the rest, potential accomplices of the crime industry itself. "*Events* means death." As soon as she went through *Events*' enamel-painted door, Stephanie's heightened and no doubt congenitally morbid awareness, exacerbated by Odile Allart's recent monologue, conjured up the formaldehyde smell of an autopsy lab. Her colleagues looked as if they were expecting the homicide squad to arrive at any moment to grill them about unsolved crimes.

As good or bad luck would have it, the news that day was less complicated. The illicit trade in radioactive materials that had been preoccupying everyone for a year had suddenly come to the fore, and Santa Varvara was in the process of becoming its center. Some twelve ounces of plutonium had been intercepted there. And the international secret services, infiltrating the local underworld, had discovered a sort of atomic Mafia. True, AFP, the official French press agency, had just identified the intercepted sample as being 87 percent enriched plutonium, unsuitable for making an atomic bomb. Still, everyone on the paper agreed or pretended to agree that uranium and plutonium shouldn't just be bought and sold like iron bars. And so, as it was summer and some news items had to be fabricated to fill the political vacuum and make people forget the rising unemployment figures, the collapse of the Left and the implosion of the Right, *Events* ran the headline: "Why the Sudden Increase in Black-Market Plutonium?" The editor himself explained that while it took almost eighteen pounds of plutonium and fifty-five of uranium to make an atomic bomb, and the present illicit trade involved far smaller amounts, "plutonium itself is an extremely dangerous poison." Enough said! How many unexplained poisonings, past or to come, could now be put down to plutonium?

Psychosis was mounting. "Our special correspondent" must go to Santa Varvara right away. "The Atomic Mafia," by Stephanie Delacour! Yet another scoop: she had all the luck! And so, despite the natural jealousy of her female colleague on the paper's literary supplement—who knew, as everyone else had for a long time, that books were no longer regarded as events, despite her attempts to persuade her not-so-gentle readers of the contrary—Stephanie was to fly off again, with much more personal reasons than plutonium, to rejoin Northrop Rilsky.

◆ CHAPTER TWENTY-THREE ◆

"Don't go thinking Santa Varvara's becoming a nuclear power, my dear! But I'm sure you know us well enough not to believe that for a moment. The enriched plutonium only passes through here in transit to somewhere else; we're a legal and political sieve, so full of loopholes we're a paradise for business and other deals. The real destinations? Pakistan, North Korea, maybe Iraq, Iran. They all buy fissile material. And of course scientists ready to flee the former Soviet bloc for fewer dollars than your French experts sell themselves for, but still infinitely more than they get back home. One of these days we may see a little atom bomb in Baghdad, why not? For my part, I try to put a stop to it when I can."

Rilsky adapted to the new situation with his usual intelligence and phlegmatic calm. The atomic Mafia was at once more naive and more flexible, easier to detect but harder to pin down than the usual suspects, those who sooner or later always ended up in the Medellín cartel. Russian and Ukrainian scientists who had nothing in common with a crook like Michael Fish but who'd been humiliated by poverty and underemployment sold themselves to the services of paranoid countries large and small: dictatorships and fundamentalist states alike exploited these cold war castoffs in order to pursue their dreams of world domination. A handful of cash was enough to infiltrate the networks of these escapees from ex-communist nuclear power stations, and none of the newly rich renegade scientists disporting themselves on the Santavarvaran beaches escaped the vigilance of Rilsky and Popov. But it got more complicated when they tried to trace the itinerary of a stolen nuclear sample, for then they came up against geopolitics: the government of Santa Varvara was just as anxious as any other to avoid having to choose between bearded Islamists and former Red soldiers. It played along first with one bunch and then with the other, shielded now one group and now a different setup, and thus let stocks of enriched uranium build up on all sides, just so long as they didn't exceed the critical threshold. This policy meant that many a sorcerer's apprentice risked getting his fingers burned.

"So now you're a supercop, my dear Northrop! And as all this is well outside the scope of the crime squad, I presume you work for the Ministry of the Interior now? Or is it the Secret Service?" (Stephanie, sincerely admiring.)

"You'll find out sooner or later, but the truth's not nearly so amusing as you think. The people concerned are just corruptible children; they don't have the same vices as genuine psychopaths. Unless you happen on some delinquents: then they're the crime squad's business. Because the atomic Mafia doesn't draw the line at much, you know, when it comes to getting rid of a member who's turned out to be a double agent. The same old story? Not always. The body of a former director of Chernobyl was found at Burgas in Bulgaria; he'd been poisoned by the plutonium they'd put in his mattress. You never thought of that one? Neither did I. The most expensive poisoning ever." (Rilsky grinned and smoothed the lapels of the jacket he was wearing over a pale yellow shirt.

"I was sure of it: you're the only man in the world who's never bored. While Fish and Brian rot in prison and the Harrison business seems finally settled . . ." (Stephanie, cautiously getting back to her pet subject.)

"Fish got ten years, but he'll be let out long before that. It's only to be expected: the atomic Mafia, which, as you may easily suppose, gets close to the government as soon as the circuit becomes international, is the child of the old Mafia of yesteryear. So it wouldn't surprise me if, for their own crooked purposes, today's atomists came and spirited

Fish out of his cell. As for Brian, he got away with only three years for corruption. But he'll probably have to serve out the whole sentence, because no one really needs him now. There are plenty of young men available these days who are just as good at that sort of thing as he is and who don't have epilepsy . . . Yes, the case *is* closed." (Rilsky and Stephanie look each other in the eye.)

"Tyson, or whatever his name is—the serial killer—can't have been responsible for the beheading." (Stephanie, poker-faced.)

". . . ." (Rilsky, equally impassive.)

"Jason Thingamabob has been cleared because at the time of the 'guillotining' he was cutting some other unfortunate woman's throat. As for Tyson's cherubic stabbing, it was carried out at least twelve hours before the decapitation. I read the lab reports, you see." (Stephanie, pretending she was being forced to say what in fact she was volunteering. She'd forgotten Rilsky didn't like having his conclusions challenged.)

"I'll tell you what I think. Any woman who wants to survive has to prostitute herself in some way, become the little tart of her circle, as Popov would say. [The captain didn't mind using cop's jargon in a really serious situation.] One solution is for her to act as if she has a vocation and hide behind the rules of her profession. If she's a success people say she's a genius. If she fails they laugh at her as a would-be saint or martyr, suffering from repression. Or they dream up some other caricature of voluntary servitude. Mrs. Harrison escaped both these extremes because she was, as you may imagine, a typical *mater dolorosa*. But in my view she took her role as a mother so seriously it deprived her of both success and failure, both genius and ridicule. In short, it reduced her to platitude, which is the height of bad taste. [Rilsky was concentrating so hard on his argument he was almost squinting.] Did she really aspire to such an unattractive fate? Possibly. But if so she'd have needed to know how to cope with prostitution and crime—and there you have it! Gloria was quite incapable of that, to put it mildly. And when you're too ignorant of such things you're more likely to end up a victim than an executioner. So much so that anyone can settle your hash, my dear Stephanie." (Rilsky had assumed the air, familiar to Stephanie, of a suave and well-informed spy.)

"You're quite right, but that doesn't get us anywhere. What I'm saying is simply that the serial killer who may have stabbed Gloria can't have been responsible for the severing of the head." (Stephanie, disappointed at such vulgar showing-off on Rilsky's part.)

"There's something in what you say. It might even contain the germ of a plausible new theory. But in the absence of proof I honestly think we may stick to my hypothesis." (Rilsky, deciding at last to take up the challenge as if that were all he'd been waiting for.)

"Are there any other blanks in your investigations?" (Stephanie, the cheeky little girl.)

"Not that I know of." (Rilsky, sarcastic but hesitant.)

"Really!" (Stephanie, suddenly blasé.)

"You love to catch me being careless or incompetent; it's rather charming. Right. If you say so. We haven't got very far. [After all, the young snooper might be useful, and there was no risk involved: the Harrison case, embarrassing as it had been, was closed now, and everyone suitably dealt with.] Your friend Gloria was suffering from the effects not only of the Rohypnol she was in the habit of taking but also of Elavil, which was never prescribed for her." (Rilsky, casting the fly.)

"It's an antidepressant." (Stephanie, neutral.)

"There's no keeping anything from you. But there's nothing surprising there; in Santa Varvara it's easy to get such things without a prescription provided you know your pharmacist. You don't even need a well-meaning friend or relation who's depressed himself to put his own medicine in your drink." (Rilsky, more neutral still.)

"Pauline Gadeau was on antidepressants for a long while when she was in her teens. After a bereavement. In France." (Stephanie, seizing the bait.)

"Was she? How amusing. The things you know! In that case I can tell you she's needed them again recently. Popov was told about it by her pharmacist, as a matter of fact. But be that as it may, let's change the subject. As you know, Gloria Harrison's will was set aside by the court. Fish lost his share of the estate, and Bob is trustee for the whole amount. Young Jerry was lucky. Pauline Gadeau has turned out to be a real mother to him, if you catch my meaning. With Bob's approval, Pauline and Jerry live together in the Harrison house; everyone agrees that's the most practical arrangement for the speech therapy classes. I'm sure you agree, my dear Stephanie, needless to say. You ought to go and see them: they're sweet." (Rilsky, innocent, jumping at the chance of passing on to his female colleague the remains of the uncomfortable affair. Atomic mafia or no atomic mafia, it was starting to weigh on his conscience.)

◆ CHAPTER TWENTY-FOUR ◆

My laptop had broken down. What better excuse could there be for asking Bob to invite his nephew to the laser cube I was staying in as usual in Santa Varvara? After his mother's death Jerry's enthusiasm for video games had changed into an obsession with computers. Like many of his contemporaries he'd already got the general hang of them, but it wasn't long before he became an absolute expert.

I'd never been alone with him before. His huge dark eyes looked strange with that fair hair, and the disturbing impression created by his appearance was intensified by his labored but extraordinarily clear speech. And probably exaggerated further by my memory of the murder.

I find it easier to be natural in difficult than in ordinary situations, maybe because it's more effective. I told him right away how sorry I was about his mother. He didn't flinch but didn't seem too upset either.

After a year and a half, Jerry Novak was no longer a little boy. In front of me now was a teenager who must already be shaving some fluff off his flaxen cheeks, taking an interest in the cut of his leather jackets, and attracting the girls. He was silent for a moment, not looking at me, as if trying to avoid giving the same answer to me as to all the other friends and acquaintances of Gloria's who'd inflicted the same ordeal on him. He believed if he'd stayed at home during the night of Saturday the fifteenth to Sunday the sixteenth of October the tragedy would never have happened. And for very different reasons I'd come to the same conclusion. But I wanted to know why *he* thought so. It was very simple, he said: if he'd been there his mother wouldn't have had so much to drink. Nor, knowing he was in the house, would she have taken so many sedatives. She still liked to watch over him when he was asleep as she had done when he was a baby, and delicate. And lastly Michael Fish would have taken into account his and Pauline's presence in the villa: Ms. Gadeau always slept in Stan's studio the night before she took Jerry to spend a vacation in the country with her. So if he, Jerry, had been there, a serial killer wouldn't have got into his mother's room.

My own version of the facts didn't square at all with Jerry's theory, but I didn't want to upset him. I was very impressed by the way he handled death. His youth had stitched horror away under a tissue of reasons, transforming grief and guilt into obstinate logic. Error was equated with dysfunction. A mistake in logic is serious but comprehensible; unforgivable, perhaps, but one can dissociate oneself from it. Left to itself the reasoning consciousness is like a computer system: it may make irremediable blunders, but they're not part of itself. I wondered if the boy's attitude was typical of a whole generation or the paradoxical consequence of Gloria's devotion. It wasn't difficult to see how an anxious overprotective mother might cause her son to construct a carapace of coldness, using neurotic rituals and intellectual prowess to ward off his mother's clinging possessiveness but thereby branding himself as indifferent. Jerry must have suffered terribly because of his mother's brutal death, but instead of enduring it in his own flesh or his own mind—take your choice—he'd chosen to *understand*: to understand how he should have acted before, and how he still ought to act now. Unless of course he hadn't suffered at all, or very little, because his mother's death merely involved a few changes in his habits—and not all that many, since Pauline was there to take over. It was quite possible, if, as I was ready to do, you agreed that Jerry had escaped Gloria's emotional influence by sheltering behind his video interests, his skill at producing false Picassos, and now his computer skills. What did it matter? Was the unobtrusive grief of Gloria's son, so elusive people might think it didn't exist at all, just one more of Gloria's defeats? Or, on the contrary, was it her greatest success? After all, her handicapped son didn't need her anymore. Down with grieving, and instead of passion and death, or the passion of death, long live the robots! In short, Gloria had bestowed a supreme gift on her son when she freed him of the burden of the woman-as-mother. Death as a gift, our ultimate present to those we love, who are bound then to love us a bit less.

I decided to leave these uncertain meditations till later and made an effort to follow Jerry's monotonous drone. It was the sort of voice that doesn't grip your attention, but it was what I'd come for. He was telling me about the forty-eight hours that wouldn't have been what they were if he and Pauline hadn't left some time before dinner was over. Jerry had met Rilsky shortly after the murder, and the captain, to be fair to him, questioned the boy very briefly, realizing he was still in a state of shock. It would have been crazy to go on at length about so painful an experience. And logically speaking—and all Jerry's teachers agreed that he had a very logical mind—what else could he have told Rilsky except that he and Pauline left his mother's house at about 10:30 to spend the Halloween vacation in the country?

"You left at around ten thirty?"

"Yes. Pauline had promised to have me to stay with her in Bourgas for the vacation. That was convenient, because Mother had some urgent work to finish. We got there well after midnight, maybe around one o'clock, I couldn't say: Pauline's nervous and drives very slowly. Especially at night. We'd had an exhausting week, with the dinner party and everything. So we slept through Sunday morning and had a late lunch: we *were* on vacation." (His words are strung out, mechanical and awkward. An artificial voice from beyond the grave, shrill and inquiring.)

"Nothing particular happened? I mean, that Sunday, before they told you about . . ." (I hesitate.)

"The murder. [*He* doesn't hesitate.] I don't think so. Raphael came in the afternoon as usual—he lives near Pauline's place. We

always get together during vacations. He's as keen on video games as
I am, but not so good at them: he doesn't have as much equipment as
I do. So he comes over to my place as usual, I go to get my cassettes
and stuff, and what do I find? No VDU, no cassettes, nothing. I didn't
know if it was I or my mother who'd forgotten to put them in my
bag—we always packed my bag together—but anyhow we'd left
everything out. Disaster! Pauline realized right away this was going
to spoil my vacation. So she drove back there and then to get my
stuff. She knows where I keep it, and anyway I explained it to her all
over again just to make sure." (The thought sounds right, but the
mouth is slightly twisted. The synthetic-sounding voice makes our
conversation seem unreal. I feel as if I'd been misled, trapped.)

"What time did Pauline leave to go back?"

"I don't know. Let's see. Raphael must have come over at around
three o'clock. So I suppose she left at around four. A real bore for her,
having to cope with the weekend traffic. Almost two hundred fifty
miles round-trip. She didn't show up until eleven that night. I'd gone
over to Raphael's place for supper, and we were all getting anxious
about her." (Jerry relates everything logically. His handicap doesn't
seem to bother him. I go on observing him suspiciously. His gestures
strike me as spasmodic. Is he really all that well balanced?)

"So you were all worried about Pauline?"

"We certainly were! She was absolutely whacked when she got
back. She was as white as a sheet and shivering too, I think. Being tired
always makes her feel cold. Especially in her hands. That's why she
wears gloves."

I wanted to say, But it wasn't from the cold that Pauline was pro-
tecting her hands, my poor Jerry. It was from the blood that spurts out
when a scalpel severs an artery.

"Was she wearing gloves when she got back from Santa Varvara
that Sunday?" (I, as casually as I can.)

"I think so. She was so cold she'd even put her raincoat on over her
T-shirt."

"Maybe she wanted to hide her clothes?" (I abandon caution in order to try him out.)

"Eh? Oh, I see what you mean. Pauline doesn't dress very well. But she doesn't try to hide it: she doesn't care. No, she was just pale and shivering. I *think* . . . Though the weather was still warm then; we were having a sort of Indian summer. But Pauline's always cold when she's tired, as I said. I was delighted at getting my game equipment back . . . After a good night's sleep Pauline was all right again. But then, about midday on Monday, somebody phoned. They didn't explain right away, but I realized something must be wrong at home. Mother wasn't answering the phone. I thought there might have been an accident. We wondered about Fish: perhaps Mother had gone off to find him. Then Lieutenant Popov came, and we knew."

He thinks like an adult. Why do people say he's strange? In his position I'd have thought as he did. With one difference, perhaps. But I can hardly ask Jerry to think like me.

"Did you cry?"

"At first I didn't understand. Then, yes, I cried. After that I don't remember."

"What about Pauline?"

"Pauline? Everyone said she was perfect. Perfect. She's all I've got now, you see."

I saw. That was the trouble. For all his logical mind Jerry was only a little boy. No, he hadn't thought what I thought. Not for a moment. He hadn't thought anymore at all.

I can stand up to men, but I can't resist a child. My skin becomes porous: the child seeps into me and vice versa. Through an osmosis of feelings and words, affection becomes a solution of pure childhood. But this handicapped little nerd, with his great vague eyes like satin embers, standing there in front of me, shattered me even more than mingled sea and sun.

The genetic malice that had struck him now attacked me: I felt threatened by deafness, feeble-mindedness, incurable idiocy. Only threatened, for he was managing wonderfully, young Jerry the nerd. Hadn't you noticed? Yes, I'm the one who's handicapped. You've only to look at me to see me as I am, as Jerry shows me to be. I, like him, might be, *am* the prey of the vengeance of some ancient gods. But enough! That's no reason for abandoning him.

My skin resumes normal service, I'm solid again; the little wounded puppet can lean on me. Love has driven out fear, which crystallizes into a caress. Silence. I caress the wound in Jerry's voice. He's got me.

◆ CHAPTER TWENTY-FIVE ◆

My head can't stay empty. Morning with its vast green aroma brings me an oppressive but luminous hallucination. A face tries to fill my thoughts, and my anxieties give it the power to conjure up images. Added to all this, a sense of fatality presents the case to me laid out on a shell of certainty.

I can only remember Pauline vaguely, but I know what she looks like. She has a face made of dust. Eyes dull and waxy as little balls of soap. Her gnarled hands, with veins outstanding, old before the rest of her, hang down beside the body of a forgotten girl. Her mouth rises up before me like an animal, all on its own. A mouth that moves, that is agile but dumb. But it won't say anything. This story is mine.

She's been dead for twenty years. A synthetic image lives in her stead, in another language, another country. But the synthesis has been made flesh through love. Love for Jerry has turned Pauline into a mother. In Gloria's shadow. No matter: resentment is one more experience, and jealousy surmounted can fill a woman with pride. In Santa Varvara a foreigner is a supplicant. But Pauline doesn't mind imploring, effacing herself, playing second fiddle. So long as no one encroaches on her love for Jerry, so long as Gloria doesn't deprive her of the blessing of bringing about Jerry's second birth. But no, he is born again a thousand times, every time he learns a new word. But thwarted love is a wave conveying hate.

Fish tries to get Jerry sent away, to a school in Switzerland, any-where. All he wants is to get hold of the mother's money, even marry her. And maybe—why not?—disinherit the son. Gloria, in love and indecisive, is ready to give in. Pauline overhears the negotiations and knows a threat is approaching. The synthetic image disintegrates. A part of it gets hold of some Elavil and substitutes it for the sleeping pills. Of all the guests at the dinner party on Saturday, October 15, Pauline was the only one with access to Gloria's medicine cabinet. She might gradually drain Gloria's strength away, poison her slowly, or— with luck—kill her outright. Anything to make sure Jerry's life wasn't disturbed, to take his fate into her own hands, without a rival, free from quarrels, just the two of them, Pauline and Jerry, mother and son: brother and sister, resurrection! She doesn't know what she's doing. When you're virtual you never quite know if what you do is really done, if you're doing things or imagining them, if you're being seen or not: seeing or being, neither seeing nor being, both at once or neither. The hatred of which Pauline is ignorant doesn't ignore her rival. Taking advantage of the bustle of the dinner party and the packing of the bags for the vacation, she slips into the bathroom and replaces the sleeping pills with the Elavil tablets: she'll strike Gloria in the mouth, the stomach, in her very blood: she'll stifle her, strangle her, drown her. She sits at the foot of the long table among the less important guests, Jerry's gray speech therapist, she, I, the synthetic image born of both love and hate.

To drive for two hours there and another two hours back on the freeway just for a video game and some cassettes: ridiculous. No mother would do it; she'd get her son to occupy himself more usefully: reading, for instance. But Pauline Gadeau isn't a mother; Jerry is more than a son to her. She has given him speech, in other words a soul, and now she lives only for him.

An unconsummated passion made up of sounds and looks, of lips and throats articulating together with unremitting attention has secretly bound her to the child. Pauline introduced herself into his silent being and opened his ears for him. And out of the silent world of the boy she'd become she began to speak as if she were Jerry himself. It was a kind of underwater osmosis, a communion of dolphins in ultra-sounds inaccessible to human beings. Pauline's mouth is in Jerry's eyes. Day after day the little optical glutton eats up the various shapes of her lips, imprinting them on an almost inaudible voice. But in it you can hear the breath brush against the palate to produce the vowels and consonants that make up "Pauline." For him it's a drawing done by the mouth; for her an outline in sound. "That's it," "You've got it," "I'm smiling at you," "You're smiling at me," "I'm receiving you, Jerry." The mouth listens, the eye absorbs the mouth: mouth and eye together replace the dead ear and modulate the voice, and Jerry makes himself heard. He needs Pauline in order to trace the strange paths from lips to eyes and vocal cords and then, using this mute map, to utter words. Before a word can come forth, Jerry has to capture an incredible number of contours made by Pauline's lips, together with landscapes made by her throat, and then reproduce them in his own body. His deaf ears are aware only of confused silence. But through an impulse of the senses his mouth and eyes re-create the music of the perceptions: you can actually see the melody being embodied. Two mouths, two throats, two pairs of eyes, but only one pair of ears between the two of them. An antlike task? Speech isn't innate; it's born of a love that listens.

The speech therapist exists only if she's a sensory mirror to the half-deaf patient. She feels his breath, his larynx, his chin, his cheek-bones, his chest, his nasal cavity, the movements of his tongue: she shows them to him, makes him savor them. They vibrate, he discovers them, uses them; and this territory of flesh that starts to move for her, through her, emits sounds, speech, for him and for her. He can't hear himself properly, perhaps not at all. But she has received him, got his message, and Pauline, the mirror, reflects her understanding back to him. And he's a shrewd reader. He looks, feels, reads his reflection. In this way he learns that speech has taken place, that a language is devel-oping in him via a reading that replaces hearing. The reading is a visible understanding between them. Jerry reads better than he speaks. Pauline has won.

The vacations are the best time for her to have Jerry all to herself. No more putting off or canceling lessons. Instead, a long unbroken sequence, the link between them unthreatened by interruption. She can live with him from day to day, between grass and water, garden and beach, in time with the salt that's maturing in the marshes and the ducks dotting the quivering surface of the ponds. For years a family of mallards has crisscrossed the pond in front of the little holiday home that Pauline Gadeau goes to every weekend and on vacations, far away from the harassments of the city and the speech therapy department at St. Ambrose's. She's sure they're the same mallards, handing down from generation to generation the secrets of the warm currents and the sodden earth beneath the wild fennel. When you have no family yourself it's easy to imagine the families of others, even of ducks. Especially in the case of the mallards, which seem inhabited by a kind of cosmic peace, the mixture of detachment and unity to be seen on Chinese scrolls, where birds share an air of divinity with ideograms both broad and slender, enigmatic and empty. The male and female mallard—she slightly larger than her mate—escort their four offspring from a distance. The ducklings were quite small when Pauline first saw them, in June. But now they're almost as big, and as placid, as their parents. Silence. The whole flotilla's taking a nap on the surface of the water; suspended time takes the place of brush strokes and afternoon light. They'd be a foretaste of heaven, these two weeks of vacation with Jerry, shared as usual with her neighbors the ducks, with the shutters open wide onto the creek.

This communion was scarcely ruffled when Jerry discovered that his video games had been left behind in his bedroom in Santa Varvara. "I forgot to pack them, Pauline: how awful!" She knows he really needs his games. They're a harmless drug, too childish for him perhaps, but they help restore his strength for the efforts Pauline asks of him in order to do what comes automatically to other children.

Without a second thought she gets into the car and drives back to Santa Varvara, as if the hundred or so miles were nothing at all. On the crowded freeway, sweltering in the Indian summer, she realizes she's going away from the mallards and Jerry, that a crazy sense of duty has made her take to the road, that she's dead tired. Gloria Harrison must be a really careless mother, with her mind on other things—which has been obviously, shockingly, the case recently—to forget to pack her son's favorite toy when he goes away on vacation. It's clear she doesn't think about Jerry anymore. She's mainly concerned with other things, her own life for instance—if you can call it a life when it fails to concentrate on a mother's true business of promoting her son's happiness and sharing in his progress. Gloria no longer has any conception of what a genuine mother's life should be. Did she ever have one? You can't help wondering. Anyhow, she doesn't think of anything now but herself, her work, her love affair—and, to be fair, just a bit about Jerry. But in a way that's so utilitarian, dogmatic, and possessive it can't be of any help to a child who needs relaxation, affection, and a refuge rather than Gloria's ceaseless agitation. She's a hard woman, Gloria Harrison: fickle, capricious, selfish. What use is a mother like that to a child with Jerry's difficulties, Jerry's intelligence and need for love?

The Harrison home seems strangely deserted after the frenzy of the freeway. Cool and empty in the shade of the silvery poplars. The trees in Santa Varvara emanate a sense of youthfulness. Not like in France, where the trees think. Here they radiate innocence, at least to Pauline, who contrasts them with the harshness of the road, of life, and of all the people ruled by passion. She has the key to Jerry's study and goes straight up to the second floor. She knows the drawers and closets by heart and has no trouble finding the box containing the video games. Really, what a desultory and heartless mother you'd have to be to pay so little attention to your child's amusements and so much to your own pleasures! Primitive pleasures too, and more and more so. Pauline can feel her anger rising and a flush spreading over her neck.

How many times have Gloria Harrison and her lover sunk to shouting at each other, perhaps even come to blows, forgetting that Pauline and Jerry are working just overhead and the speech therapist can hear everything even if her patient can't? Thank God, Jerry has never known anything about it; he's got enough problems without that. But Pauline has deliberately eavesdropped on the impossible Fish as he insists on something she doesn't understand. A lot of incomprehensible words, Gloria refuses, he returns to the charge, then Gloria explains, and he grows more violent still. Pauline guesses it's all about disinheriting Jerry. "How do you imagine he'd cope? He's not up to managing anything! He can't concentrate, he's handicapped: just face the facts and send him to Switzerland!" The voice rises, shrill and implacable. Gloria weeps, refuses, promises to sort it all out, to do what Fish wants, anything, anything so long as he stays with her. He slams the door to show he's serious; Gloria's sobs can be heard up in Jerry's study. Pauline can tell Gloria's going to give in. And that day, for the first time, the speech therapist realizes she hates Jerry's mother. She's never liked her much: all those outbursts of emotion, those floods of caresses followed by an avalanche of slaps. Mrs. Harrison's an undisciplined hysteric, poor woman. You can understand it, really; after all, a speech therapist is supposed to be a bit if a psychologist. So Pauline did understand. But it mustn't continue. Gloria had gone too far; she was putting her own pleasure before Jerry's future, and that deserved worse than contempt: hatred. Jerry had only Pauline to defend him. Well, she was ready. He could rely on her. The red flush flooded her neck, her head. Time no longer existed. Pauline had lost track of it.

No sound from inside the house. She goes to the door opening into Gloria's study and knocks. No one there. Another door nearby is ajar. The bedroom. She knocks again. No one. She opens the door and goes in. A body. A wound on one breast. Blood. Gloria unconscious.

Pauline is horrified, but a hidden camera could have recorded a smile on her face. Surprise? Shock? Secret pleasure? Cameras don't interpret. And anyhow from now on Pauline is a robot. She doesn't know she's smiling. Her lips are twisted in a grimace reflecting a far-off anguish unleashed. She acts. The heat mounts from her neck to her cheeks. Her legs carry her outside, she goes back to the car, gets out her surgeon's bag: a souvenir of former skills but useful in an emergency, especially when you're looking after children. Pauline has always kept it with her since that time in another life, the time of Aimeric. The stethoscope confirms the outward evidence. Pointless precautions, but Pauline goes through with them, an overgrown little girl tending her dolls. The heart has stopped beating. Perhaps it did so more than twelve hours before: rigor mortis has set in. Rigor mortis: the rigidity of death. But is death the right word? Has the pallid face of this envied, hated woman really been reduced to nothingness? Pauline is overcome again by the blind anger that crushed her out of existence twenty years ago and that was then, inadequately, described as a breakdown.

Aimeric's body brought back to the holiday home in Brittany, cheerful and festive as the Harrison house. Aimeric drowned. Pauline drowned too. Pauline is no more . . . Her brother's death is a silent fury, her strangled sobs implode: I'll kill myself. No more words, no more deeds, you're nothing, I'm nothing, I'm dying. For a long time I was a corpse; I am a corpse. Like this obscene woman lying there in front of me, sprawled on the floor in a pool of blood, her flesh cold, like meat on a slab. She made Jerry, she took him away from me, she threatens him, she's going to drag him away with her into her own crazy life. She's going to drown him. Her or me, Aimeric or Jerry, a knife cleaves us; I hate her, I hate death. A mother destroying her son. Whose son? My mother's? Aimeric or Jerry? Her son. My son. Aimeric wasn't my brother, I carried him about in my arms when he was a baby, I fed him when Mother was at the lab, I taught him to walk, to talk, to read. Like Jerry. Her son. But Gloria's not fit to be a mother. No mother is. And it's not just because she's ready to disinherit him, slaps him, and forgets to pack his games. No, it's more serious. She doesn't understand, a mother never understands: she's frivolous, quick-tempered, too this or not enough that, intellectual, unrealistic, too realistic, not intellectual enough, always unreal. A woman who's helpless and depressed, that's what a mother is, that's where the mystery lies. Like me. I hate. And hatred doesn't only implode, a white-hot furnace consuming me for twenty years: tears, sleepless nights, longings denied, jealousies shrugged off, anger changed into caring. Hatred also decides, strikes, cuts the Gordian knot. The scalpel opens the flesh, the vertebrae are parted by its precision, the bones give way: I make the incision. I cut myself off from her, sever myself from the mother who drowns her son, detach myself from the corpse that I was but am no longer. I amputate her power, remove her distinguishing marks. She'll be stupidly, cruelly bereft of both her observation post and her crowning glory, poor old Gloria. Her supreme ornament will end up in the garbage, in a plastic trash can on the freeway, even her son wouldn't recognize her remains. Are you really yourself when you haven't got a head? A headless body has nothing, it has no self anymore so it can't own anything, it knows neither mine nor thine. Nor hers. Her what? Her son, your son, my son? Aimeric, Jerry.

◆ CHAPTER TWENTY-SIX ◆

The blade compresses the rigid flesh of the neck. The first sign of age in a woman appears in the skin of her neck. Every morning Pauline pinches hers, feels a varying mixture of affection and annoyance as she sees the baked apple grow browner, more withered, slacker. Gloria's complexion is—was—fresher, although she and Pauline were much the same age. But the youthfulness that was so proud of itself yesterday is today stiff and frozen. Heaven knows why it's the neck that ages first. Lovers smell the subtlest perfumes there, musky from inner juices but lightened by the influence of the eyes and the sun. Infants cling there, preferring these open curves even to the sibylline warmth of breast and belly. The weight of the head rests there: a vertical aberration perched in supernatural equilibrium on a stem that defies both gravity and the horizontal litheness of quadrupeds. Impossible to express how tiring it is to stay upright despite lovers, babies, and a head that has to think of everything! Sometimes the combination of tasks is pleasant, even glorious, but it's tiring, very tiring. The neck feels the effect of it, but it steadies, takes the strain. The neck is the most insidiously and monstrously feminine of organs. Unlike the big toe, which in both sexes bears the brunt of the body and betrays weakness of character, the neck—though only in women—shows not only wear and tear but also signs of spiritual weakness and life unfulfilled. And in the end it reveals the permanent tendency to cave in that's called stupidity: the triumph of inertia and passivity. It can't be disguised by makeup; it would take a face-lift to cure it, a process of cutting open and sewing up again. Or else it could just be removed, lopped off.

The skin splits neatly but doesn't retract as the lips of a living wound would do. There are no jagged edges pointing inward. The blade shears on, cold and clean, through the lifeless, stiff, but docile muscles of Gloria's almost bloodless corpse. After breaking the skin the steel hews through the larynx, the carotid arteries, and various veins. The blood flows sluggishly, soaking Pauline's gloves but not splashing onto the big gray T-shirt that comes down to the thighs of the jeans she always wears in the country. A few little splashes at the most. Hardly noticeable. Still, she'd better cover herself up with a raincoat or something and change into clean clothes later on.

Pauline dislikes her hands. Her fingers are short and stubby, her nails break easily; she's got peasant's hands that remember having been hen's claws in another life. She hates them. They are sensual enough but roughen at the touch of cleaning liquids or soil, and chap if they're put in either hot or cold water or exposed to the wind or the sun. They're hands that need to be hidden, protected. But people don't wear gloves these days, especially in summer, and not often in spring or autumn either. Never mind: Pauline does wear them, and in Santa Varvara too, if you please. They make her look like an old maid, but that doesn't bother her. You have to coincide with some type or other, so why not that? The spinster's as dead as a doornail, and the real Pauline was drowned at the same time as Aimeric, even if Jerry has grafted a new shoot on to the withered trunk.

The neck bones don't present any problem: the scalpel skirts them and slips between the cartilage, probing and piercing until the last shred of skin is severed. The swollen purplish head falls coolly away. Pauline doesn't see it: it's merely waste to be got rid of. The blue of the trash bag covers it up: "my sexual organ," "the tool of my trade," as poor Gloria jokingly used to call it. Rather a sinister object really, though, only fit to be ground up in a garbage truck. The mindless energy of the speech therapist handling the corpse has just rid us of death, of her death.

Needless to say, when performing such decisive acts one doesn't ask oneself questions. And no one is likely to come and bother Pauline. Michael Fish, after strangling his difficult mistress, made off early in the morning with the forged *Woman with Collar*, not to mention some genuine Stanislas Novaks. At the present moment Hester Bellini, with her silver spoons, her disheveled curls, and her black uniform, is wandering distraught through the mountains near her native village. Brian Watt, enjoying the Eisenstein program on TV, is indulging at last in pleasures within his scope. And the serial killer took himself and his knife off long ago, disappointed at having met with a woman beautiful but dead. No witnesses. The silence of the grave. Pauline drives away. Her legs warm up, beads of dusty sweat trickle into her eyes. Sweltering in traffic jams on the freeway, she can feel the blood pulsing through her veins again. She must throw the garbage bag away somewhere, put on another pair of gloves. What time is it? Eight in the evening already! She hadn't remembered how crowded the roads are on Sundays. It's past Jerry's dinnertime; he'll be anxious. Never mind, they'll eat late, she'll make him an omelette. He'll have his games, anyhow.

It's easy to cut up a woman's body if you're a woman. Nothing to it. You know it all so well! It doesn't call for either grief or pity. You know how to set about it, which flap of skin to lift off, which joint to go for, which bit of cartilage to destroy. You know what shame to awaken, what suffering to revive, what susceptibility to trample on, what jealousy to exacerbate, what longing to thwart, what desire to frustrate, what death to repeat—to go on repeating endlessly, not letting the pain ever ease. You're attacking yourself, but from a distance. You protect yourself and survive while the other dies, disappears into the void to which she seems always to have belonged. You yourself are reborn, set off again. More impersonal than before, and more assured. "I" is dead, long live no one! No one is cruel. No one gloats. What might seem like carnage is merely the act of a surgeon: quite impartial. The acting-out of a breakdown cancels out cruelty:

it's merely a kind of thought, a substitute for thought, and just as cold and efficient.

A woman looking visibly relieved throws a blue plastic bag into the trash can at a service station. All she has to do now is bring Jerry his games.

◆ CHAPTER TWENTY-SEVEN ◆

I go to see Jerry too. I'm really eager to see his painting, his new Picassos, his new computer. He invites me. Yes, he insists. Yes, he means it: he'll be delighted. We've got through to one another.

He was using some program—or some process he'd invented himself, I wasn't quite sure—that allowed him to reproduce on the screen the famous sham Picasso that caused Michael Fish's downfall. The young forger, now also a computer whiz kid, was turning out quantities of *Women with Collar*. He could print out as many copies as he liked, each more authentic than the original itself. No matter how much I tried to be modern and Rimbaudesque and cool the poetic ardors of my female colleague on the literary supplement by maintaining that "Art is foolishness!" I couldn't help being rather shocked by the mass production of those Picassos. You can do anything on your computer these days, so why not the mosaic depicting the beheading of St. John in St. Mark's in Venice or Rodin's headless *Walking Man*—or, while you're at it, the decapitation of Gloria herself? There's no more art, no more crime; we live in the age of artificial intelligence: the computer knows everything, can do everything, does do everything. It invents, thinks, has ideas; it's the creator now, there's no such thing as a creator anymore. It's only to be expected, isn't it? Oh, I know, for the moment we still need an intermediary, a programmer, Jerry himself, but for how long? Jerry, having made his escape from Gloria's death and Pauline's lips, forges Picasso's *Woman with Collar* and thereby foils all of them—women, his mother, the speech therapist—quite calmly, in accordance with the rules of the computer, the logic of the software. He's a logical demon.

Pauline stands in the doorway of Gloria's study, upright and white in her gray dress. A domelike, sculptural brow offsets the ash-colored hair arranged in a bun. Only her mouth is really alive, the lips pursed as if about to emerge from the dead husk of the rest of her face. Untouchable. But this is not the dignity of a clear conscience. No, she's on the frontier that an articulate being passes through on the way from having no conscience to being hard as a stone. What's blindingly obvious is the power of usefulness: Pauline is indispensable. And she knows it. I know she knows it, but there's nothing I can do about either her knowledge or mine. Whatever she's done, whatever she might have done, whatever I think she's done, whatever she certainly did do, this now allows life to go on after death. Her life, of course, for I'm sure she's free now, emptied of the hatred that once built up under her synthetic image. But even more the life of Jerry, whom I too am beginning to love (wonders will never cease!). The indispensable speech therapist replaces Gloria's passion with a useful and rational love that the act of decapitation has purged of its festering morbidity. At least, that's how it seems to me, that's what I hope, that's what ensures the continuing life of the race. Or, more to the point, the life of Jerry Novak. Her brother is her son. It's as simple as that. But is it true or false? That is *not* the question. There is no question. Life goes on. That's life.

But I'm ashamed for Pauline: I often do feel embarrassed on behalf of people incapable of feeling shame themselves. I feel the humiliation they can't feel; their typically human impenetrability affects me like a kind of arrogance, deals me a mortal blow. Some hormone that runs warmly in my veins starts to throb: yes, that's it—revulsion turns not my stomach but my blood.

Pauline's still standing in the doorway of Gloria's study. As she speaks to me I watch her eyes: is it insolence I see there or reserve? Or perhaps a certain mildness. I see that, as if nothing had happened, she's wearing her pointless black gloves. I finally realize Northrop Rilsky is on the phone. Mr. Bob Harrison told him Ms.

Delacour was going to see Jerry, and he's taken the liberty of calling up to ask if she could go a concert with him this evening. Pauline is being meek; she knows her place as a member of staff. I wonder if she's laughing up her sleeve at me or if this role is already almost second nature to her. Part of the nature that replaces the real nature of a foreigner.

Again that feeling, dating back to my youth, that everything is appearance, delusion, hallucination. Not that there ever *was* any certainty somewhere governing the inessential and eventually justifying it. On the contrary, the semblance that stealthily surrounds us, that is constantly creating us, may well be mere foam on the surface of something that seems threatening but turns out to be serene; the fallout of a vast, hidden, advancing spirit, separate forever from appearances. Speaking, doing, traveling, supporting causes, writing and so on . . . you can do these things: why not? I did them, sometimes with ease and always without undue fatigue. But without conviction, either, not really. For the secret plenitude that vibrates the senses makes everything else seem hopelessly insipid. That's reason enough to doubt, question, probe. Or else just let it all go. But as I don't like giving in, I analyze.

I go to answer the telephone, looking forward to the pleasure of telling the violin-playing captain the results of my own investigation. Later, after the concert, perhaps. First I'll let him bark up the wrong tree a while longer; he's always so sure he knows best. Unless he's already guessed the truth for himself, which would explain his ambiguous remarks and awkward manner. But no, he can't possibly have found out what Stephanie herself has discovered. What does the worthy Rilsky know about a woman's secret world? About a child borne by a woman, an abnormal child to whom she gives life every day, day after day her whole life long? All that has nothing to do with Existence, Man, Humanity, Society, all their subtle verbiage. You either feel it or you don't; it's different, another world at the other end of the earth. At best, if he'd come anywhere near the truth when he offered his necessarily shaky conclusions to the courts in Santa Varvara, he could only have been governed by humanist considerations and his sense of measure and what's right. His restraint couldn't have had anything to do with an understanding of passion, either Gloria's or Pauline's. It couldn't have any connection with the crazy truth, the confounded tenderness that paralyze me now as I contemplate Jerry's huge eyes and the ex–medical student's ridiculous gloves.

I'm still going to answer the telephone. I think about Gloria, about her lonely existence as a translator, about my own loneliness, about the meanness and dislike that dogged her all her life, and about the ferocity of the attack on her dead body. A mature body like a statue by Phidias, so stupidly ill-used by fate it aroused a universal desire for a real beheading . . . But why?

Charm, which is also a more attractive face of helplessness, made people find her lovable, attractive, at first. "I am her," Hester might have thought, and so might Pauline and a lot of others. But my polyglot friend seemed quite unaware of what went on around her. And her fierce devotion to Jerry and Michael made her look so self-sufficient, almost happy, that it cut her off from the rest of the world. "She's not one of us, she really isn't," people said. To the Santavarvarians, who like everyone else did all they could to be "one of us," the duplicity they thought they saw in Gloria must have been insufferable. As a woman both disturbing and unprotected, she was to them like some exciting but powerless mirage. A classic victim. Is that the normal fate of a female foreigner? Maybe, but that in itself wasn't enough. She must have made some mistake, some mistakes. What were they? Who could say? Could I consult Larry Smirnoff? Igor Zorin? I already had. A real psychoanalyst? A female psychoanalyst? In Paris? But who? It must be someone incapable of hatred. That must be it. As a woman translator who, by definition, trained herself to love, she must have been more or less incapable of hate. That was her weakness, I imagine. No, I'm sure of it. For it's a rare and incurable defect, a negative demon, the absence of hatred that delivers you defenseless into the hands of all the others.

"Captain Rilsky would like to speak to you on the phone." (Pauline Gadeau had clasped her gloved hands and seemed to be smiling. Invulnerable. She'd assumed her slight air of superiority, the one that belonged to Camaret-sur-Mer and the days of Aimeric.)

Stephanie Delacour wondered if perhaps after all she shouldn't start hating this innocent usurper. Yes indeed, she would go to the concert this evening; it was very kind of Rilsky to ask her. Mozart? Of course: you can never hear too much Mozart! And I'm especially fond of the violin concertos! An excellent excuse for not talking or asking questions or analyzing one another.

Stephanie wouldn't tell Rilsky anything anyway. Was it up to a journalist, a young woman from Paris, to imagine us, to plunge again into the quagmire that was Santa Varvara? All in all, Rilsky was right, and there simply wasn't anything to be said. But what luck, in this vale of tears, to be able to listen to a bit of music. When you come right down to it, music . . .

The world of music that Jerry will never know, or scarcely. Can you love someone who doesn't belong to the same world as you? It seems crazy, but it must happen. She kissed the huge eyes of the teenager so different from the others. A lump came into her throat, one of those painful lumps made up of forgiveness, mawkish emotion, and cursed kindness. And she left the Harrison villa as fast as she could, without another word.

The reality of the rue du Cherche-Midi would soon reassert itself, but Stephanie knew that from now on there'd be two of them living there: the journalist-cum-detective and a virtual caress for the wound in Jerry's voice. Pauline's demon already possessed Ms. Delacour, and it was in this apparently indifferent but secretly passionate guise that he was preparing to descend on the logical landscape of Paris.